BEAUTY AND THE BEAST

By Ed McBain
THE 87th PRECINCT NOVELS

Cop Hater • *The Mugger* • *The Pusher* • *The Con Man* • *Killer's Choice* • *Killer's Payoff* • *Lady Killer* • *Killer's Wedge* • *'Til Death* • *King's Ransom* • *Give the Boys a Great Big Hand* • *The Heckler* • *See Them Die* • *The Empty Hours* • *Lady, Lady, I Did It!* • *Like Love* • *Ten Plus One* • *He Who Hesitates* • *Eighty Million Eyes* • *Hail, Hail, the Gang's All Here!* • *Sadie When She Died* • *Let's Hear It for the Deaf Man* • *Hail to the Chief* • *Blood Relatives* • *So Long As You Both Shall Live* • *Long Time No See*

AND

Ax • *Bread* • *Calypso* • *Doll* • *Fuzz* • *Ghosts Heat* • *Jigsaw* • *Shotgun*

THE MATTHEW HOPE NOVELS

Goldilocks • *Rumpelstiltskin Beauty and the Beast*

OTHER NOVELS

The Sentries • *Guns* • *Where There's Smoke*

BEAUTY
and the
BEAST

by
ED McBAIN

HOLT, RINEHART and WINSTON
NEW YORK

First published in the United States in 1983 by
Holt, Rinehart and Winston,
383 Madison Avenue, New York,
New York 10017.
Published simultaneously in Canada by Holt,
Rinehart and Winston of Canada, Limited.

Library of Congress Cataloging in
Publication Data
McBain, Ed, 1926–
Beauty and the beast.
I. Title.
PS3515.U585B4 1983   813'.54   82–11896
ISBN: 0-03-062198-4

First American Edition

Designer: Amy Hill
Printed in the United States of America
1 3 5 7 9 10 8 6 4 2

ISBN 0-03-062198-4

This is for Mike Peretzian
and Irene Webb.

BEAUTY AND THE BEAST

1

In Calusa, Florida, the beaches change with the seasons. What in May might have been a wide strand of pure white sand will by November become only a narrow strip of shell, seaweed, and twisted driftwood. The hurricane season here is dreaded as much for the damage it will do to the condominiums as for the havoc it might wreak upon the precious Gulf of Mexico shoreline.

There are five keys off Calusa's mainland, but only three of them—Stone Crab, Sabal, and Whisper—run north-south, paralleling the mainland shore. Flamingo Key and Lucy's Key are situated like massive stepping-stones across the bay, connecting the mainland first to Sabal and then to Stone Crab—which had suffered most during autumn's violent storms, precisely because it had the *least* to lose. Stone Crab is the narrowest of Calusa's keys, its once-splendid beaches eroded for decades by water and wind. In September, Stone Crab's two-lane blacktop road had been completely inundated, the bay on one side and the Gulf on the other joining over it to prevent passage by anything but a dinghy.

Sabal Beach suffered least—perhaps because there *is* a God, after all. It was on Sabal that the law enforcement officers of the City of Calusa looked the other way when it came to so-called nude bathing. Well, not *quite* the other way. The women on Sabal were permitted to splash in the water or romp on the beach topless. But let one genital area, male or female, be exposed for the barest fraction of an instant, and suddenly a white police car with a blue City of Calusa seal on its side would magically appear on the beach's access road, and a uniformed minion of the law would trudge solemnly across the sand, head ducked, eyes studying the terrain (but *not* the offending pubic patch) to make an immediate arrest while citing an ordinance that went all the way back to 1913, when the city was first incorporated.

My partner Frank is a transplanted New Yorker who stubbornly insists that the police interpretation of this particular ordinance is merely another indication of Calusa's lack of true sophistication. Nudity is nudity, Frank maintains, be it partial or otherwise. Calusa would like to consider itself sophisticated enough to allow beachgoers to enjoy the sun *au naturel*, Frank says, but at the same time the city fathers feel they must appease all those Puritanical citizens who migrated south from such unimaginably unenlightened places as Ohio, Indiana, and Illinois. Hence the compromise, according to my Big Apple partner Frank Summerville. I don't think Frank even knows where Ohio, Indiana, or Illinois *are*. Somewhere up there. Somewhere to the left of New York. He knows, of course, that I myself am originally from Illinois—a native, in fact, of that incredibly unsophisticated and unbelievably dull small town called Chicago. Perhaps that is why I am gauche enough to appreciate the sight of naked breasts in the sunshine, and to thank God for small favors. Frank and I are both lawyers. So is Dale O'Brien.

Dale is a woman. That's an understatement. She's a woman with a scalpel-sharp mind that has reduced to whimpering incoherency the bravest of unfriendly witnesses in many a Calusa courthouse. Moreover, she's an extraordinarily beautiful woman, five feet nine inches tall, with red hair (she prefers to call it auburn), glade green eyes, and a fair skin that, contrary to old wives' tales, stubbornly refuses to turn lobster red in the sun but instead tans graciously and gorgeously. I had known her since January, when we'd met professionally. Our relationship had survived the seasonal onslaught of the northern snowbirds, their departure early in May, the oppressive heat and humidity of Calusa's summer months, and the torrential autumn rains that had all but washed away what remained of Stone Crab's beaches, but had miraculously spared Sabal's. We had spent last night together in my rented house on the mainland, had awakened at noon, and had gone to lunch together at a new restaurant called (prophetically, we both agreed) Custer's Last Stand, doomed to close before the end of the month if the runny eggs Benedict were any measure of success. Now, in bright mid-November sunshine, we strolled along North Sabal, grateful for the capricious whims of hurricane Gloria, grateful too for a glorious Saturday that was somewhat unusual for this time of year.

Dale was wearing a green bikini a shade darker than her magnificent eyes, which were shielded from the sun now by oversized prescription glasses. I was wearing white cutoffs; I had no intention of going in the water even though the air temperature was still quite warm for November, sixty-two that morning (or seventeen Celsius, as the television forecaster had insisted on informing us) and the temperature of the Gulf water was only two degrees higher than that. I had lived in Calusa long enough to begin thinking like one of the natives: autumn came on September 21, and only the snowbirds were crazy enough to go in the water after that.

"I'm a sissy, is what it is," Dale said.

"No, you're very brave," I said.

"Matthew, please. If I had a single ounce of courage in my body, I'd take off my top."

"It has nothing to do with courage," I said.

"Then what? Never mind, don't tell me. I'm going to do it."

"So do it."

"I will. Just give me a minute."

"Take all the time you need."

"A minute is all I need."

"Okay, fine."

"I'm really going to do it, Matthew."

"I know you are."

"You don't believe me, but I am."

"I believe you."

"No, you don't."

"I do. Believe me, I believe you."

"You'll see."

"*Everyone'll* see."

"Now you're scaring me again."

"Sorry," I said.

We were walking close to the shoreline, the better to avoid dog shit; in Calusa, the ordinance against dogs on public beaches is somewhat less stringently enforced than the one against total nudity. Everywhere around us there were bounding, panting, untethered dogs: Labrador retrievers and German shepherds, dachshunds and poodles, huskies and goldens, Scotties and spitzes, bassets and beagles, Dobermans and Chihuahuas, mongrels of every persuasion—a veritable veterinarian registry of canine diversity. And everywhere around us, too, there were naked breasts: breasts shaped like apples and breasts shaped like pears, breasts the size of grapefruits and breasts the size of plums, breasts the color of eggplants and breasts the color of sweet young corn, breasts as firm as pomegranates and breasts as wrinkled as prunes, breasts with nipples like cocoa beans and breasts with nipples like cherries—a veritable vegetarian feast of mammillary proportions.

"If *she* can do it, *I* can do it," Dale whispered.

She was referring to a woman who came splashing topless out of the water, wearing only bright red bikini panties that struggled valiantly to cover her truly enormous watermelon belly and wide canteloupe buttocks. Her breasts (to abandon the greengrocer metaphor) were dun-colored dugs that hung halfway to her waist and flapped unabashedly in the sunshine. As she collapsed on a blanket some three feet from where the waves were nudging the shore, she clasped both prized possessions in her hands as though delighted she hadn't lost them in the ocean.

"I'll do it," Dale said.

"So do it."

"I will."

She was actually reaching behind her to untie the straps of her bikini top, when something stopped her. I could not see her eyes, hidden as they were behind the dark lenses of the sunglasses, but she was unmistakably looking up the beach, her attention caught by something there, her hands still behind her back, her arms bent at the elbows, frozen, like the wings of an elegant water bird poised for imminent flight. I followed her hidden gaze and saw the most spectacularly beautiful woman I'd ever seen in my life.

I thought at first that she was entirely nude.

And then I realized that the triangular black patch below her waist was not a pubic echo of the long black hair that trailed to her shoulders but was instead the minuscule bottom half of a string bikini. She could not have been more than twenty-two or twenty-three years old, easily as tall as Dale, and so voluptuously curvaceous that by comparison Dale (a beautifully proportioned woman in her own right) seemed almost angular. On a beach populated with women displaying bodies tanned to various degrees of bronzed perfection, the woman who approached us appeared carved of alabaster, pale white exquisite face framed by ebony cascades of hair, the flesh of her naked breasts almost translucent, lustrous in the hot rays of the sun, wide hips flaring above the restraining strings of the bikini patch, a shimmering mirage in black-and-white that came closer and closer, pale gray eyes in that incredibly lovely face, the scent of mimosa as she passed and was gone.

"There oughta be a law," Dale said.

The woman we'd seen on the beach came to my office on Monday morning at a quarter past ten. She was wearing tight-fitting blue jeans, a white T-shirt, sandals, and sunglasses. Her arms, where they showed below the short sleeves of the shirt, were covered with black-and-blue marks. The bridge of her delicate nose was plastered with adhesive tape. When she took off the glasses, I saw that both her eyes were discolored, one of them puffed almost entirely shut. Her lips were swollen and bruised. As she parted them to speak, I saw empty gaps where once there had been teeth.

"My name is Michelle Harper," she said. "You must forgive me, please, my English."

Her English was unmistakably tinged with a French accent, her voice low, rather huskier than one might have expected from a woman so young.

"You were recommend," she said, "by Sally Owen."

I nodded.

"You made for her a divorce," she said.

"Yes, I remember."

"She says to me you will know what to do."

"What is it you want me to do?"

"I want to have arrest my husband."

I pulled a lined yellow pad in front of me. I picked up a pencil. "What's his name?" I asked.

"George Harper."

"H-a-r-p-e-r?"

"*Oui. Mais le 'George,' il est sans . . . pardòn.* The 'George', it is without an *S,* he is *américain.*"

"George Harper."

"*Oui, exactement.*"

"Why do you want him arrested?"

"For what he has do to me. *Il a* . . . he has broke my nose, he has knock from my mouth three teeth . . . *dents?* Teeth?"

"Yes, teeth. When did this happen, Mrs. Harper?"

"Last night. *Regardez,*" she said, and suddenly pulled her T-shirt up over her breasts. She wasn't wearing a bra. The breasts I'd seen naked and unblemished on the beach Saturday were covered now with brutal black-and-blue marks. "He do this to me," she said, and lowered the shirt.

"Did you call the police?"

"When he is leave, do you mean?"

"What time was that?"

"Two o'clock."

"Two o'clock in the *morning*?"

"*Oui*. I did not call the police, I was afraid he would come back, I did not know what to do. So after I have my breakfast, I go to see Sally."

"What time was that?"

"Nine o'clock. I don't know what to do, *vous comprenez*? She says to me I must have a lawyer. She says George is gone, you know, so I do not have the proof . . . proof?"

"Yes, proof."

"*Oui*, that he is the one who does this to me. She says I must first see a lawyer."

"Well," I said, "Sally may be a good beautician, but she's not a very good lawyer. You should have called the police at once. But it's not too late, don't worry. I'm not a criminal lawyer, you understand . . ."

"*Oui*, but Sally says to me . . ."

"And in any event, this isn't something that requires one, not for *you*, anyway. If what you tell me is true, your *husband's* the one who's going to need . . ."

"Oh, it is true, *bien sûr*."

"I have no reason to doubt you."

I was reaching to the bookcase behind me for the index to the four-volume *Florida Statutes*, known familiarly down here as the F.S. As Michelle watched, I thumbed through the pages, searching out first Assault and then Battery and then Spouse Abuse, jotting onto the lined yellow pad the related volumes and chapter numbers. I read to her first from Section 901.15.

" 'A peace officer may arrest a person without a warrant,' " I said, " 'when the officer has probable cause to believe that the person has committed a battery upon the person's spouse and the officer finds evidence of bodily harm . . .' " I looked up. "We certainly have evidence of that. And at least a hundred witnesses can testify you didn't look this way Saturday."

"Pardon?" she said.

"On North Sabal."

"Ah, oui," she said.

"So we've got cause for arrest without warrant, and we'll go to the police as soon as I see what . . ." I was thumbing back to Section 784.03, which defined Battery. I read the brief description silently, and then looked up and quoted it to her. " 'A person commits battery if he (a) Actually and intentionally touches or strikes another person against the will of the other . . .' "

"Yes, he has do this."

" 'Or (b) Intentionally causes bodily harm to an individual.' " I looked up again. "Battery's a misdemeanor, let me see what he can get for that."

"Get for that?"

"The punishment."

"Ah, oui."

I flipped the pages back to Section 775.082, which defined the punishment for a misdemeanor of the first degree. "Here it is," I said. "Definite term of imprisonment not exceeding one year."

"Only one year? For what he does to me?"

"Let's see what we've got under Assault," I said, and thumbed forward again to Section 784.011. I read it silently, and then quoted it to her. " 'An assault is an intentional, unlawful threat by word or act to do violence to the person of another . . .' "

"Yes, he has made this threaten."

" 'Coupled with an apparent ability to do so . . .' "

"He is very strong, George."

" 'And doing some act which creates a well-founded fear in such other person that such violence is imminent.' "

"He is a *monstre,*" she said. *"Un monstre véritable."*

"In any case," I said, "it's only a second-degree misdemeanor. If he's convicted on *both* charges, the assault would add only sixty days to his sentence."

"And when he is out from the jail? When the year goes by? And the sixty days? He will *kill* me then, no?"

"Well . . . let's get him arrested first, okay? And let's make sure he can't hurt you again after they set bail for him."

"What is this, this bail?"

"After he's charged, the judge can set him free until trial . . ."

"*Free?*"

"Yes, if he puts up the amount of money the court in its own discretion decides upon. As assurance that he'll appear for trial. It's called 'bail.' I'm sure you have this in France."

"In France, we do not have these men who do these things," she said.

I remembered that France was the land of the Marquis de Sade, but I was gracious enough not to mention it. "Come on," I said, "we've got work to do."

The police station in Calusa is known as the Public Safety Building. According to my partner Frank, this is another of the city's attempts to lend respectability to everything under the sun. A euphemism, plain and simple. Frank insists that a spade should be called a spade, and that calling a police station a public safety building is like calling a garbage man a sanitation engineer.

In any case, that's what it's called, the Public Safety Building, the words lettered discreetly in white on the low wall outside. Less conspicuously lettered to the right of the brown metal entrance doors, and partially obscured by pittosporum bushes (as though to prove my partner's theory) are the words *Police Department*. The building itself is constructed of varying shades of tan brick, its architecturally severe face broken only by narrow windows resembling rifle slits in an armory wall. This is not unusual for Calusa, where the summer months are torrid and large windows produce only heat and glare.

At the main desk, Michelle filed a complaint charging that

her husband, George N. Harper, residing with her at 1124 Wingdale Way had on Sunday, November 15, at 11:45 P.M., committed upon her person assault and battery in the following manner: he broke her nose, he blackened both her eyes, he split her lip, he knocked three teeth from her mouth, and he bruised her arms, legs, and breasts. The officer who took the complaint told us that they would start looking for her husband at once, and would inform us if and when he was apprehended.

We left the police station ten minutes later, driving back to the office where Michelle had left her car—a Volkswagen Beetle of uncertain vintage—in the parking lot. Before she got out of my car, she said, "*Merci, monsieur, vous êtes très gentil.*" I assured her that everything would be all right, and that it would only be a matter of time before the police picked up her husband and held him to account for what he had done. When she asked me what would happen if they set him free on bail, I told her we would file a petition for an order restraining an abusive spouse, which could be granted when a divorce action was pending or if criminal charges had been filed. I promised I would call her the moment I had any word from the police, and in any event early in the morning, if only to see how she was.

I never got a chance to call her.

Detective Morris Bloom called me first, at home, at seven o'clock on Tuesday morning, to say that a woman identified as Michelle Harper had been found dead on the Whisper Key beach, some thirty yards from the pavilion there. Her hands and legs had been bound with wire hangers, and she had apparently been burned to death.

2

I had never before now been inside a morgue.

In the movies, an attendant dressed entirely in white rolls out a drawer and a relative of the deceased looks down at the body while the attendant gently pulls back the sheet covering the face, and then the relative sobbingly makes identification, and the attendant rolls the drawer back in, and that's that. In the movies, that is a morgue. In real life, a morgue is a handful of medical examiners in blood-stained green surgical gowns, sawing open skulls, or studying the contents of a stomach removed from a corpse; a morgue is dead meat on cold steel surgical tables with blood running down narrow troughs into a basin at the end; a morgue is total exposure, the human being reduced at last to a beast of the field, three pounds of brain and twelve ounces of heart; a morgue is the permeating stench of decomposing flesh, a faintly sweet putrescent aroma that seemed to invade not only my nostrils but every pore of my body.

Michelle Harper had struggled mightily against the wire

hangers binding her hands and feet and the flames that had consumed her. It would seem contradictory to use the word *frozen* in describing the posture of a body burned to death, but frozen she was, her large frame contorted and stiffened into a position one would have thought the human body incapable of achieving. She had died in anguish; her body expressed that anguish more completely than any autopsy report would ever reveal.

"Found an empty five-gallon gasoline can maybe ten feet away from her," Bloom said. "We've got it at the lab now, see maybe we can find some latents on it. Whoever did this must've doused her real good."

Morrie Bloom was six feet three inches tall, and now that he'd abandoned his diet, he had to weigh at least 230, a heavyset man with the oversized knuckles of a street fighter, a fox face with a nose that had been broken more than once, shaggy black eyebrows, and dark brown eyes that almost always seemed on the imminent edge of tears, a bad failing for a cop.

"Are you sure it's her?" I asked.

"Found her clothes and her handbag in the sand, wallet and driver's license in it. That means she went out there under her own steam. Lady doesn't take her bag with her if she's being dragged someplace. We're still looking for the husband, this George N. Harper. I understand you were in yesterday to file a complaint. We can't find hide or hair of him. Do you know what the N stands for? Did she happen to mention it?"

"No. Why? Is it important?"

"I'm just curious," Bloom said, and shrugged. "I can't think of many men's names beginning with an N. Norman? Nathan? Can you think of any? Beginning with an N?"

"Nelson," I said.

"Yeah, Nelson, that's right," Bloom said.

I could not believe we were having this conversation here in this place with the charred and grotesquely contorted body of Michelle Harper on a steel table before us, and open cadavers everywhere around us, and the stench of death in my nostrils and in my throat.

"And Neil, I guess," Bloom said.

"Yes, Neil."

"Anyway," Bloom said, "I sure as hell would like to find him. From what I read in the complaint . . ."

"Do we have to talk in here?" I asked.

"What? Oh, you mean the stink. I'm used to it, I guess. I spend a lot of time in morgues, occupational hazard, huh? When I was just starting as a detective, out on Long Island, I used to wash my hands a lot. I'd get back from the morgue, I'd wash my hands ten, twelve times, trying to get the stink off. You'll see, Matthew, you'll wash your hands a lot today. Come on, let's go outside."

We sat on a low white wall outside the hospital. The sunshine was bright, the air was balmy—but the stench lingered.

"I must be coming down with a cold," Bloom said, reaching for a handkerchief in his back pocket. He blew his nose, blew it again, and then said, "I moved to Florida because you're not supposed to get colds down here. I catch more colds down here than I ever did up north. Goes to show." He put the handkerchief back in his pocket. "I called you because you were in the office with her yesterday . . ."

"That's right."

"To file the complaint."

"Yes," I said, nodding.

"So she was one of your clients, am I right?"

"After yesterday morning, yes."

"But not before then?"

"No."

"First time you ever saw her was yesterday morning?"

"Yes. Well, no. I'd seen her on the beach Saturday."

"Oh? Did you talk about her problem then?"

"No, no. I didn't even know who she was. She was just walking by on the beach."

"But you remembered her when she came in yesterday, is that it?"

"Yes. She was a very beautiful woman, Morrie."

"Yeah," he said, and shook his head. "That's the shit of it, ain't it? From what I get from the complaint, she was beaten up real bad. So now she turns up on the beach, burned to death. Does that seem like a coincidence to you?"

"No."

"Me neither. Which is why I'm anxious to find this wonderful husband of hers. Guy disappears from the face of the earth, there's got to be a good reason, am I right?"

"Yes."

"Murder's a very good reason," Bloom said. He was thoughtful for a moment. Then he said, "What I'm going to do, Matthew, when I release this to the papers and the radio and television stations, I'm not going to mention that Sunday-night beating, okay? I'd appreciate it if you kept it quiet, too. *Whoever* killed her—the husband or whoever—he won't know anything about the beating unless he's the one who did it. And we don't want him working up an alibi because *he* knows *we* know, okay? For the murder, he'll have an alibi. But for the beating, maybe not—unless we tip him off. So let's keep it our little secret, okay? Not a breath about that beating Sunday night."

"Okay," I said.

"Good," he said.

He did not call me again until four that afternoon, while I was in conference with my partner Frank. There are people who say that Frank and I look alike. These are undoubtedly the same people who insist that married couples begin looking like twins after they've been together for any substantial period of time. I do not believe I look at all like my former wife, to whom I'd been married for fourteen years, nor do I believe there is the slightest bit of resemblance between Frank and me.

I'm an even six feet tall, and I weigh 190 pounds. Frank is two and a half inches shorter than I am, and 30 pounds lighter. True enough, we both have dark hair and brown eyes, but Frank's face is rounder than mine. Frank maintains that there are only two types of faces in the entire world—pig faces and fox faces. He classifies himself as a pig face and me as a fox face. The designations have nothing to do with character or personality; they are only intended to be descriptive. But it seemed to me that Frank was behaving in a decidedly pigheaded way that afternoon as he paced the office, telling me that it was one thing to take a young lady to the police to file a complaint, but it was quite *another* matter to get involved in a homicide case, which Frank felt I was doing with alarming frequency these days.

"Why did Bloom find it necessary to call *you* this morning?" he asked, pacing. "Why did he want *you* to see the body? We handle a routine matter for somebody who walks in off the street, and the next thing I know you're at Calusa General looking at a corpse!"

"Do you think I *wanted* to look at a corpse?"

"Then why'd you *go* look at it?"

"Because Michelle Harper was a client . . ."

"Some *client*," Frank said, rolling his eyes. "Two more clients like Michelle Harper, and we can retire. Popular belief to the contrary, Matthew, this is a *business* we're trying to run here, and your time is very valuable. If you choose to fritter it away by running around town looking at dead . . ."

That was when Cynthia buzzed from outside.

Cynthia Huellen is a native Floridian with long blond hair and a glorious tan that she works at almost fanatically; never a weekend goes by that does not find Cynthia on a beach or a boat. She is easily the most beautiful person in the law offices of Summerville and Hope, twenty-five years old, and employed by us as a receptionist. Frank and I keep telling her to quit the job and go to law school instead. She already has a B.A. from the University of South Florida, and we would take her into the firm the minute she passed her bar exams. But each time we raise the possibility, Cynthia grins and says she doesn't want the hassle of school again. She is one of the nicest young people I know, and she is blessed besides with a keen mind, an even-tempered disposition, and a fine sense of humor. She told me now that Detective Morris Bloom was on six. I pressed the button in the base of the phone and said, "Hello, Morrie."

"Matthew, hi," he said. "We got him."

"Good," I said, and glanced across the room. Frank had begun scowling the moment he heard me mention Bloom's name. He stood now with his hands on his hips, staring at me. "Where'd you find him?"

"He walked right in off the street. Said he'd been in Miami for a few days, heard the news on the radio while driving back. I'm just about to ask him some questions here, but there's a slight problem."

"What's the problem?"

"He doesn't have an attorney, and he wants one here during the Q and A. I told him we could have one appointed for him, but he thinks there might be something fishy about that. So I was wondering . . . if you have the time . . . maybe you could come down and talk to him, maybe he'd find you acceptable. Just for the Q and A, Matthew. What you do later, if we charge him with anything, is entirely your own business. What do you say?"

"When did you want me?"

"Soon as you can get here."

I looked at Frank again.

"Give me ten minutes," I said.

"Good, see you," Bloom said, and hung up.

I put the receiver back on the cradle. Frank was still staring and scowling at me.

"What'd he want?" he asked.

"They've got George Harper. Morrie asked me to represent him during the Q and A."

"Shit," Frank said.

It had never occurred to me that George N. Harper might be a black man. Sally Owen, the woman for whom our firm had handled a divorce a year ago, the woman Michelle had called for advice before coming to see me, was black—but even in Calusa, there are white people who have black friends. Nor had Michelle's address, 1124 Wingdale Way, triggered any immediate insights. Wingdale Way was in the heart of the city's black section, still called the "colored" section by many of the older white residents here, and referred to as "New Town" by Calusa's polite society. I simply never made a connection.

I have always felt uncomfortable with the descriptive label blacks have chosen for themselves. I suppose it is no less accurate than the "white" label, or the "yellow" label, or the "red" label, but I had never before that Tuesday afternoon met any so-called black man who was anything but one or another shade of brown. George N. Harper was the color of coal, the color of midnight, the color of mourning. George N. Harper was the blackest black man I had ever seen in my life. And the biggest. And the ugliest.

He was pacing the floor of the captain's office at the Public Safety Building when I opened the door and entered. He turned to face me at once, a startled hulk of a man some six feet four inches tall and weighing 350 pounds if he weighed an ounce. He was wearing blue overalls with shoulder straps, a blue denim shirt, and high-topped brown leather workman's shoes. He had huge shoulders and a barrel chest, a pockmarked face with flaring nostrils and thick purple lips, an Afro haircut and rheumy brown eyes that peered at me from beneath a wide brow, huge hands clenching as he turned, Neanderthal surprised.

"Mr. Harper?" I said.

"You the lawyer?" he said.

"I'm Matthew Hope," I said, and extended my hand. He did not take it.

"Whut I need a lawyer for?" he said. His eyes kept searching my face.

"Mr. Bloom said you'd requested . . ."

"I dinn kill her."

"Nobody says you did."

"Then why I need a lawyer?"

"You're entitled to one if you want one. Didn't Mr. Bloom explain your rights to you?"

"Yeah."

"You can have a lawyer if you want one. Or you can refuse to answer questions entirely, if that's your choice. It's up to you."

"You a cop lawyer?"

"I don't know what you mean."

"You one of them lawyers they said they could get for me?"

"No, I wasn't appointed."

"You think I need a lawyer here?"

"That's entirely up to you. If you had anything to do with your wife's murder . . ."

"I didn't."

"Are you sure about that?"

"I'm positive."

"Because if you did . . ."

"I'm telling you I didn't."

"You realize that anything you say to the police can be used later in evidence, don't you? If you're lying to me, Mr. Harper, I'd advise you to remain silent, I'd advise you not to answer any of their questions."

"I ain't lyin. I dinn kill her."

"You're a hundred percent sure of that?"

"A hunnerd percent."

"So what do you want to do?"

"If I *doan* answer them, they goan think I killed her."

"Not necessarily. I'll make it clear on the record that you claim to be innocent of the crime and are answering questions of your own free will. If that's what you want. They're waiting, what do you say?"

"Yeah, let's do that," Harper said.

The interrogation (or the "interview" as it is euphemistically called in genteel Calusa) was held in Bloom's office, adjacent to the captain's. In addition to Bloom, Harper, and myself, there was a man sitting behind a Sony tape recorder. Harper looked at the instrument, and then looked at Bloom and asked, "You gonna tape this?"

"Yes, sir," Bloom said.

"Ev'ythin I say?"

"Everything. Has your attorney informed you that this may possibly be used as evidence?"

"Yeah, he tole me. Is it okay to have them tape it?" he asked me.

"If you choose to answer their questions, there has to be a record of what you say."

"Well, I guess it's okay," Harper said.

The man sitting behind the recorder pressed both the Play and Record buttons. He said a few words into the mike, testing, played them back, and then rewound the tape and pressed the buttons again. Bloom read Miranda-Escobedo, as required by law, and elicited from Harper the responses that made clear he had been informed of his rights, understood what they were, and was willing to answer the questions about to be put to him.

"Detective Bloom," I said, "I want it made clear on the record that my client denies any knowledge of the murder of his wife, and is answering your questions here voluntarily and in a spirit of cooperation."

"It's on the record," Bloom said, and the interrogation began. "Mr. Harper, when did you last see your wife alive?"

"Saturday night."

"What time Saturday night?"

"Long about two."

"A.M.?"

"Yessir."

"Then that would've been Sunday morning."

"Felt like Saturday night."

"Where was this?"

"Home."

"Can you give me the address, please?"

"1124 Wingdale."

"And that's the last time you saw her alive?"

"Yessir. Juss before I left for Miami."

"At two in the morning?"

"Yessir."

"Isn't that an odd time to be traveling?"

"Nossir. Wanted to get an early start."

"Why'd you go to Miami?"

"Wanted t'see my mama. Also to drop off a load."

"A load of what?"

"Junk. I'm in the junk business. I buys an' sells junk."

"And you went to Miami . . ."

"To sell some junk. To a man I does business with down there."

"What's his name?"

"Lloyd Davis. Turns out it was a wasted trip, though."

"What do you mean?"

"Lloyd wun't there. His wife tole me he was out with the reserve that weekend. He got to put in so much time with them, y'know. The army reserve. I was in the army with Lloyd overseas. Thass how we got to know each other."

"But he wasn't there when you got there Sunday."

"Nossir, he was not. My mama wun't there neither. Neighbor tole me she'd gone up t'Georgia, t'see my sister."

"What time was all this, Mr. Harper?"

"Oh, early in the mornin sometime. Took me six hours or so to get down there, musta been, oh, I'd say, eight, nine o'clock sometime. Somewheres in there."

"So what did you do when you discovered neither Mr. Davis nor your mother were in Miami?"

"Went to have some breakfuss."

"Where?"

"I don't recollect the name of the place. Little place off the road there someplace."

"Did you eat alone?"

"Yessir."

"Then what?"

"Called another ole army buddy of mine. He's a recruitin sergeant there in Miami."

"What's *his* name?"

"Ronnie Palmer."

"You phoned him . . ."

"From the place where I had breakfuss."

"What'd you talk about?"

"Oh, juss how are you, how's things, like that."

"Then what?"

"I went up to Pompano."

"Why?"

"Figgered I was up that way, might as well do some sight-seein. It's ony juss outside of Lauderdale, y'know."

"How long were you in Pompano?"

"Oh, juss long enough to look aroun a little."

"Then what?"

"Kept on drivin north to Vero Beach."

"Why'd you go *there?*"

"Still sightseein."

"All the way up to Vero Beach?"

"Ain't too far."

"Something like a hundred miles north of Pompano, isn't it?"

"That ain't so far."

"How long did you stay there?"

"Oh, coupla hours, no more'n that."

"Then what?"

"Drove back down to Miami."

"And what'd you do there?"

"Got me a bite to eat, then went to the beach. T'get some sleep. Woulda gone to my mama's house, but she was away, and I dinn have a key."

"So you slept on the beach."

"Yessir."

"In Miami."

"Miami Beach, yessir."

"Were you on the beach at eleven forty-five P.M.?"

"Slept on the beach all night, yessir."

"Were you there at eleven forty-five P.M.?"

"Morrie," I said, "I think he's answered the question."

"I'd like to pinpoint the time, Matthew, if that's all right with you," Bloom said.

"Mr. Harper, would you have any objection . . . ?"

"None a'tall. I was on the beach at eleven forty-five P.M., yessir. All night. Juss like I said I was."

"Miami Beach, is that right?" Bloom asked.

"Yessir, Miami Beach."

"Then you weren't here in Calusa, is that right?"

"Morrie," I said, "he's just *told* you, at *least* four times . . ."

"Okay, okay," Bloom said, and turned again to Harper. "Mr. Harper," he said, "are you aware that on Monday morning your wife filed a complaint with the Calusa Police Department charging that you had physically abused her at eleven forty-five P.M. on Sunday night, November the fifteenth?"

"Whut?" Harper said, and turned away from Bloom to look at me.

"Are you aware of that?" Bloom asked.

"Nossir, I am *not* aware of it," Harper said. "How could I . . . *whut* did you say I'm spose to have done to her?"

"The complaint charged that you broke her nose and . . ."

"Nossir, that complaint is wrong."

"Your wife made the complaint."

"Nossir, she couldn'ta done that. Nossir."

"Mr. Harper, when did you leave Miami?"

"This mornin."

"What time this morning?"

" 'Bout ten o'clock, musta been."

"And you came directly here to the police station when you got back to Calusa, is that right?"

"Directly."

"Why didn't you come back home yesterday? Your business partner was away . . ."

"Lloyd ain't my partner. He's juss an ole army buddy I does business with, thass all."

"But he was away."

"Thass right."

"And so was your mother."

"Thass right."

"So why'd you stay in Miami? Why didn't you just turn around and come back yesterday morning?"

"I thought Lloyd might come back."

"*Did* he come back?"

"Nossir."

"So why'd you stay there?"

"Thought he might."

"Uh-huh. How long have you been married, Mr. Harper?"

"Woulda been two years come nex' June."

"Your wife was a foreigner . . ."

"Yessir."

"Where'd you meet her?"

"In Bonn, Germany. I was stationed with the military police in Bonn."

"When was this?"

"When I met her, you mean?"

"Yes."

"Two years ago this month. Met her in November, married her the followin June."

"Were you married in Germany?"

"Nossir, right here in Calusa."

"What kind of a marriage would you say it was?" Bloom asked.

"I loved her t'death," Harper said, and suddenly buried his face in his hands and began crying. In the stillness of the office the only sound was the whirr of the tape as it relentlessly recorded Harper's grief. He sat in a hardbacked chair, dwarfing it, his wide shoulders shaking, the sobs coming up out of his barrel chest, his huge hands covering his pockmarked face, sobbing uncontrollably. Bloom waited. It seemed that Harper would never stop crying. His sobs reverberated through that empty room like the moans of a wounded animal deep in a secret jungle glade where nothing else might hurt it and only the moon bore witness. And then, at last, the sobbing stopped, and he reached into his back pocket and took out a soiled handkerchief and dried his eyes, and then blew his nose and sat very still in the chair, sniffing, his shoulders slumped, all life and spirit seemingly drained from that enormous body.

"Mr. Harper," Bloom said gently, "you say you were in Miami on Sunday morning, and then you went up to Pompano and Vero Beach, and then came back down to Miami later in the day, is that right?"

"Yessir." His head was still lowered, he seemed intent on studying his high-topped workman's shoes.

"Did anyone see you while you were in any of those places?"

"Lots of people seen me."

"Anyone who might be able to say with certainty that you were actually *where* you were when you *say* you were?"

"Juss Lloyd's wife, an' the lady lives nex' door to my mama."

"But that was on Sunday morning."

"Yessir."

"How about Sunday night?"

"No, I dinn see nobody I know Sunday night."

"Or Monday?"

"Nobody."

"No one at all?"

"Nossir."

"Mr. Harper, are you sure you weren't here in *Calusa* on Sunday night? Are you sure you didn't drive back here to . . . ?"

"I'll have to object to that, Morrie. You've got his answer to that already. He was in Miami on Sunday night, he's already told you that."

"Then how do you account for the complaint his wife filed on Monday morning?"

"Are you questioning me, *too*, Morrie? If so, you'd better read me my rights."

Bloom sighed.

"Mr. Harper," he said, "did you kill your wife Michelle Benois Harper?"

"Nossir, I did not," Harper said.

"Okay, thank you very much. Is there anything you'd like to add?"

"I dinn kill her," Harper said directly into the microphone.

Dale and I have never exchanged the words *I love you*.

I know that Dale was once passionately in love with an artist she'd met in San Francisco when she was practicing law out there. I also know that she lived with him for two years, and that the parting was painful for her because it came as the result of a sudden recognition that seemed to negate everything they had previously shared. Last January, when we were first getting to know each other, she used to talk about him a lot. She never talks about him now. But neither has she ever told me she loves me.

For my part, I have used those words often and with varying degrees of sincerity. I'm thirty-eight years old, and when I was growing up in Chicago, I had none of the sexual advantages today's young people enjoy. I was seventeen when the sixties were just starting; I missed out on the permissiveness that followed. A goodly amount of my adolescent energy was spent feverishly scheming on how to plunder the treasures inside a laden blouse, each button the equivalent of a Vietcong division guarding the road to Hanoi, how to slide a wily and preferably unsuspected hand along the inside of a thigh and onto those cherished nylon panties beneath a fortress skirt, how to hide from the eyes of a shocked citizenry the erections that bulged the front of my trousers whenever any girl of reasonably modest good looks (and, quite frankly, even some very ugly ones) sashayed into view. I loved legs, I loved breasts, I loved thighs, I loved asses, I loved girls with a passion that was all-pervasive and overwhelming. And on that perilous road to hopeful consummation, I discovered that the words, *I love you*, sometimes worked wonders: "I love you, Harriet, I love you, Jean, I love you, Helene, I love you, Melissa," my fingers frantically working those maliciously obstinate buttons and those diabolical brassiere clasps invented by a mad woman scientist, "I love you, Joyce, I love you, Louise, I love you, Alice, I love you, Roxanne!" Those were the days of garter belts and nylon stockings, soon to give way to panty hose (invented by that same madwoman in her boiling laboratory), and *God*, the delirium of actually *touching* those secret mysterious undergarments, the windows of my father's Olds fogged with the exhalations of singular male intent and determined female resistance, "I love you, Angela, I love you, Shirley, I love you, Ming Toy, I love you, *Anybody!*"

I used the words as cheap currency in a market without buyers.

I later learned, when I met and fell truly in love with Susan—the woman who would later become my wife—that the words I had until then considered the three cheapest words in the English language were indeed the three most expensive in any language. I'm not referring now to the alimony payments I still make to Susan each and every month, $24,000 a year with a built-in cost-of-living increase—but who's counting? I'm referring only to the pain of total exposure, the loss of a private entity to a partnership. We were good partners for a good many years; many divorced men and women tend to discount the happiness they once shared, remembering only the bad times. But perhaps that was the trouble; we became partners and stopped being lovers. And yet, as partners, we made it work for fourteen years, and we did, after all, produce together the light of my life, my darling daughter Joanna, long-legged and beautiful and mightily resembling her mother—Joanna whom I love to death but whom I only get to see every other weekend and for half the duration of her school vacations.

When a wife becomes a partner and nothing more than that, and when another woman suddenly materializes as an apparition from a bygone time of hand-in-hand moonlit walks along Lake Shore Drive, reviving memories of all that steamy adolescent sex in the front and back seats of automobiles, when "love" once again enters a man's life with all the heart-lurching suddenness of a lightning flash at midnight, well then, the partnership goes down the drain, the tweed and corduroy you've been cutting for that Seventh Avenue manufacturer surrenders to the silken secret of whispered liaisons, and the marriage dissolves, the marriage ends—"I love you, Aggie," for such was her name, Agatha Hemmings, now herself divorced and living in Tampa, so much for that ozone-stinking lightning bolt that left behind it nothing but a withered landscape.

So our wariness—Dale's and my own—with the words *I love you* is perhaps understandable. Or perhaps we have no need for saying them out loud. If what we share together isn't "love" (whatever the hell *that* may be), it is at least a reasonable facsimile. We are enormously glad to see each other. We chatter like magpies when we're together, not only about the profession we happen to share, but about everything under the sun—and there is a lot of sun in Calusa, Florida. Moreover, I find it more and more difficult to keep my hands off her. I want to touch her all the time. I find it almost impossible to be anywhere with her—a public place and most certainly a private one—without longing for some sort of physical contact. I will sometimes reach across a restaurant table to brush a strand of auburn hair away from her cheek. I will touch her fingernails, I will touch her arm, I will cop a covert feel as I am helping her into her coat, I seem to absorb from her flesh the very essence of her, and the simple knowledge that she is still and simply *there*. My partner Frank says that the world is divided into Touchers and Tapdancers; Frank tends to make sweeping generalizations about everything. I know only that never in my life (discounting those delirious adolescent forays when I would have touched even an iguana if the contact served to still the longings of that raging tumescent creature in my pants) had I been a particularly demonstrative person. My need to touch Dale remains bewildering to me.

Dale insists it's because of the sunrise-sunset coloration of her hair; the hair on her head is a lovely burnished shade of red, the hair between her legs is blond. Since I am privy to her secret, she says, since I know that her "golden snatch," as she sometimes calls it, had in her own tumultuous adolesence inflamed more than one energetic swain to heights of unprecedented passion by its very contradictory and surprising existence—why naturally, then, I burn with desire to touch not the passive flesh of cheek or elbow but rather the responsive slit buried behind those gilded portals, the touching here and there *above* serving as a sort of out-of-town tryout for a Broadway opening *below*, so to speak. Dale is thirty-two years old, a true child of the sixties, and is often more candid about matters sexual than the Tapdancers of the world are. (Frank defines a Tapdancer as anyone who glides and clicks away from true contact with another person.)

Lying in bed with Dale that night, I told her all about the encounter the day before with Michelle Harper and her subsequent murder (which she'd read about in the Calusa *Journal*, without connecting the story to the beautiful woman we'd seen on the beach Saturday) and the Q and A with her husband, and the fact that he had no real alibi for where he might have been when Michelle was first being beaten and next being killed. Dale listened—I love the way she listens, those magnificent green eyes intent on my face—and then rolled over naked to light a cigarette, nodding, absorbing what I was telling her, weighing it with the keen mind of a lawyer searching for a case that could possibly be made in Harper's favor. She blew out a stream of smoke (I realized all at once that she was smoking pot) and then said, "If he *really* did it, you'd think he'd have a ready . . ." and the telephone rang.

I have always regretted the moment of insanity that prompted me to give Morrie Bloom the telephone number at Dale's house on Whisper Key. She answered the phone now, listened for a moment, said, "For you, Matthew," handed me the receiver, and then sat cross-legged on the bed, closing her eyes and puffing on the joint.

"Hello?" I said.

"Matthew, it's Morrie. Sorry to disturb you so late at night."

"No, that's okay," I said, and Dale pulled a face.

"Few things I think you ought to know," he said. "You remember I was telling you about that empty five-gallon can we found on the beach?"

"Yes?"

"Well, we checked with the gas station where Harper brings in his truck, and also where the woman used to get her Volks serviced, it's right around the corner from where they live. We figured it would be the most likely place, and we got lucky. Place called A&M Exxon on Wingdale and Pine. Anyway the attendant there—black guy named Harry Loomis—filled Harper's gas tank on Saturday morning, around seven, seven-thirty, sometime in there. He *also* sold Harper an empty five-gallon gasoline can. Filled it for him. A red can like the one we found at the scene." Bloom hesitated. "Matthew," he said, "we had him up here looking at the can, he's identified it as the one he sold to Harper on Saturday morning."

"How can anybody tell one red can from anoth—?"

"That's not all of it. I got a call from the lab ten minutes ago—well, let me go back a few steps, okay? You remember that before Harper left the station house this afternoon, he agreed to let us print him, said he had nothing to hide, you remember that, don't you? You were there when the guy downstairs was printing him."

"Yes, I remember."

"Well, we sent those prints over to the lab, where they were working on the latents they lifted from the can, and I got a call from them ten minutes ago. The prints on the can match Harper's. And, Matthew, they were the *only* prints on the can. Harper's and nobody else's."

"Are you calling for my advice, Morrie? Then here it is. Harper first bought that gasoline can . . ."

"And had it filled, Matthew."

"Yes, at seven, seven-thirty Saturday morning. He then went back to the house and was home all day Saturday.

There's nothing to say he didn't leave that can in the garage or wherever *before* he left for Miami at two A.M. *Sunday*. If he left the can home, *anybody* could have found it and used it to . . ."

"His fingerprints are on it, Matthew."

"They'd naturally be on it. If he handled the can . . ."

"What happened to Loomis's prints? The guy who sold him the can, the guy who filled it for him?"

"Are you suggesting that Harper wiped off the attendant's prints, and then committed murder and neglected to wipe off his own? Come on, Morrie."

"People panic, Matthew. I had cases before where the killer left incriminating evidence behind. I had one guy, he strangled this hooker to death while he was fucking her, he was naked when he did it, you know? And he left behind a monogrammed shirt, ran out of there barefoot with only his pants on, left behind a shirt with his initials on it, R.D., I can still remember the initials. So it's not too unusual, Matthew. Even the pros panic. And murder isn't a professional crime unless the mob has it done for them."

"This is all circumstantial, Morrie. A man buys a gasoline can, he has it filled . . ."

"I got a witness who saw them on the beach Monday night, Matthew."

"What witness?"

"A fisherman anchored just offshore. Saw a white woman and a black man struggling on the beach."

"Has he identified Harper?"

"Close enough. Big black guy struggling with a naked white woman."

"But has he specifically identified *Harper*?"

"We're bringing Harper in. I expect identification will be made at that time."

"So why are you calling *me*, Morrie?"

"Because if we get a positive make, we're going to have to charge Harper. I mean, Matthew, I know it isn't the strongest of cases . . ."

"What does the state's attorney think?"

"He thinks if this guy can identify Harper, we've got a case."

"And if he can't?"

"We keep looking. Those prints on the can, the fact that he bought the can two days before the murder was committed, the fact that his wife filed a complaint the day she was killed—that may not be enough for a sure conviction, but it's enough to keep us working. That's if this guy who was out on the water . . ."

"A fisherman, did you say?"

"Yeah. Claims he saw them struggling, heard the guy yelling her name. He didn't pick that out of the air, Matthew. Michelle isn't that common a name."

"No, it isn't. I still don't know why you called me."

"If we get a positive make, the state's attorney will have a whack at him this time, and *this* time we'll be charging him, Matthew. So I thought you might want to represent him during the formal Q and A. This is serious this time, Matthew."

"I'm not a criminal lawyer, Morrie . . ."

"I know you're not."

"But I know damn well what I'd advise him this time. If it's serious this time."

"If that guy identifies him, it's very serious this time."

"Then I'd advise him not to answer any further questions."

"That's what I figured you'd advise him. But shouldn't somebody be here to tell him that?"

"Me, you mean?"

"Well, you, yes, if you want to come down. It's just, this fucking Miranda-Escobedo, the law says we've got to appoint a lawyer if the man requests one, but we don't *have* lawyers just hanging around here at the station house, you know, the law's got a jawbone but no teeth, do you follow me? So since you already know the man, and did such a good job this afternoon, which by the way I'm sorry I hassled you so much . . ."

"That's okay, Morrie."

"So if you wanted to pick up here where you left off, it might not be a bad idea. For Harper, I mean. 'Cause the way I look at it, he's in bad trouble here, and he's going to need all the help he can get."

"When will you have him there?"

"Pete Kenyon's already on the way to Wingdale. Unless Harper's skipped, he should be back here within . . ."

"Do you think he may have skipped?"

"My guess? No, he'll be there at the house when Pete pulls up. No, I don't think he's skipped."

"So when will you have him downtown?"

"I suppose maybe five minutes, unless he gives Pete trouble." Bloom paused. "Pete didn't go alone, Matthew. I sent two cars with him. If Harper murdered his wife . . ."

"*If*," I said.

"Well, I know, that's what we've got to prove. But if we get that positive I.D., we'll have enough to charge him, and that's what we'll do. Would you like to be here, Matthew?"

"I'd like to be *here*," I said. "I like it *here*, where I am. I like it very much right *here*."

Dale blew me a kiss.

"Well, it's entirely up to you," Bloom said.

"Don't ask him anything until I get there," I said.

"Would I do that?" Bloom said.

"No, but some of those guys in the State's Attorney's Office can be very cute."

"No questions, I promise."

"And you understand, don't you, that I'll advise him to remain silent?"

"Sure. Exactly what I would do." Bloom paused. "So are you coming down?"

"Yes," I said, and sighed.

"Thank you, Matthew," Bloom said, and hung up.

I looked at Dale.

"One of these days," she said dreamily, "I'm going to buy myself a flesh-colored vibrator."

3

Benny Weiss is perhaps the best criminal lawyer in all Calusa. My partner Frank says that this is because Benny himself looks like a criminal. I don't know what criminals are supposed to look like. I once thumbed through a psychological text in which there was a series of photographs, some of which were of schizophrenics, others of normal people like Frank and me. When these photos were shown to real-life schizophrenics who were asked to pick out the ones they preferred, they invariably picked out the pictures of schizophrenics like themselves. I don't know what the test was supposed to prove.

But assuming Frank is correct about Benny looking like a criminal, then perhaps this accounts for the great number of criminals who seek his services when they run afoul of the law. I personally think Benny looks like a cocker spaniel. He is a smallish person—five feet eight inches at the outside, I would guess—slight of build, with a narrow face and soulful brown eyes and unruly brown hair that he rakes with his fingers every three or four minutes. He smokes incessantly. In his office that Wednesday morning at 10:30 A.M., he sat alternately smoking and raking his hair. He looked as if he had not slept much the night before. That was because I'd dragged him out of bed at 11:00 P.M. and asked him to meet me downtown, where a man named Luther Jackson—the fisherman who'd been anchored just off the Whisper Key beach on the night Michelle was murdered—had positively identified George Harper as the man he'd seen struggling with her. The identification had been made from a lineup of six men, all of them black, five of them policemen working for the Calusa P.D. The state's attorney had questioned—or attempted to question—Harper soon after the identification was made. Both Benny and I had advised him to remain silent.

At nine this morning, I had accompanied Harper to court for what is known as a "first appearance hearing," normally held on the morning after an arrest, to request bail for him. Ever since last November, when Florida's Supreme Court had made its new ruling, even a person accused of a capital crime was entitled to bail. The ruling stated that before release on bail could be denied, proof of the crime had to be evident or presumption of the crime had to be great; it was the state's attorney's burden to oppose bail by showing that the evidence he possessed was legally sufficient to obtain a verdict of guilty. The court, in its sole discretion, had the right to grant or deny bail.

The County Court judge presiding over the hearing immediately informed me that I would have to take the matter before a Circuit Court judge who would later have trial jurisdiction. The Circuit Court judge hearing me could have set an impossible bail like half a million dollars, but he chose instead to deny bail completely, citing as his reason (not that he needed any) the particularly heinous nature of the crime. George Harper was taken to the Calusa County jail to await the grand jury's decision as to whether it would indict or dismiss. The grand jury was scheduled to meet on the following Monday, November 23.

"Let me tell you something about the practice of criminal law," Benny said, and dragged on his cigarette. "Criminal law involves guilt or innocence. You may argue that divorce also . . . or is that a touchy subject?"

"It is not a touchy subject," I said.

"In which case, you may argue that divorce—at least in many states of the union—*also* involves guilt or innocence. But a man or a woman seeking a divorce, even if one or the other of them has broken the sacred vows of marriage . . ." (and here Benny, a confirmed bachelor, looked heavenward and smiled) ". . . is in no particular jeopardy, unless one considers onerous alimony a peril."

"One might consider it a peril," I said.

"Even so, however guilty one or the other party in a divorce action may be, neither is facing a prison term *or* death in the electric chair, which is the maximum penalty for first-degree murder in this state, which crime our friend George N. Harper has been charged with. What does the N stand for, do you know?"

"No," I said.

"Now, Matthew," Benny said, stubbing out his cigarette, and raking his right hand through his hair as though trying to remove the nicotine stains from his fingers, "I'm sure you'll recall the Canons of Professional Ethics, which grant to a lawyer the right to undertake a defense *regardless* of his personal opinion as to the guilt or innocence of the accused . . . where did you go to law school?"

"Northwestern," I said.

"Then I'm sure you're familiar with the Canons."

"I'm familiar with them."

"And the professional right to undertake a defense even if you feel the accused is guilty."

"Yes."

"Otherwise, of course, an innocent person might be *denied* a proper defense, and then our entire judicial system would go to hell in a handbasket, and there'd be no more lawyers and no more law in this equitable land of ours. Where law ends, there tyranny begins, quote, unquote. Oliver Wendell Holmes, I believe."

"What are you trying to tell me, Benny?"

He took another cigarette from the package on his desk, struck a match, held the flaming end to the tip, and exhaled an enormous cloud of smoke. As an afterthought, he blew out the match. "Now, Matthew," he said, "if you *do* take on a client in a criminal case, whether or not you believe he's guilty, then you are *bound*—and this is also in the Canons, Matthew—you are *bound* to present, by all fair and honorable means, every defense the law of the land permits, so that no person will be deprived of life or liberty except by due process. I believe that's an exact quote, but I have the Canons here if you'd like to check them."

"I'll take your word for it."

"Thank you."

"What are you saying, Benny?"

"Matthew, I appreciate your getting me out of bed last night, I truly do. I always enjoy going down to the police station at two in the morning . . ."

"It was only eleven."

"It felt like two. But no matter, who needs sleep? I also enjoy listening to those assholes from the State's Attorney's Office, they really do give me great pleasure, Matthew. But, Matthew, whereas the Canons grant me the *right* to defend somebody I believe is guilty, they do not impose upon me the *obligation* to undertake such a defense. I believe George N. Harper is guilty. I have made it a policy over the years never to defend a person I believe is guilty. That's why I'm such a good criminal lawyer. If I defend only the innocent, how can I *help* getting so many acquittals?"

"Benny . . ."

"I've also made it a policy never to defend a person I don't like, even *if* I believe he's innocent. I don't particularly like George N. Harper, don't ask me why. Therefore, ever grateful for the opportunity to get out of bed in the middle of the night and to go downtown without a shave, I must nonetheless decline your offer to represent Mr. Harper in this case."

"Benny, he needs a good lawyer," I said.

"You're a good lawyer, Matthew."

"I know very little about criminal law."

"Then let the public defender handle it."

"I think he's innocent."

"The Public Defender's Office," Benny said dryly, "has also been known to believe in the innocence of an accused party."

"That's not the point. I *know* they've got some very good people up there, and I personally like Dick Jorgenson, but—damn it, Benny, they've got so *many* cases to handle, I'm afraid he'll get lost in the shuffle."

"Then defend him yourself," Benny said simply.

"I wouldn't know where to begin."

"Begin where the state's attorney will begin," Benny said, and stubbed out his cigarette. "He's going to be building a case to prove beyond reasonable doubt that Harper did, in fact, murder his wife. He's going to assemble whatever he can to show Harper had the means, the motive, and the opportunity. I don't know when this thing will come to trial, the docket's jammed right now, it might not be till early next year. So you'll have plenty of time to assemble facts that will show he did *not* have the means, the motive, or the opportunity. If you believe he's innocent, that's what you'll have to show, Matthew. And you'll have to show it convincingly enough to keep your man out of the electric chair."

"I don't know if I can do that."

"Then maybe you don't believe in his innocence strongly enough."

"I think I do, Benny."

"Then take the case. Convince the jury."

"You won't help me?"

"I think he's guilty," Benny said simply, and put another cigarette in his mouth.

There were several very good reasons why I should not have undertaken the defense of George N. Harper.

To begin with, I was *not* a criminal lawyer, and I felt I might be doing him more harm than good. Section 782.04 of the F.S. reads: "The unlawful killing of a human being, when perpetrated from a premeditated design to effect the death of the person killed . . . shall be murder in the first degree and shall constitute a capital felony, punishable as provided in s. 775.02." The section defining the penalty referred to yet another section titled "Findings in Support of Sentence of Death," and listing "aggravating circumstances" as one such supportive finding. Under a subheading that read "Aggravating circumstances shall be limited to the following," there was a list that included "The capital felony was especially heinous, atrocious, or cruel," and lastly, "The capital felony was a homicide and was committed in a cold, calculated, and premeditated manner without any pretense of moral or legal justification."

If the state's attorney could prove that Harper had, in fact, bound his wife's hands and feet with wire hangers before dousing her with gasoline and setting fire to her, there could be no question that the crime had been "cold, calculated, and premeditated," and that it had also been "especially heinous, atrocious, or cruel." Harper was facing death in the electric chair, and whereas he had specifically asked me to represent him, I wondered now if the better part of valor would not be to make a request to the court for an attorney more experienced in such matters.

Secondly, like Benny Weiss, I did not particularly *like* Harper. I tried to understand this unreasoning antipathy to the man. Was it caused by a lingering prejudice, the aftermath of a Chicago childhood that separated blacks and whites as effectively as a barbed-wire fence? I did not think so. I learned my first lesson in tolerance when I was seventeen and avidly chasing girls of any persuasion, color, or stripe. There was a gloriously beautiful black girl in my high-school English class, and I took her to the movies one night, and for ice-cream sodas later, and then led her into my father's multi-purpose Oldsmobile, and drove to a deserted stretch of road near the football field, and plied her with kisses and my ever-reliable "I love you" (her name was Ophelia Blair, "I love you, Ophelia," my hand fumbling under her skirt), and then pleaded that she let me "do" it because I'd never in my life "done" it with a black girl.

Never mind that I'd never done it with a *white* girl, either. That was my supreme argument: she was black and I was white, and oh what a glorious adventure awaited us if only she'd allow me to lower her panties and spread her legs, a latter-day Stanley exploring Africa. It never occurred to me that I was reducing her to anonymity, denying her very Ophelia-ness, equating her with any *other* black girl in the world, expressing desire for her only because she was black and not merely *herself*, whoever that might have been, the person I had not taken the slightest amount of trouble to learn. I was baffled when she pulled down her skirt and tucked her breasts back into her brassiere, and buttoned her blouse, and asked me very softly to take her home, please. I asked her out a dozen times after that, and she always refused politely. I was learning. I have learned well over the years. I may not be color-blind (that would be too much to expect of any white man) but neither do I ever base my personal response to any man or woman on an accidental, at best, tinting of the flesh, preferring instead to seek out the person within the shell.

So why didn't I like George N. Harper?

Maybe it was because he was so damn ugly. I have never won any beauty contests myself, but the size of Harper, the intimidating hulk of him, the gorillalike slouch of him, the menace—yes, *menace*—inherent in his eyes and in his stance and in the huge hands that dangled at the ends of his powerful arms, the sheer primeval power of him, the frightening *look* of him caused me to back involuntarily away from him whenever we were in the same room together, as though I were convinced that he was capable of committing against me the very crime he'd been accused of committing against his wife. And yet if the color of his skin didn't matter to me, then why should his physical appearance have constituted a handicap? Did due process apply only to the beautiful people in the world? Wasn't Harper entitled to the same fair and honorable defense Robert Redford might have enjoyed? Or did I secretly believe he *was* guilty, and was I looking for excuses to avoid advocating his cause, depriving him beforehand of his life or liberty without benefit of the due process required by the laws of the land? No, he was innocent. I knew it with every fiber in my body. He was *innocent*, damn it. I should defend him, I *would* defend him.

But there was yet another reason why I should have told him no. Discounting my inexperience, discounting my aversion to the man, discounting even the selfishness of the last reason, it remained nonetheless a true and valid reason for begging off.

I had planned a vacation.

Selfish, yes, I admit it.

Or perhaps *not* quite so selfish when one considers that Dale had planned her own vacation for the same period of time, or that both our vacations coincided with Joanna's Thanksgiving break, when all three of us planned to go to Mexico together.

We had been working on the trip for months, consulting the best travel agent in Calusa (no great shakes, but really the only game in town) and were scheduled to leave for Puerto Vallarta nine days from now, on Friday, November 27, to spend almost four days as guests of Samuel Thorn, a retired Calusa Circuit Court judge, in a villa he'd owned for the past year, after which we planned to go to Mexico City, flying back home again on Saturday, December 5. True enough, this would only be nine days. And assuming, as Benny had guessed, that we would not be coming to trial till after the new year, nine days of preparation would not be sorely missed.

Unless one considered the indisputable fact that the state's attorney would be working during those days to compile the evidence he hoped would put Harper in the electric chair. I supposed Dale would take the news of a canceled vacation like the adult she was. But Joanna had just turned fourteen, and she had already planned a term paper on her "Mexican Adventure," and had bought a new bikini to wear poolside at the Camino Real, where she planned to exhibit breasts that, after a prolonged delay, were at last maturing at an alarming rate—alarming at least to a father who would have beaten off with a stick any pimply-faced teen-ager who dared openly ogle them. When she'd modeled the bikini for Dale and me, I commented mildly and with some embarrassment that it was, ah, a bit revealing, didn't she think, for someone who was only fourteen? Joanna, with her customary candor, said, "You should see the one I *didn't* buy, Dad." End of argument. But how was I to tell her that I was thinking about canceling our Mexican trip in favor of defending a man I didn't like, a man who'd been accused of murdering his wife in the most horrible manner, a man I "felt" was innocent ("Never feel," Benny had told me just before I'd left his office. "*Know!*") when all the signs indicated that he was guilty as hell?

By Friday of that week, I still hadn't decided whether to represent George N. Harper (as he had asked me to do) or to advise him either to find another lawyer who would accept his case or request the public defender to appoint one for him. Joanna was supposed to be with her mother that weekend, but at the last minute my former wife called to ask if I would mind having her two weekends in a row because she, Susan, had been invited to attend the Tampa Bay Bucs football game that Saturday, and she and Arthur planned to spend the weekend up there, not returning till late Sunday night—so would I mind?

I *never* mind seeing my daughter two weekends in a row; I would like to see my daughter every day of my life. Neither do I mind Susan's apparent need to tell me just which eligible bachelor she is currently seeing and presumably sleeping with. Earlier in the year, she had enjoyed a brief but doubtlessly torrid fling with a man named Georgie Poole, reputedly the richest man in all Calusa, a bachelor in his mid-forties who, it was rumored, had a penchant for television cuties in situation comedies, hence his frequent "business" trips to Los Angeles. The romance had cooled by March, at which time Susan promptly informed me that she had taken up with "a very dear man" named Arthur Butler, the one who would be taking her to Tampa this weekend.

In one of her brighter moments, Susan mentioned wittily that not only had the Butler done it, but he'd done it exceedingly well, and was, moreover, continuing to do it on a regular basis. I don't know why Susan keeps reminding me that she's a desirable woman; I knew she was desirable when I married her, and I even thought she was desirable when at last I divorced her. (I also don't know why so many divorced women seem to drift into selling real estate, which was what my former wife now did.) I wish she would keep her various relationships to herself. So long as none of them is harmful to my daughter, so long as she doesn't frighten the horses, so to speak, I really don't care *what* she does with her own life. But I *do* object to hypocrisy.

Susan was poised to spend the weekend with Arthur Butler in Tampa, there to enjoy the football game and, I was certain, sundry indoor sports as well. On her block (as my partner Frank would put it), this was perfectly acceptable behavior. But the first words my daughter said to me when I picked her up after school that Friday were, "Mom won't let me go to Mexico if Dale's coming with us."

I must tell you, first, that Joanna is blond and blue-eyed and long-legged and easily the most beautiful child in all Calusa, and perhaps the entire state of Florida, or maybe even the world. She is also a scientific genius. Or, at least, she gets A's in biology and provides fierce B-plus competition for the boys in her geometry class, even though *some* unenlightened sexists would maintain that these subjects would best be left to the male of the species.

On the other hand, Joanna does very poorly in English, and she cannot boil an egg properly, and I have never caught her knitting or tatting or playing the harpsichord or doing any of the little feminine curtseying things that used to be considered the mark of a domesticated American female back when Abraham Lincoln was president.

Joanna wants to be a brain surgeon.

She read somewhere that a famous surgeon in Indianapolis used to practice tying one-handed knots inside a matchbox. Whenever Joanna and I dine out together, she prays that the matches on the table will not be of the book type, but rather of the box type. Often, she sits by the pool at the house I am renting, and ties knots inside a matchbox while simultaneously reading Freud's *Psychopathology of Everyday Life*. She finds Freud "neat."

The next thing you should know about Joanna is that she absolutely adores Dale. Her sudden infatuation came as a total surprise to me; before Dale, Joanna had been known to demolish in her tracks any lady I had the audacity to introduce. Her *sotto voce* nicknames for these hapless unsuspecting beauties were in themselves devastating: she secretly labeled one woman "Bubbles La Tour," merely because she was as magnificently endowed as a burlesque queen; she privately called another "Houdini the Great" only because she had a not-unsurprising habit of vanishing whenever Joanna put in a surly appearance; she dubbed yet another "El Dopo," because her name was Eleanor Daniels and she made the mistake one bleak October afternoon of wearing a sweater monogrammed with the initials E.D. (In all fairness to my daughter, Eleanor really *wasn't* too terribly bright.) Joanna's smoldering gaze could reduce to steaming ashes the strongest of suitors for her cherished father's attention; she once grew extravagantly jealous of a twice-weekly cleaning woman who was in her sixties, and about whom I made an unfortunate and idle comment to the effect that she was "a nice person." Electra had nothing on my daughter Joanna. But all that was before Dale; Joanna would walk through fire for Dale O'Brien.

So now she was telling me that my beloved former wife

would not allow her to go to Mexico if Dale would be accompanying us.

"Why not?" I asked.

"She says she has custody."

"I know she does. What's that got to do . . . ?"

"She says she's responsible for my moral rectitude."

"That's redundant."

"Huh?"

"Rectitude means 'moral uprightness.' Is your mother saying she's responsible for your moral moral uprightness?"

"Whatever. She won't let me go, Dad."

"Do you *want* to go?"

"Are you kidding? I've been planning on this for *months*!"

"So have I. I'd better call her."

"I think she's already left for Tampa," Joanna said.

"I'll try her, anyway."

She had not already left for Tampa. She was, in fact, still packing when I phoned her at the house I used to share with her.

"What is it?" she said. Her tone of voice was the one a mother might have used on a wayward child who'd just stamped into the kitchen while a soufflé was in the oven.

"You tell *me*," I said.

"Oh, it's riddle time, right?"

"No, it's Q and A time. What's this about Joanna?"

"What's *what* about Joanna?"

"Did you tell her she can't go to Mexico with me?"

"Oh, so *that's* it."

"Yes, that's it, Susan."

"If you have any questions about custody, I suggest you call my lawyer. I'm busy right now, and I . . ."

"I have no intention of calling that mealymouthed shyster you . . ."

"I'm sure Eliot McLaughlin would enjoy knowing you think of him as a mealymouthed shyster."

"He already knows it. This has nothing to do with custody, Susan. You had Joanna for Easter, and you'll have her again for Christmas. *I* get her for Thanksgiving. And I'm taking her to Mexico with me, period."

"Not if the redhead goes with you."

"If by the redhead . . ."

"You know exactly who I mean."

"Are you referring to Dale O'Brien?"

"Oh, is *that* her name? And here I thought Dale was a *man's* name."

"Susan, cut it out."

"Cut what out?"

"This bullshit about Dale."

"I certainly hope you don't use that kind of language in Joanna's presence. It's bad enough . . ."

"I'm trying to tell you there's no legal way you can prevent me from taking her any damn place I *want* to take her!"

"No? How about corrupting the morals of a minor?"

"Don't be absurd."

"Taking a fourteen-year-old to Mexico, where you'll be living in sin with . . ."

"Living in *sin*? Come on, Susan, this isn't the Middle . . ."

"What do *you* call it, Matthew? You'll be in the same house with Joanna and what*ever* her name is . . ."

"Her name is Dale O'Brien."

"For four days, isn't that what Joanna told me? Four days in Sam Thorn's cozy little villa, with you in one bedroom screwing your brains out with the redhead while across the hall Joanna . . ."

"What I do in private has nothing to . . ."

"Public is more like it."

"There are four bedrooms in the villa. Joanna will have her own . . ."

"How kind of Sam to provide such luxurious surroundings for you and your little bimbo."

"This *must* be the Middle Ages! I haven't heard the word *bimbo* since . . ."

"What would you *prefer* calling her, Matthew?"

"What do you call Arthur Butler?"

"What*ever* I call Arthur is between . . ."

"Where will you be sleeping with *him* this weekend?"

"Wher*ever* we'll be sleeping is none of your business. And besides, Joanna won't be with us."

"Who says?"

"What?"

"I said who *says* Joanna won't be with you?"

"What's that supposed to mean?"

"It's supposed to mean I'm taking her home to you right this minute. Back to your *custody*, darling. So you can protect her *rectitude*."

"What?"

"I said . . ."

"You told me she could stay with *you* this weekend."

"That was before your started pulling all this stuff about Mexico. Will you be there for the next ten minutes or so? I wouldn't want Joanna coming home to an empty house. Might not look too good when I challenge your custody."

"What?"

"Let me spell it out for you, Susan. One, we're divorced. I don't like being dragged into your personal life, and I wish to hell you'd keep out of mine. Two, I don't enjoy these screaming contests on the telephone. Anger is a form of intimacy, and I don't *want* to be intimate with you. And lastly, you've got a choice. Either Joanna goes with me to Mexico next week, just as she's supposed to, or else I take her back to you as soon as I hang up, and you can decide *then* whether you want to stay home this weekend or take her to Tampa with you, where you'll be 'living in sin,' as you choose to call it, with a man named Arthur Butler, an act the courts might consider unfit behavior for a woman who has custody of a fourteen-year-old."

"This is blackmail," Susan said.

"Nonetheless, what's your answer? Does she come to Mexico with me, or to Tampa with you? Or do you stay right here in Calusa this weekend? I'm sure your friend can find someone to take those football tickets off his . . ."

"You are a son of a bitch," she said.

"Decide, Susan."

"Take her to Mexico."

"Thank you."

"A *rotten* son of a bitch," she said, and hung up.

I felt as if I'd just successfully pleaded a case before the Supreme Court of the land.

Oddly and surprisingly, it was my daughter Joanna who helped me make up my mind about George N. Harper. Her reaction to the news that her mother had "reconsidered" the stand she'd taken on Mexico was completely ecstatic, but she fell almost immediately into a blue funk that indicated to me she had something more important on her mind. I have learned over the years that it's never wise to pry when Joanna is mulling a problem. If she wants to tell me about it, if she wants my advice or my solace, she'll eventually spill it all out, often quite suddenly, as she did that night after dinner.

In Calusa, the temperatures at night sometimes drop alarmingly, even in the best of months. November is not one of the better months, although we'd been blessed these past few weeks with benign temperatures and sunny skies while my partner Frank's pals back in New York were suffering through ten-below-zero temperatures. The house was chilly tonight. I had set fire to one of those fake logs you buy in a drugstore, and I was pouring myself a cognac when Joanna said, without preamble, "Do you think Heather is a slut?"

For a moment, I had difficulty remembering just who Heather was. Ever since Joanna first entered nursery school, there had been a constant parade of young girls in the house, all of them with chic, sophisticated names like Kim, Darcy, Greer, Alyce (with a *y*), Candace, Erica, Stacey, Crystal, and yes, Heather. I sometimes wondered what had happened to all those good old-fashioned names like Mary, Jean, Joan, Nancy, Alice (with an *i*), and Betty.

"Heather?" I said.

"Yeah, Heather."

I dimly recalled a plump little girl with mousy brown hair and dark brown eyes who—at the age of six, anyway—had an alarming habit of bursting into tears whenever she was supposed to spend the night at our house. I could not reconcile this sobbing little tyke with the image Joanna's word had conjured: a slut was somebody who stood on a street corner in Frank's beloved New York City, swinging a satin handbag, skirt slit to her thigh, winking at passing strangers and asking them if they'd like to have a good time.

"Everybody's saying she's a slut," Joanna said.

"Who's everybody?"

"Everybody."

In Joanna's lexicon, "everybody" meant all the girls in the eighth grade.

"Do *you* think she is?" I asked.

"Well, she may be fooling around a little, but who cares? So's everybody else."

In Joanna's lexicon, "fooling around" meant being intimate with a member of the opposite sex; "everybody else" meant a handful of girls who were precocious.

"Not me," she said quickly, and grinned, and then became immediately sober again. "That's not the point," she said, "whether she is or she isn't. I just don't like them *saying* she is without knowing for sure, I mean."

"Is she a close friend of yours?"

"No, not close."

"But a friend?"

"Not even a friend, really. I mean, I know her to say hello to, that's all. I mean, she's not a very attractive person, Dad. She's fat, and . . . well, she's sort of dumb for a place like Saint Mark's, which is pretty hard to get into, even if it *isn't* Bedloe. And her language . . . well, she curses a lot, even more than any of the other girls do—that's normal for Saint Mark's, cursing a lot, the whole 'shit, piss, cunt, fuck' routine, you know? But Heather really goes *over*board with it, like she's trying to prove how *mature* she is, you know what I mean?"

I was still reeling over the string of profanities my fourteen-year-old daughter had casually dropped into the conversation.

"Dad?" she said.

"Uh-huh."

"You know what I mean?"

"Sure, she . . ."

"Sort of shows off, you know what I mean?"

"Uh-huh."

"But that doesn't make her a slut, does it?"

"Not necessarily."

"I mean, even if she *is* fooling around a little. Which nobody knows for sure."

"What's a little?"

"Well . . . with more than one boy. More than the boy you're going steady with. Maybe two or three boys. Or maybe four."

"Uh-huh." I was afraid to ask what "a lot" might be.

"Dad? Are you okay?"

"Yes, fine," I said.

"So everybody's giving her the cold shoulder, as if she's some kind of . . . pariah? Is that a word?"

"That's a word."

"Yeah, pariah. Which, even if she *isn't* as gorgeous as some of the other kids, and curses a lot, or whatever, that's no reason to treat her as if she doesn't exist, is it? Or calling her a slut behind her back, even sometimes to her face? Garland called her a slut to her face today."

"Garland."

"Yeah, Garland McGregor. You know Garland, she slept over once."

"Right, Garland."

"Who, I mean, was only fooling around when she was thirteen. Garland, I mean. With this boy from Bedloe, even if he *was* stunning. I almost burst into tears when it happened today, when Garland called her a slut to her face. I mean, *she's* got feelings, too, hasn't she? Heather, I mean. Hasn't *she* got feelings, too?"

"Yes, darling, she has feelings, too," I said.

"I'm going to go up to her on Monday and tell her to ignore what all those assholes are saying."

"Okay," I said.

"Do you think that's the right thing to do? I mean, Dad, I don't even *like* her. And suppose . . . well . . . suppose she really *is* a slut, like everybody's saying she is?"

"But you don't know that for sure, do you?"

"No, I don't."

"And neither do the others."

"No, they don't know it for sure, Dad."

"Then, yes, it's the right thing to do."

"Yeah, I guess," Joanna said.

I had already decided I would try to defend George N. Harper.

4

Section 905.17 of the *Florida Statutes,* in describing who may
be present during a grand jury session, unequivocally states:
"No person shall be present at the sessions of the grand jury
except the witness under examination, the state attorney and
his assistant state attorneys, designated assistants as provided
for in s. 27.18, the court reporter or stenographer, and the
interpreter."

This may seem to be loading the dice against the defen-
dant, but such is not the case. He does not have to testify if
he chooses not to, but when he *is* invited to testify, and
assuming he accepts the invitation, he will once again be read
his rights and he may at any time interrupt the questioning
to consult with his attorney, who is waiting just outside the
door to the sealed chamber.

On Monday morning, November 23, I was waiting in the
courthouse corridor while George Harper was inside listening
to the testimony of the doctor who had done the autopsy on
Michelle Harper, and the garage attendant who had sold him

the empty five-gallon gasoline can and subsequently filled it for him, and the laboratory technician who had lifted Harper's prints from the can, and the police officer who swore that he had taken Michelle's criminal complaint on the morning of November 16, and the fisherman who had positively identified Harper as the man he'd seen struggling with a white woman on Whisper Key beach that same night. Harper did not once come out to the hallway to summon me for assistance or advice; that was because I'd told him to decline any invitation to testify.

The grand jurors finished hearing the state's attorney and his witnesses by a quarter past ten, and retired to deliberate their decision. When Harper joined me in the corridor outside, I asked, "How'd it go?"

"They gonna try'n fry me," he said.

"Well, we'll see. We don't know *how* they'll vote yet, do we?"

"Whut's all this gonna coss me?" he asked.

"We'll worry about that later."

"I ain't a rich man. I don't wanna be in hock to you for the ress of my life."

"I promise you won't be."

"How 'bout this *other* lawyer you said you're gonna try'n find to hep you? Whut'll *he* charge me?"

"First I have to find him."

"You tell him I ain't no rich man."

"I'll be sure to tell him."

At a quarter past eleven, the jurors returned a true bill signed by the jury foreman and requesting the state's attorney to prepare an indictment for first-degree murder. George Harper was taken back to the county jail, and I went to see James Willoughby, a criminal lawyer who had worked for the State's Attorney's Office before entering practice with the firm of Peterson, Pauling, and Merritt—familiarly known in Calusa as Peter, Paul, and Mary.

Willoughby was a man in his early forties, fox-faced and blue-eyed, reportedly as shrewd and as clever as a murder of crows, the one attorney who—if speculation in Calusa's legal shops proved valid—would one day replace Benny Weiss as the town's dean of criminal lawyers. Unlike Benny, Willoughby brought to each of his defenses an intimate knowledge of the way the state's attorney—his erstwhile employer—prepared his cases, and he coupled this inside information with an unremitting desire to humiliate his former boss ("that son of a bitch," as Willoughby cheerfully called him) whenever the opportunity presented itself. It was the state's attorney himself, Willoughby claimed, who had hindered his career in public service because of the fear that Willoughby would one day unseat him in a public election. Willoughby went after the State's Attorney's Office the way a terrier goes after a rat. Nothing pleased him more than to overthrow a case carefully prepared by whichever prosecutor "that son of a bitch" assigned to his latest murder, arson, armed robbery, burglary, or merely spitting-on-the-sidewalk case. Willoughby was just the man I needed.

"But I don't want you fucking it up," he said at once.

"What do you mean?"

"I mean I'll join you in the defense if you promise me your role will be a limited one. I don't want to lose a case to that son of a bitch because some real-estate lawyer . . ."

"I'm not a real-estate lawyer."

"Your firm handles a great many real-estate transactions."

"Our firm also handles . . ."

"Does it handle homicide cases?"

"No, but . . ."

"The defense rests," Willoughby said, and spread his hands, and grinned at me—somewhat ghoulishly, I thought. "My point, Matthew, is that whereas I have a great deal of respect for your expertise in sundry other areas of the law, I cannot have you bumbling about underfoot where a man's life is at stake."

"That's why I came to you in the first place," I said. "I don't need to be lectured . . ."

"Forgive me, no lecture was intended."

"I'm well aware of my limitations."

"Fine, then. Just remember that we're in *my* ball park."

"I realize that," I said. "In fact, if you'll take the case, and if my client agrees to it, I'll step out entirely."

"No, no," Willoughby said.

"Why not?"

"Well, from what you tell me, your man is a virtual pauper who . . ."

"No, I didn't say that. He's gainfully employed, he has his own junk business."

"Can he afford the services of the best criminal attorney in Calusa?"

"Benny Weiss is the best criminal attorney in Calusa."

"That's an unkind cut, Matthew. If Benny's such a hotshot, go to Benny."

"He turned me down."

"Why, may I ask?"

"He thinks Harper's guilty."

"So what? You'll pardon me, Matthew, but that's amateur night in Dixie. Who *cares* whether your man is guilty or not? Either you're a gladiator or you aren't. Either you're willing to go into that arena and risk your reputation—*even* for a cause you don't believe in—or else you get fat and lazy and that son of a bitch gets to send more and more people to jail or to the chair. I don't care if a *thousand* witnesses saw your man carve up his wife with a butcher knife . . ."

"She was incinerated."

"Who cares *what* she was? Stabbed, shot, strangled, hanged, who *cares*? The fun is in convincing a jury that your man couldn't possibly have done it in a million years. That's the fun of it, Matthew."

I could hardly equate the attempt to save Harper's life with unbridled joy, but I said nothing. I needed Willoughby, and he knew it.

"But to answer your question," he said, "the reason . . ."

"I forget what the question was," I said.

"The question was, in effect, 'Why do I need you?' I need

you because my normal fee would be well beyond what your pauper client can afford."

"If you get so much 'fun' out of it," I said, "maybe he ought to charge you."

"That, too, is unkind, Matthew. You may be willing to turn *your* shop into a charitable organization . . ."

"You should talk to my partner sometime."

"Does he share my view? The point is, the grand jury's brought in a true bill. Once Harper is served with the indictment, we'll have two, three weeks to enter a plea. Our plea, of course, will be 'not guilty,' and we'll request a trial by jury. Considering the jammed docket, that may not take place till the beginning of the year sometime. The *point*, Matthew, is that I could not normally expend the time and energy essential to an aggressive defense unless the fee were commensurate with my efforts. Since the case is nominally yours, I can only assume you'd be willing to do all the preparation necessary for . . ."

"Well, wait a minute . . ."

"Under my supervision, of course. I'll tell you what we need, you'll go after it. Are we agreed on that?"

"Well . . ."

"We would have to agree on that, Matthew. Otherwise, count me out. I'm not suggesting that you have to do the legwork yourself. You can hire investigators to track down your witnesses, you can have some lackey in your office take depositions—unless, of course, you choose to do all that yourself, in which case you can consider it on-the-job training."

"Thanks," I said.

"I'll base my modest fee on however many hours I put in before trial, and however much time I actually spend in court."

"How much time do you think that'll be?"

"In court? On a routine homicide? A week, ten days."

"What's your hourly charge, Jim?"

"The same as yours, I'm sure."

"I don't think Harper can afford that."

"Then find another champion," Willoughby said.

"I'll make a deal with you," I said. "If you get him off . . ."

"No deal," Willoughby said. "This isn't a collection case, this is murder." He looked at his watch. "I've got someone coming in at one," he said. "Are we agreed? Your firm handles the preparation—under my supervision—and I handle the trial itself. I get paid my usual hourly fee for whatever time I put in before the trial, and however long the trial may actually run. Does that sound fair?"

"Do I have a choice?"

"There are other lawyers in town," Willoughby said dryly. "Not as good as Benny Weiss perhaps . . ."

"Okay, okay," I said.

"Good," he said. "Here's where I'd like you to start."

"Start? He hasn't even been served yet."

"He *will* be served, so why not get a jump on the state's attorney? None of this'll be wasted motion, Matthew, believe me. Any edge we can get will be worth the effort. The prosecution's case will undoubtedly rest on (a) the fact that Michelle Harper made a formal complaint to the police charging that her husband had knocked her around on the night before the murder, (b) the fact that Harper bought a five-gallon can and had it filled with gasoline two days before the murder, (c) the fact that his fingerprints are on the can, and (d) the fact that someone has identified him as the man struggling with his wife on the night the murder was committed. I'm sure that guy at the garage really sold him the can and filled it for him, he has no reason to be lying about that. But how come *his* fingerprints aren't on it, together with Harper's? Talk to him, Matthew, find out in detail how he handled that can, how he filled it, and so on. Talk to Harper, too. Find out whether or not he took that can with him when he went to Miami. If he did, we've got trouble because that means it was in his possession and not laying around where anybody could have got hold of it. Fingerprints impress a jury, Matthew, they read too many detective novels and see too many movies. So get after that gasoline can and find out where it came from and where it went and how many people could have got hold of it before it ended up on the beach where the body was found."

I looked at him and sighed.

"As for this fisherman, whatever the hell his name is . . ."

"Luther Jackson."

"White or black?"

"White."

"No matter. The point is, did he *really* see Harper on the beach or can we show that his identification can't be trusted? He's the *first* guy you've got to talk to, Matthew."

"Okay," I said, and sighed again.

"Now about Michelle," Willoughby said, "who, unfortunately, is unavailable for further comment. She said her husband was the one who beat her black and blue. But how do we *know* he was?"

"Well, she came to my office . . ."

"Yes, and you took her to the police. But whose word do we have except Michelle's—who now happens to be dead? How do we know it wasn't some *other* guy who beat her up? And incidentally murdered her the following night?"

"She went to a neighbor for advice," I said. "It was the neighbor who suggested she come to me."

"After she heard Michelle's story, right?"

"Right."

"From Michelle's mouth, and nobody else's. Go see this neighbor—what's her name again?"

"Sally Owen."

"Sally Owen, right. Go talk to her, find out *exactly* what Michelle told her that Monday morning after her husband allegedly beat her up. Maybe Michelle said something we don't yet know about."

"All right," I said.

"But first find this guy Luther Jackson and ask him what he saw and heard on that beach. He's the prosecution's star witness, Matthew. Without him, they can flush their case down the toilet."

"Okay," I said.

"So much for shooting down the prosecution's case," Willoughby said. "That's only half the battle. *Our* case relies solely on alibi. Harper claims he was in Miami—with a short excursion to Pompano and Vero Beach—from sometime Sunday morning till sometime Tuesday morning. Okay, if he was really in Miami on Sunday night, then he couldn't have been here beating up his wife, the way she claimed he did. And if he was really in Miami on *Monday* night as well, then he couldn't have been here on the beach with her, where Mr. Luther Jackson says he saw him. If his alibi stands up, we're home free. Talk to him, Matthew, pick his brain for whatever he can remember about the time he spent on the east coast, locate some guy who saw him pissing off a pier on Sunday night, locate some dame who went to bed with him on Monday night, dig around, get the facts and get the people—*especially* the people—we'll need to establish that he couldn't have been here getting in trouble when he was actually someplace else. Have you got that?"

"I've got it," I said.

"Okay," Willoughby said, and smiled, and extended his hand. "Good luck," he said.

I had the feeling I was shaking hands with the devil.

By law, the State's Attorney's Office must supply to defense counsel the names and addresses of any witnesses it will call to testify at a trial. Even though I was getting an early start, I had no reason to believe that I'd have any trouble with them now. Whatever Willoughby's opinion, there wasn't a lawyer in town who did not believe that Skye Bannister—the unfortunate name with which the state's attorney had been blessed—was anything but a fair and decent man sworn to uphold the laws of the state. A man in Bannister's office immediately told me the name of Luther Jackson's boat and the marina at which it was docked, and then threw into the pot as well the names and addresses of Lloyd Davis and Harper's mother in Miami. Surprisingly, he wished me good luck before he hung up. Everybody was wishing me good luck today. I began thinking that maybe I would need it.

I did not get to the Sandy Pass Marina until a little after one o'clock that afternoon. I had called ahead to the marina office, but the man who answered the phone sounded dubious about getting a message to Jackson before my intended arrival. He told me he'd "try," and in my experience anyone who tells me he'll "try" is really intending to go out to lunch. But the boat (named *Luther's Hammer*, presumably in reference to the protest nailed to the door of All Saints Church in Wittenberg in the year 1517) was there in one of the slips, and a man I presumed to be Jackson himself was squatting on the fantail, mending a fishing net. He looked up as I approached.

"Mr. Jackson?" I said.

"Yep," he said.

"Matthew Hope. I'm representing George Harper, the man you . . ."

"Come aboard," he said, and rose from where he was squatting. He was, I guessed, somewhere between sixty and seventy years old, a man whose face seemed eroded by sun, sea, and water, his nose bulbous and veined, his flinty blue eyes set deep in leathery weathered skin. He did not extend his hand. Instead, he reached for a pipe resting on the transom, shook the dottle out over the side, filled it with tobacco, and was lighting it as I stepped onto the deck.

"If you're here to say I didn't see him," he said, "I seen him, and that's that."

"That's what I'd like to talk about," I said.

"You'll be wasting your time."

"It's my time," I said.

"And mine, too. I already spent close to two hours with the grand jury this morning, I don't appreciate having to spend *another* two with you."

"Mr. Jackson," I said, "a man's life is at stake here."

"I ain't about to change my mind about what I seen and heard. I already told this first to the police, and next to the grand jury. Ain't no reason for me to go back on what I already said."

"Except that when we subpoena you for deposition, you'll have to tell us what you plan to say at the trial."

"Who says?"

"That's the law, Mr. Jackson. That's what protects the innocent in this country."

"Your man ain't innocent," Jackson said. "I seen him and I heard him. He's the one killed her, all right."

"In any case, can you tell me now what you think you saw or heard that night?"

"It ain't what I *think*, Mr. Hope. It's what I *know*."

"And what's that, exactly?"

"If you're gonna get all this later in a deposition, why do you need it now?"

"Mr. Jackson, we're spending more time *arguing* about talking than we'd be spending if we just plain *talked*."

"Well, I suppose we are," he said.

"So? Can I stop pulling teeth? I'm a lawyer by trade, not a dentist."

Jackson smiled.

"Okay," he said. "What do you want to know?"

"I want to know what you saw and heard on the night of the sixteenth. First, tell me what time this was."

"Along around ten o'clock."

"Where were you?"

"Anchored just off the beach."

"On Whisper Key?"

"Yep. Heard the redfish were working in the shallows. Dropped the hook and put two lines over the side."

"What kind of night was it?"

"Full moon, if you're thinking I couldn't see to the beach. Check the newspapers. They'll tell you it was a full moon that night."

"How far off were you anchored?"

"Just past the shallows. Maybe twenty feet from shore. No more'n that."

"And you say you could see the beach clearly?"

"Clear as I'm seein you right this minute."

"What exactly did you see, Mr. Jackson?"

"Black man and a white woman come runnin up the beach. The woman was naked."

"What did she look like?"

"Long black hair, skin as pale as the moonlight."

"And the man?"

"Big and husky. And *black*. Blackest nigger I ever seen in my life."

I made a mental note to ask Luther Jackson, when we took his deposition, to discourse a bit on his attitudes about "niggers." I also made a note to check with Morrie Bloom about the various shades of brown on the faces of the five policemen who'd been in the lineup with Harper; were any of them as black as he was? Or had Jackson made his identification based solely on *how* black Harper was?

"Did you see the man's face?" I asked.

"I seen it, all right."

"From twenty feet away?"

"My eyes are fine, Mr. Hope. If I can spot a school of fish three hundred yards off the bow, I can sure as hell see a man's face from twenty feet offshore."

"What kind of hair did he have?" I asked.

"Same as Harper's."

"What color were his eyes?"

"Couldn't see his eyes. Most niggers have brown eyes, same as Harper's."

"When you say a big man . . ."

"Like Harper."

"How tall would you say?"

"Like Harper."

"How much did he weigh, would you guess?"

"Same as Harper."

"Then there's no question in your mind that the man you saw on the beach was George Harper."

"None a'tall."

"And you say you saw him at ten o'clock or thereabouts?"

"Around then. Him and the woman both. Was the woman first caught my eye, naked the way she was. Hard to see niggers in the dark, you know," he said, and chuckled. I said nothing, but I made another mental note to ask him again, when we took his deposition, all about how difficult it was to see "niggers" in the dark.

"Did they just walk onto the beach, or what?" I said.

"Came *runnin* up the beach. Woman ahead of him, Harper following her."

"Was she carrying anything?"

"Nothing that I saw."

"No handbag, nothing like that?"

"Naked," Jackson said, and nodded. "Big tits shining in the moonlight."

I remembered that the police had found Michelle's handbag in the sand, had in fact been able to make positive identification from the driver's license in her wallet. It was the handbag that had led Morrie to believe she'd gone out onto the beach voluntarily. Had she dropped her bag on the sand near the pavilion before running from her murderer?

"How about *him*? Was *he* carrying anything?"

"Who? Harper?"

"The man you saw running after her."

"Nope. Nothin I could see."

"How long had you been out on the water before you saw these people, Mr. Jackson?"

"Couple of hours. Left here around six-thirty, figure it took me forty minutes to get to Whisper. Let's say I was there, anchored there with my lines in the water, since from about seven-thirty on."

"That would make it two and a half hours."

"Like I said, a coupla hours."

"Was the tide high or low?"

"High. Couldn't a been sittin only twenty feet offshore

with *my* draft if the tide had been low. Check with the papers, you don't believe me. High tide, full moon."

"What were you doing during those two and a half hours?"

"Fishing. What d'you think I was doin? That's what I am, is a fisherman."

"Catch anything?"

"Yep. Not as many as I hoped, but I pulled in a few."

"What'd you do when you weren't pulling in fish?"

"Had a few beers, whiled away the time. Fisherman gets used to being alone out on the water."

"How many beers?"

"Just a few. If you're thinkin I was drunk, Mr. Hope, forget it. Ain't a fisherman in all Calusa can drink me under the table."

"How many beers did you have, actually?"

"Drank me a coupla six-packs."

"Twelve beers?"

"More or less."

"Which was it, Mr. Jackson. More or less?"

"Maybe broke out another six-pack, started on that. Ain't much to do out on the water when they ain't bitin."

"So you drank something between twelve and eighteen beers in the two and a half hours before you saw the man and the woman on the beach."

"Which don't mean I was drunk."

"Nobody says you were. Did you see a fire on the beach?"

"Nope. Didn't see no fire."

"But you *did* see the man and the woman struggling."

"Yep. Grabbed her by the arm, yanked her off her feet. Started slapping her, seemed like, I couldn't see too clear when they were rolling around there in the sand. But I could hear the slaps, and I heard him yelling her name, too."

"What name did you hear?"

"Michelle."

"What else did you hear?"

"Called her a no-good whore. Said she always *was* a whore, said a whore wasn't to be trusted."

"You heard all that from the boat?"

"Yep. Wind was carrying from the east, you check the papers. Wind from the east, high tide, full moon."

"What did the woman say?"

"Nothing. Just kept whimpering while he was hitting her."

"Then what?"

"Dragged her off."

"Dragged her through the sand?"

"Yep. By the hands, it looked like. Her hands were together, he was draggin her by the hands."

"What'd *you* do?"

"Same thing."

"What do you mean?"

"Dragged ass."

"Why?"

"Fish weren't bitin, no sense hangin around there. Pulled up the hook, went on my way."

"Did you report what you'd seen to the police?"

"Not till after I heard about the murder."

"When was that?"

"Tuesday sometime. Heard it on the radio. Figured maybe that was what I seen on the beach Monday night."

"But you didn't see any fire on the beach?"

"Nope."

"Not after you saw the people there, and not while you were under way, either."

"Nope. Went south, anyway. They were heading north, toward the pavilion—where they found her body, you know."

"Mr. Jackson, I'd like to have you come to my office to repeat under oath what you just told me. Would you have any objection to signing a deposition?"

"None a'tall. Ain't going to help your man none, though. I seen him on that beach, I heard him calling her them dirty names, I heard him slapping her, I seen him dragging her off through the sand. It was *Harper* I seen and nobody else, and I'll swear to that on a stack of Bibles."

"Thank you, Mr. Jackson," I said.

"For what?" he said.

I phoned Sally Owen from the marina office, and caught her between customers at the beauty parlor where she worked. She told me she had somebody coming in at two, and asked if I could possibly get there at two-thirty, by which time she should be finished. As it turned out, she was still working on her customer when I got there at twenty to three.

Sally was a good-looking black woman in her early thirties, dressed for work in tight-fitting slacks, high-heeled sandals, and a white work smock that flared out over the slacks like a short miniskirt. She wore her hair in the sort of Afro cut Angela Davis had made famous, and she wore as well a pair of dangling ruby earrings that seemed more suited to a night out on the town than to the somewhat sterile decor of her surroundings. The shop was in New Town, the black section of Calusa, not too far from where Michelle had lived with her husband. Sally asked me to take a seat, and I watched as she continued twisting the woman's hair into the countless number of slender braids Bo Derek had popularized in the film *10*.

The woman upon whom she labored was a "6" at best—if one insists on rating women by their looks alone. Dale had despised the film. She asked me afterward, with some justification, how *I* would enjoy being rated by a numbers system. She insisted that Blake Edwards, the director, had to be some kind of a male chauvinist pig at heart. I told her I'd found the movie only slightly amusing, but that Bo Derek certainly was a beautiful woman. In an amazing turnabout, Dale asked me—somewhat shyly and a trifle coyly—how I would rate *her* if given the opportunity. Ever nimble on my feet (we were, in fact, supine in Dale's bed at the time) I told her she surely rated a "20" on looks alone, plus another "20" for the purity of her mind. Dale said, "Liar," but she snuggled closer to me.

The braiding was only half-finished when Sally came to where I was sitting. "Didn't tell me *this* was what she wanted," she said. "Gonna take another hour at least. I don't want to keep you waiting. We'd better talk now."

We moved to a corner of the shop away from the chairs and the hair dryers and the sinks. An end table between us was covered with back issues of *Vogue, Harper's Bazaar*, and *Ebony*. Sally offered me a cigarette, and then lit one for herself.

"So," she said. "Something, huh?"

She had, I realized all at once, extraordinarily beautiful eyes, a pale amber against the smooth tan of her complexion. Her left eye turned in ever so slightly, in what the British might have called "a bit of a squint," not enough to make her look truly cross-eyed, but lending to her face a somewhat out-of-focus, smoky, and oddly sexy appearance. She was perhaps five feet six inches tall, a well-proportioned woman who sat with her legs crossed, the ruby earrings suddenly seeming appropriate with the high-heeled sandals she was wearing.

"You get to know a person, and then something like this happens," she said, and shook her head, and dragged on the cigarette.

"How well did you know her?" I asked.

"Pretty well. For neighbors, we got along better than most. She lived only three houses down the street, you know. Only white woman in the neighborhood."

"And that's how you knew her? As a neighbor."

"Well, a friend, too. I suppose we were friends. Considering."

"Considering what?"

"She was white, I'm black. Aren't too many whites and blacks who're *real* friends in this town, are there?"

"Did you consider her that? A *real* friend?"

"I was a shoulder to cry on, let's put it that way."

"How so?"

"Whenever King Kong started up, she called me."

"King Kong?"

"George. Her husband."

"Started up how?"

"Well . . . hassling her, you know?"

"What do you mean by that?"

"The green-eyed monster is what I mean."

"He was jealous of her, is that what you're saying?"

"That's putting it mildly. Well, look, figure it out for yourself. You get a woman who looks like Michelle, and she's married to an *ape*, he's going to believe whatever he *wants* to believe, am I right?"

"I don't think I'm following you. What, exactly, *did* he believe?"

"He was crazy, that's all."

"Crazy how?"

"Well," Sally said, "let's say the man was hypersensitive to any other man she even glanced at."

"*Did* she glance at other men?"

"No, no, pure as a lily, Michelle was. It was all in his *head*, you understand?"

"You're saying he accused her of . . ."

"Well, 'accused' might be too strong a word."

"What word would you prefer?"

"Let's say he *suspected* she was paying too much attention to other men."

"Is that what she told you?"

"Used to come to the house in tears, complaining about the way he hassled her all the time."

"Uh-huh. Confided all this to you, is that right?"

"Confided it to me, right."

"How often did this happen?"

"Did what happen?"

"Her telling you he'd accused her . . ."

"Well, not accused."

"Sally," I said, "I'm having some difficulty getting this straight. *Did* Harper, or did he *not*, accuse his wife of paying too much attention to other men?"

"She said he *suspected* her of it, that's right."

"And hassled her about it?"

"Right."

"That's accusing her, isn't it?"

"Well, if you want to put it that way," Sally said, and shrugged.

"How often did this happen?"

"You want this exact?"

"Please."

"It was at least three or four times."

"She came to your house on at least three or four occasions . . ."

"Right."

"In tears . . ."

"Right."

"To confide that her husband had accused her of paying too much attention to other men."

"That's what she told me."

"Had you ever witnessed any of this?"

"Witnessed what?"

"Michelle paying attention to other men?"

"No, no. Like I said, it was all in his head."

"Had you ever been with them socially?"

"Oh, sure."

"And you never saw Michelle behave like anything but a model wife?"

"That's right."

"How did Harper behave on those occasions?"

"He was his usual self."

"And what was that?"

"Never said a word to anybody you didn't have to drag it out of him. He'd come to the house sometimes with Michelle, just sit quiet the whole night long, like something was eating him up alive. I mean, this would be like a party, you know, six or seven people in, he'd sit there without saying a word to anybody. All bottled up inside, you know? I'm telling you, I'm not surprised he killed her. It's the ones who're all bottled up inside who finally let it out in ways you don't expect."

"Did he seem like a violent person to you?"

"Well, he beat her up, didn't he?"

"You have only Michelle's word for that."

"What are you talking about?"

"When she came to see you last Monday morning, she was the one who told you her husband had abused her."

"And I wasn't surprised, I'm telling you."

"That she told you this?"

"No, that he finally got around to hitting her. It was what she was afraid of all along. That one of these days, when he got in these jealous fits of his, he'd hurt her somehow."

"She told you that?"

"Right, that one of these days he'd hurt her. In fact . . ."

She shook her head.

"Yes?"

"She told me she was afraid he'd kill her one day."

"When did she tell you that?"

"It was Halloween night. I remember because when she knocked on the door, I thought it was some trick-or-treaters coming around. Instead, it was Michelle again, in tears, telling me Kong was on another rampage, yelling at her, threatening her . . ."

"Threatening her?"

"Right, telling her if she ever *looked* at another man, he'd fix her good."

"And she interpreted this to mean he'd kill her?"

"That's what she said."

"That he'd kill her?"

"Or mess her up some way. The morning she came here, last Monday morning, her breasts were all black and blue, her nose broken, teeth missing from her mouth. Hurting her *that* way, you know? So she wouldn't be attractive to other men."

"Uh-huh. But you heard all this only from Michelle, isn't that right?"

"That's right."

"Which would make it hearsay."

"What does that mean?"

"It means you never actually *saw* or *heard* any indication, in public, that Harper actually *was* a jealous person. Or that he might be capable of doing such extreme violence."

"Man's about to beat up his wife, he doesn't go inviting a crowd in to witness it, Mr. Hope."

"I realize that."

I was silent for a moment. Sally took this as a cue that our conversation had ended. She stubbed out her cigarette and then glanced up at the wall clock. Across the room, the would-be "10" was beginning to show signs of impatience.

"How long had you known Michelle?" I asked.

"Since from when they got married."

"Which would've been about a year and a half ago, is that right?"

"Right. I've known her about that long."

"Were you at the wedding?"

"No, I didn't really get to know her till afterward."

"The wedding took place here in Calusa, didn't it?"

"Yeah. Had a big reception afterward. At the house. Cars lined up all over the street."

"But you weren't invited."

"Nope. Kong and I never *did* get along, and like I told you, I didn't know Michelle at the time."

She looked at the clock again.

"Just a few more questions," I said.

"Sure, it's just my customer's getting itchy."

"There's one thing I don't understand."

"What's that?"

"If, as you say, Harper had threatened Michelle on several previous occasions . . ."

"That's what he did."

"Why do you suppose that *this* time his threats erupted into actual physical violence?"

"Go ask *him*," Sally said. "Not that I think you'll have much luck. Like I told you, Kong isn't the kind of man who goes opening his heart and soul to you."

I was thinking of what George Harper, sitting in Bloom's office during the Q and A, had told us openly and with seeming honesty: "I loved her t'death." I was thinking of him bursting into tears immediately afterward, and then burying his face in his huge hands, and sobbing as though his heart would burst.

I thanked Sally for her time, and stepped out of the shop into brilliant sunshine that was painful to the eyes.

5

My partner Frank is a firm believer in his own variation of Murphy's Law, which states that if anything can possibly go wrong just before a planned vacation, it will most certainly go wrong. Your healthy cat—or in this case *Dale's* healthy cat—will suddenly come down with a 104-degree fever that the vet will assure you is not particularly high for cats, whose normal temperature range is somewhere between 100 and 103, but that nonetheless will necessitate a battery of tests in order to determine the cause. Normally—the vet told Dale, and she reported to me on the phone late Monday night—a cat's fever will be directly related to a fight he or she has just had with some other cat or a dog or, in Calusa, a raccoon. But Sassafras, Dale insisted, was the sort of benign feline who never got into even a spitting contest, much less a bonafide battle. Nonetheless, Sassafras was now at the vet's, and Dale would have to call tomorrow to find out what the story was, and tomorrow was Tuesday, two days before Thanksgiving, three days before we were to leave for Mexico, and she hoped it was nothing serious because she couldn't bear the thought of leaving a sick cat behind while she went off on a holiday.

That was on Monday night at 11:00.

On Tuesday morning, at around 8:00, a loudspeaker in the Calusa airport crackled with the news that my 8:30 A.M. Sunwing Shuttle flight to Miami had been delayed and would not be leaving till 9:00. It is sometimes difficult for nonresidents of Calusa to believe that we have so much trouble flying from here to Miami, a scant 165 air-miles away. There are four major airlines servicing our modest city, but three of them—Delta, Pan Am, and United—don't fly from here to there at *all*. Eastern has five daily flights to Miami; only one of them is nonstop, and that leaves at 9:48 P.M. The rest require changing planes either at Orlando or Tampa. It is easier to take Sunwing's Shuttle (which my partner Frank—accustomed to the more sophisticated shuttles from New York to Boston or Washington, D.C.—calls the Sunwing *Scuttle*), a tiny airline with three scheduled flights to Miami and back every day of the week. The flight takes an hour and twenty-five minutes—when it's on time. My 8:30 A.M. flight that morning did not, in fact, leave until 9:20, confirmation—if any was needed—of the Murphy-cum-Summerville Law.

I arrived in Miami at a little before 11:00, an hour after I *should* have arrived, and immediately placed a call to my office. Cynthia Huellen informed me that the state's attorney had already served Harper with the indictment (he was wasting no time, that son of a bitch) and that Karl Jennings of our office had appeared before the same Circuit Court judge who'd earlier denied Harper bail; unsurprisingly, he had denied it once again, setting a date two and a half weeks away for appearance, at which time we would have to enter our plea. The taxi I caught at the airport was driven by a Cuban who did not know Miami half as well as he had known Havana. It took him a full hour to find the address I had carefully lettered onto the sheet of paper I handed him, and then another ten minutes making change for a twenty-dollar bill in a grocery store two doors up from the house in which

Lloyd Davis lived and conducted his business. It was 12:15 when finally I got out of the cab.

Davis's house was small and constructed of wood shingles painted green. The front lawn was patchy and strewn with what appeared to be the overflow debris of the junk piled against the side of the house and visible in the backyard, a flotsam-and-jetsam collection of automobile parts and radiators and refrigerators and bottles and lawn furniture and plumbing fixtures and you-name-it, Lloyd Davis seemed to have it. A dog of uncertain origin sat on the rickety front porch of the house, scratching his ear. He barely glanced at me as I mounted the steps and approached the screen door.

A record player was going someplace inside the house—Billie Holiday singing the blues. There was no doorbell. I rapped gently on the wooden frame surrounding the tattered screening. There was no answer. I rapped again, and then called, "Hello!"

"Who is it?" a woman's voice said.

"I'm looking for Lloyd Davis," I said.

Billie's voice reached for a high note, found it, teased it, slid down the other side of it.

"Hello?" I said.

"Just a minute," the woman answered.

The record ended. I heard only the sound of the needle caught in the retaining grooves, clicking endlessly, and then silence. I waited. She appeared suddenly behind the screen door, a woman of about thirty, I guessed, wearing a faded silk wrapper, her hair done up in rags, her eyes studying me suspiciously.

"You here about the bike?" she asked.

"No, I'm not."

"Oh," she said.

"I'm a lawyer representing George Harper," I said. "I'd like to see Mr. Davis, if that's possible. Is he home?"

"He's out back. In the garage," the woman said. "I'm his wife."

"All right for me to go back there?"

"Don't see why not," she said.

"Mind if I ask you a few questions first?"

"What about?"

"About Mr. Harper's visit here on the fifteenth."

"Uh-huh," she said.

She did not open the screen door. She stood just inside it, a vague filtered figure in the gloom beyond.

"*Was* he here?"

"He was here."

"Looking for your husband?"

"Looking for Lloyd, yeah."

"What time was this, would you remember?"

"Sometime in the morning."

"Can you be more exact about that?"

"Around eight o'clock, I guess it was. Eight-thirty. Around there."

"How long did he stay?"

"Five minutes, is all. Said he wanted to see Lloyd, told him Lloyd was off with the army."

"Did he say where he was going next?"

"Nope. Just said thanks and went on his way."

"Thank you, Mrs. Davis," I said.

She did not answer. One moment she was there, and the next she was gone again, disappearing as suddenly as she had materialized. As I walked toward the garage at the back of the house, I heard the Billie Holiday record starting again.

Lloyd Davis was a man in his late twenties, I guessed, some six feet tall and weighing two hundred pounds, give or take. He was wearing blue jeans and a white tank-top shirt, his chest and arm muscles bulging as he carried a Franklin stove from one section of the garage to another. Despite the obvious weight of the cast-iron stove, he moved as effortlessly as a quarterback through an ineffective defensive line, gingerly picking his way across the cluttered garage floor, setting the stove down with a grunt, and then turning to face me with a sudden and surprising smile. A fine sheen of perspiration glistened on his handsome face, highlighting the distinctive cheekbones and almost patrician nose. His skin was as black as Harper's, the color of bitter chocolate, his eyes the color of Greek olives. The teeth behind the wide smile were even and white.

"You the man who called?" he asked.

"What?" I said.

"About the motor bike?"

"No," I said. "I'm Matthew Hope. George Harper's attorney."

"Oh," he said. "Well, how are you? I'm Lloyd Davis, nice to meet you." He extended his hand, took mine in a firm clasp. "Would you like a beer? I'm dying of thirst here."

"Thanks, no," I said.

He went across the garage to where three old refrigerators were standing side by side against the far wall. Unerringly, he opened the door of one that was plugged in, and reached inside for a can of beer. The garage was littered with the same sort of debris that cluttered the driveway and part of the front lawn: ancient lawn mowers, yellowing toilet bowls, gutters and leaders, lampshades, bridge tables, radios, copper pipes, brass couplings, bikes with and without wheels, roller skates, clay pots, a typewriter, a set of battered leather luggage, a floor lamp with a metal base, and more miscellaneous crap than I could hope to count in a month of Sundays, all of it vying for floor or shelf space with an assortment of cardboard cartons containing everything from old magazines to beads and souvenir ashtrays to—in at least one instance— what appeared to be a priceless collection of soiled rags.

"I thought you were the guy coming for the bike," he said. "He called ten minutes ago, said he heard I had a good used bike for sale. It *is*, too." He ripped the tab from the beer can, brought the can to his lips, and drank deeply. "Mmm, I've been *craving* this," he said. He set the can down precariously on what appeared to be an upended plaster-cast statue of a lion or a seal or perhaps the Venus de Milo, difficult to determine since it was missing its head and all of its appendages. "So Georgie got himself in trouble, huh?" he said.

"It looks that way."

"From what I can gather, he's using Miami as an alibi, right? Says he was here in Miami when it all happened."

"Well, he *was*, wasn't he?"

"He was here Sunday morning a week ago, is what he was. Spoke to Leona—my wife—and then left. I don't know where he was after that."

"But *you* didn't see him, is that right?"

"Nope. I was off with the reserve. Got to put in my drill hours, you know, if I want to keep my rating and pay. Sixteen hours a month, plus another two full weeks a year, usually sometime in the summer. Takes me away from my business, but what can you do? Anyway, I'll be finished with it come January."

"Exactly what sort of business are you in, Mr. Davis?"

"It's a perpetual tag sale here, is what it is," Davis said. "There's nothing retired old farts like better than a tag sale. Think they're getting something for nothing, you know? Every Saturday and Sunday, they come in here like I'm *giving* my stuff away. Nothing to do with their time, they go looking for crap they can clutter up their trailers with. I'll be open Thanksgiving Day, ought to be a good day for me."

"Had you known Mr. Harper would be here on the fifteenth?"

"Nope."

"He didn't call you beforehand?"

"Well, he never does. He loads up his truck, comes on down to see if there's any crap I'd like to buy. He's got a few other dealers down here, too, but I'm his main customer."

"Who are the other dealers, would you know?"

"Nope. Georgie's kind of closemouthed when it comes to business. When it comes to *anything*, for that matter. You sure you don't want a beer?" he asked, and picked up the can again.

"No, thanks," I said. I hesitated, and then asked, "Was he that way in Germany, too?"

"What way?"

"Closemouthed."

"Oh, sure. Except when he was busting some poor bastard who got drunk on a weekend pass. We'd get a lot of soldiers come to Bonn, we still got lots of troops stationed in Germany. They'd come up there for the weekend, get drunk and start howling at the moon. Georgie'd love to bust 'em. He has a mean streak in him, Georgie has. I'm not surprised it ended up this way."

"Do you mean what happened to Michelle?"

"Yeah, sure, what else would I mean? The way he used his club on some of those dogfaces over there . . . well, I'm not surprised, is all I'm saying."

"When you say 'The way he used his club . . .'"

"Well, these guys were drunk for the most part, I mean they weren't doing anybody any *harm*, you know what I mean? Okay, every now and then you'd get some guy pissing in the Rhine, or else starting up with some German girl he thought was a hooker but who turned out instead to be some honest burgher's daughter, you know what I mean? Even so, it was all harmless, guys off on a weekend toot. Georgie used to treat them like they just committed an ax murder. Beat the shit out of more damn stupid assholes . . ."

Davis let the sentence trail. He tilted the beer can to his mouth, sipped at it.

"Did you know Michelle in Bonn?" I asked.

"Sure, that's where I met her."

"Where was that?"

"In Bonn. You just asked me . . ."

"Yes, but where? Under what circumstances?"

"Oh. Georgie and I double-dated one night. I had me this white chick used to sing in a little cabaret—listen, don't mention this to Leona, okay?" he said, and winked. "I was married at the time, but I was a long, long way from home. You ever been a long, long way from home?"

"On occasion," I said.

"Then you know how it is," Davis said, and smiled.

"So you double-dated . . ."

"Yeah, we went to a little joint near the Kennedy Bridge—are you familiar with Bonn?"

"No."

"Anyway, that's where I first met Michelle. Saw her that one night, and that was it."

"How come?"

"What do you mean, how come?"

"If Harper was your friend . . ."

"Well, yeah, but . . . you know. A guy wants to be *alone* with his chick, am I right?"

"What was she doing in Bonn? I thought she was French."

"Her father's French, her mother's German. They used to live in Paris, moved to Bonn when she was—I forget what she said, thirteen, fourteen, something like that. She was maybe nineteen when I met her."

"Was that the last time you saw her? That night?"

"No, no. Saw her again here in the States, when she came here looking for him."

"Looking for Harper?"

"Right. Came to the house here, first place she came. Well, let me correct that. She went to his mother's place first, 'cause that's where she thought he was living. *Then* she came here. I was the one who gave her his address in Calusa."

"When was this, Mr. Davis?"

"A year and a half ago, little more than that maybe."

"Before they got married?"

"Oh, sure. That's why she *came* here, you see. To find him, to get him to marry her. She was crazy about him."

"But he was crazy about her, too, isn't that right?"

"Yeah? Funny way he had of showing it then. When we got our orders, when we knew we were coming back to the States, he shipped out without even giving her a dingle."

"What do you mean?"

"Didn't phone her, nothing, just packed his duffel and off he went."

"How do you happen to know that?"

"He told me, is how."

"That he hadn't called her?"

"That he didn't *plan* to call her. Said she was prime white pussy, but that was all behind him, he was coming back home to feast on some *soul* food. Those were his exact words."

"Did he have anyone specific in mind?"

"Huh?"

"This 'soul food' he mentioned."

"No, no, just the general black female population," Davis said, and grinned.

"But she followed him here anyway."

"Sure did. Real tenacious lady, that Michelle," he said, and grinned again. "Didn't find him here in Miami, went right up there to Calusa, cornered him like a rat. Said she loved him and wanted to marry him, and either he married her or she'd go drown herself in the ocean."

"Who told you that?"

"She did."

"Then you saw her again after she left Miami?"

"Oh sure. I was at the wedding, in fact. Best man at the wedding."

"When did Michelle tell you this story about drowning herself if he wouldn't marry her?"

"Oh, I don't remember. One time when I was visiting the house there. She made a big joke of it, you know, like how to hook a man who doesn't want to *be* hooked. Georgie laughed, too. It was like a joke."

"Uh-huh. So you continued seeing them after the wedding, is that right?"

"Now and then. Socially, you mean? Now and then. Business, I see Georgie every month or so, whenever he comes down with a load of stuff."

"Let me try to get this straight," I said. "Harper left Germany without even phoning Michelle, after what was apparently a hot romance between them . . ."

"That's right."

"So she followed him here and demanded that he marry her or else she'd drown herself."

"You got it."

"Was she in trouble?"

"What do you mean?"

"Was she pregnant?"

"No. What makes you think she was pregnant?"

"Woman follows an American soldier all the way here, says he'd better marry her or else she'll drown herself . . . that sounds peculiar to me, Mr. Davis."

"Peculiar or not, she wasn't pregnant."

"You know that for a fact."

"I know it for a *positive* fact. I was at the wedding, this was maybe six months after we shipped out of Bonn. A woman six months gone can't wear a tight gown like she was wearing and not show whether she's pregnant."

"Is that what she was wearing? A tight gown?"

"White satin," Davis said and nodded. "She looked beautiful. A real beauty. Lord knows what she ever saw in Georgie."

"What do *you* think she saw in him?"

"Who knows?" Davis shook his head. "It's a real pity," he said. "She was a nice lady. And I'll tell you, Mr. Hope, even though Georgie's a friend of mine, I wish he fries for this. I wish they strap him in that chair real tight and turn on eight million watts of electricity, and fry him to a crisp."

I found George Harper's mother in a storefront Baptist church in the same black section of town. I had been to her house first, and the man who lived next door told me where she might be. Except for her, the church was empty. She sat on a folding chair some three rows back from the altar, her head bent, her hands clasped in prayer. I was reluctant to intrude, but I was there about her son, and my business was urgent.

"Mrs. Harper?" I said.

She looked up, blinked, shook herself out of her reverie, and then seemed surprised to see a white man in a black man's church.

"I'm Matthew Hope," I said. "I'm the attorney representing your son."

She was a woman in her late sixties, I guessed, her complexion as black as her son's, her face wizened and weary, her eyes studying me with a suspicion bred of centuries of slavery and nurtured by another century of denial, her eyes silently asking why her son couldn't have found himself a *black* attorney.

"Yes, Mr. Hope?" she said. Her voice was almost a whisper, an echo of the frail body in the frayed black coat.

"I'd like to talk to you, if I may."

"Please sit down," she said.

I sat beside her. Behind the altar, a tall window streamed early afternoon sunlight.

"Mrs. Harper," I said, "your son is in serious trouble, he's been accused of murdering his wife."

"Yes, I know."

"I want to ask you some questions. Your answers might help us in . . ."

"I wun't in Miami when he was here," she said. "If thass whut you wants t'know, I wun't here. I was up visitin my sick daughter in Georgia. She's *still* sick, but I couldn't stay away no longer. Not with George spose to've done whut they say he done."

"Do *you* think he did it, Mrs. Harper?"

"No, sir, I do not. Ain't a gentler soul alive than my George. Loved that girl to death, wouldn'ta lifted a finger to her ever."

"Mrs. Harper, your son claims he went to your house on Sunday the . . ."

"Yes, he did."

"And was told by a neighbor that you were in Georgia."

"Thass juss where I was."

"Which neighbor would that have been?"

"Miz Booth next door."

"Could I have her full name, please?"

"Alicia Booth."

"And her address."

"837 McEwen Road."

"Did she report to you that your son had been there?"

"She did."

"When did she tell you this?"

"When I got home."

"Which was when?"

"Lass Wednesday. Soon's I learned my boy'd been locked up."

"She told you he'd been there on Sunday the fifteenth?"

"Thass ezzactly whut she said."

"I'd like to see her before I go back to Calusa," I said. "Would you know whether she'll be home during the day, or does she work?"

"She's ninety-four years old, an' she's blind," Mrs. Harper said. "You'll fine her home, I'm sure."

"Mrs. Harper, from what I understand, your daughter-in-law came here to Miami looking for your son, is that correct? I'm referring now to the time before they were married. This would've been approximately a year and a half ago, would you remember?"

"I remember."

"*Did* she, in fact, come to see you?"

"She did."

"When was that, exactly?"

"George got his discharge in January and they was married in June. So this would've been in the spring sometime, March or April, sometime in there. I remember she was wearin a coat. It's unusual you see anybody wearin a coat in Miami, even on the coldest day. But she was wearin one. All bundled up, she was, like she was expectin a blizzard down here."

"Can you tell me in detail what you remember about that visit?"

As Mrs. Harper remembered it, she had just come home from visiting a friend that day—yes, it *had* to have been in April because she recalled that she and her friend had been talking about the flower arrangement they planned to put on the church altar on Easter Sunday, this had to be just before Easter sometime. She was putting her hat on the rack in the front·hall when she heard someone knocking at the door, and she opened the door and this very beautiful woman was standing there, prettiest young woman she'd ever seen in her entire life, white *or* black. The woman said her name was Michelle Benois, and she was looking for George Harper, was this where George Harper lived?

Mrs. Harper heard Michelle's French accent, and surmised she might have been someone George had known overseas, but she wasn't about to go telling her where she could find her son because she didn't know but what this was *trouble* standing here on her doorstep and shivering in what was sixty-degree weather, holding her coat closed tight around her, asking where she might find George Harper. George had moved to Calusa by then, to start his junk business, told his mother he'd make himself a fortune buying and selling junk, fat chance of *that* happening. But she wouldn't tell this strange beautiful woman with the French accent where she could find George, not until she'd talked to George at least, which she did by telephone every Saturday, to take advantage of the lower weekend rates. She planned to call George the very next day—she remembered now that this had to be a Friday when Michelle came to the front door because she was planning to call her son the next day, and what she did was call every Saturday—and she would ask him then about whether she'd done the right thing in not telling a stranger where he was living.

Michelle then asked—and this surprised her—if Mrs. Harper knew where she might find a man named Lloyd Davis, who was a friend of George's and who, Michelle said, she had also met in Bonn. Mrs. Harper was beginning to think now that this was some kind of trouble involving both George *and* Lloyd, who she knew had been with her son in the MPs over there in Germany, and who she knew when she saw him on the street, but not really to talk to. She didn't know where Lloyd was living at the time, knew he was married and lived with his wife somewhere in this section of town, but not exactly where, and anyway she wasn't about to give away Lloyd's address, even if she *had* known it, same as she wasn't about to tell any white woman looking for trouble where she could find George.

"I was polite to her an' all," Mrs. Harper said now, "but I tole her to go try the supermarket, or one of the bars, ast them *there* where Lloyd Davis lived 'cause I juss dinn *know*."

"What kind of trouble did you feel she represented?" I asked.

"I dinn *know* whut kind, Mr. Hope. All I knew was a beautiful young woman showin up on my doorstep in the middle of Niggertown, askin for my son's whereabouts, an' that meant trouble, *white* trouble. Turns out I made a mistake, but I dinn realize that at the time."

"What kind of mistake?" I asked.

"Well, I dinn know George was in love with her. I dinn know he'd be happy to see her."

I looked at her.

"When you say 'happy to see her . . .' "

"Beside hisself with joy. I called him the next day, you know, Saturday, like I always called him, an' I tole him this woman named Michelle somethin had stopped by the day before, askin where she could fine him an' all that. Well, I tell you, I never heard him sound so excited in his life. He kept askin me questions on the phone—how'd Michelle look, whut was she wearin, did she finely cut her hair short the way she said she was gonna do the last time he'd seen her, did she leave a number where he could reach her . . ."

"Did he say when that might have been?"

"Whut?"

"The last time he'd seen her?"

"No, I don't recall as he did. But, oh my, he was juss *thrilled* t'learn she was here in the States. I tole him she'd asked after Lloyd, too, an' he told me he was gonna call Lloyd soon's he hung up with me, couldn't wait to get off the phone, didn't even ast me how my rheumatism was, which'd been botherin me somethin terrible just then."

"Do you know whether he called Mr. Davis or not?"

"Well, I *spose* he did, but that din't help him none."

"What do you mean?"

"Dinn actually get t'*see* her till almost two weeks later, when she showed up in Calusa."

"Took her two weeks to find him, is that right?"

"Almost."

"I don't understand that. Mr. Davis told me he'd given her your son's address in Calusa."

"Well, I don't know. I juss know it wasn't till two weeks later he called me an' tole me Michelle was there with him, an' he'd ast her to marry him, an' she'd said yes."

"Uh-huh."

"Nice weddin it was, too. Pretty as a picture, she was, a beautiful June bride. White satin gown, I remember. I can tell you, Mr. Hope, I wun't too keen on the idea of my son marryin a white woman, I *knew* whut kind of trouble that was askin for. But I guess it turned out all right, leastways I never heard nothin from him to the contrary. Until now, it was all right. Now someone's gone an' killed her, an' they've blamed my boy for it, an' that ain't right. He couldn'ta killed her, Mr. Hope. He loved her too much."

I barely caught the 2:30 plane back to Calusa.

I had gone directly from Mrs. Harper's house to the address she'd given me for her neighbor, Mrs. Booth, and had confirmed there that George Harper had indeed stopped by to see his mother on the Sunday he was *supposed* to have been there. Since Mrs. Booth was blind, I carefully questioned her about how she had known this was Harper, and elicited the information that she'd known him since he was a tad, and would recognize his voice and his scent anywhere. I had not until that moment known that other humans give off distinct scents to blind people. I thanked her for her time, and left secure in the knowledge that she would make a good witness when it came time to pinpoint Harper's whereabouts in Miami.

The problem, of course, was not where he had spent the morning hours on Sunday the fifteenth, but rather where he was at eleven forty-five that night, while Michelle was being brutally beaten, and where he'd been on Monday night while she was being murdered in Calusa. I did not get to the county jail until a little before four o'clock. The jailer was not happy to see me; he kept telling me as he led the way to Harper's cell that I should have called first, this wasn't a hotel they were running here.

Harper was wearing jailhouse clothing not dissimilar to what he'd been wearing the first time I met him: dark blue trousers, pale blue denim shirt, black socks. In place of the brown, high-topped workman's shoes, the county had supplied him with black shoes that looked oddly formal in contrast to the rest of his clothing, the kind of highly polished footwear one might have worn to Calusa's annual Snowflake Ball. He got to his feet the moment the jailer unlocked the cell and let me in. The ceiling seemed too low for him, the walls too confining. I felt again this aura of menace emanating from him, and experienced a chilling sense of fear as I heard the jailer twist the key in the lock behind me. His footfalls retreated down the corridor, clicking on the asphalt-tiled floor. Harper and I were alone together.

"I ast that sum'bitch jailer to call your office for me," he said angrily. "Three *times* he called, three *times* they tole him you was still out of town. Where in hell you been, man? I thought you was spose to be my lawyer."

"I've been in Miami," I said. "Interviewing people we'll need as witnesses when this thing comes to trial."

"Whut people?"

"Lloyd Davis and his wife. Your mother and the woman who lives next door to her, Mrs. Booth."

"Why'd you go botherin them?"

"To find out if you actually *were* in Miami when you said you were."

"I was."

"I know that now. At least I know where you were for an

hour or so. It's the *rest* of the time that troubles me."

"I tole you where I was the ress of the time. Pompano, Vero Beach, an' then back to . . ."

"With no witnesses."

"I dinn know my wife was bein murdered. If I'd known that, I'da made sure I got the names and addresses of anybody I passed on the goddamn street."

"Where'd you have lunch that Sunday?"

"Pompano."

"Remember the name of the place?"

"No. Fust time I'd even *been* to Pompano."

"How about dinner?"

"Miami."

"Where?"

"Little diner."

"Do you remember the name of it?"

"No."

"How about the location?"

"Downtown someplace."

"Would you recognize it if you saw it again?"

"Looked just like any other diner."

"Would you remember what the person who served you looked like?"

"I ate at the counter."

"What did the counterman look like?"

"I don't remember."

"*Was* he a man?"

"I think so."

"White or black?"

"I don't remember. I had me a hamburger an' some fries an' a Coke. Then I paid the man, an' left."

"And went to the beach?"

"Thass right."

"To sleep."

"Thass right."

"And slept on the beach all night long."

"Thass whut I did."

"And stayed in Miami all day Monday."

"Yes."

"Why?"

"I tole you. I thought Lloyd might come back."

"Lloyd told me you have other people you do business with in the Miami area."

"Coupla other people, yes."

"Did you try to see any of them on Monday?"

"No."

"Even though you had a truckload of stuff you couldn't sell to Lloyd?"

"Lloyd wun't there."

"I know that. But you didn't try any of your other customers?"

"Stuff woulda been juss right for Lloyd."

"Do you normally conduct business on a Sunday?"

"I was sure I'd catch Lloyd there on a Sunday. Weekends are the biggest time for Lloyd."

"But he wasn't there."

"No, he wun't."

"You didn't call him first . . ."

"No need to. Usually catch him there on a Sunday."

"You filled your truck with gas on the Saturday before you left, is that right?"

"Thass right."

"At A&M Exxon, at seven, seven-thirty Saturday morning."

"Yeah."

"And you also bought an empty five-gallon gasoline can, and had it filled with gas."

"I did."

"By a man named Harry Loomis."

"Harry sold me the can and filled it for me, right."

"Was he wearing gloves?"

"Whut?"

"Gloves. Was Mr. Loomis wearing gloves when he handled that can?"

"Why'd a man be wearing gloves here in Calusa?"

"Garage attendants sometimes . . ."

"I don't recall as he was wearin any gloves, nossir."

"Did he wipe off the can before he gave it to you?"

"I don't remember."

"What'd you do with that can, Mr. Harper?"

"Put it in the back of my truck."

"Did you take it with you to Miami?"

"Nossir."

"What'd you do with it?"

"Put it in my garage."

"Why?"

"Needed it there."

"For what?"

"My lawn mower."

"Are you saying that's why you bought the gas? For your lawn mower?"

"Yessir."

"What was so urgent about buying gas for your lawn mower on the morning before you were about to leave for Miami?"

"Wun't nothin *urgent*, but I was there buyin gas, so I picked me up a new can and had it filled."

"What happened to the *old* can?"

"Sprung a leak, had to throw it away."

"When did you throw it away?"

"When I foun out it was leakin."

"Was that before you left for Miami?"

"Two, three days before. Leaked gas all over the garage floor, had to wipe it up 'fore it started a fire."

"Threw it away where?"

"In the garbage."

"When is the garbage picked up at your house?"

"Mondays and Thursdays."

"So if this was two or three days before you left for Miami, the old can would've been picked up on Thursday."

"I reckon."

"And you say you put the *new* can, filled with gasoline, in your garage that Saturday morning."

"Thass what I did."

"*Where* in the garage?"

"On a shelf there. Over my workbench."

"You're *positive* you didn't take that can with you to Miami?"

"Positive."

"Okay, let's talk about Bonn a little, shall we? That was where you met your wife, isn't it?"

"Uh-huh."

"How'd you meet her?"

"In a bar there."

"And began dating her?"

"Uh-huh."

"And fell in love with her, is that right?"

"Yessir."

"Then why'd you leave Bonn without even calling her?"

"Whut?"

"Lloyd Davis . . ."

"I called her ten, twenty times the day before I leff. I kept askin her to marry me, she kept . . ."

He shook his head.

"You asked her to marry you while you were still in Bonn?"

"I did. A hunnerd times. A *thousan* times."

"And?"

"She said she needed t'think it over."

"Which apparently she did."

"I don't know whut you mean."

"I mean three months later she came here looking for you."

"Thass right."

"Insisted that you marry her or else she'd go drown herself."

For the first time since I'd known Harper, he smiled. The smile transformed his face entirely. Nothing could have made him appear handsome or even faintly attractive, but the smile brightened his eyes and changed him from a creature of hulking menace to someone suddenly very human.

"Yeah," he said, pleased with the memory. "Used t'say that all the time, Michelle. If I wouldn'ta married her, she'da gone drown herself."

"Any reason for such a threat?"

"Well, it was only jokin, you know."

"She wasn't pregnant, was she?"

"Pregnant? Michelle? Nossir, she was not."

"Had you had sexual relations with her in Bonn?"

"Well, I don't see as that's any of your business, Mr. Hope."

"Maybe it isn't. But if we're going to keep you out of the electric chair . . ."

"I dinn lay a *finger* on Michelle till after we was married."

"Uh-huh."

"Thass the truth. Some kissin, some huggin, but never nothin further'n that. Michelle was a virgin when I married her. Had to teach her like she was a chile. I swear to God, Mr. Hope, wasn't nothin funny goin on 'tween her an' me in Bonn."

"How'd you feel about her and other men?"

"Whut other men? Wasn't nobody in Michelle's life but me. She was a proper wife, Mr. Hope. Anybody says otherwise is lyin."

"But you were very jealous of her, isn't that true?"

"Had no *reason* to be jealous. Why would a man be jealous of a wife was proper in every respeck?"

"You never argued with her about what you thought might be improprieties on her . . ."

"I don't know whut that word means, impo . . . whutever you said."

"You never thought she paid too much attention to other men?"

"Never. 'Cause she *din't*, plain and simple. She loved me, Mr. Hope. Woman who's crazy 'bout a man don't go payin 'tention to no . . ."

"She was still crazy about you after a year and a half of marriage, right?"

"Yessir."

"No problems, right?"

"Well, it wun't ezz*act*ly the way it used to be, but . . ."

"What do you mean by that?"

"Well, you know how it is when two people get married, they . . . are you married, Mr. Hope?"

"I used to be."

"Then you know how it is. Things get *diff'runt*, is all. That don't mean two people don't still love each other, it means juss they's got to work out whutever it is ain't the same no more."

"What was it that wasn't the same?"

"Well, personal little things. Mr. Hope, this ain't got nothin to do with I'm sposed to've killed Michelle. Nothin at all. They wun't no trouble 'tween us that'd cause me to go killin her. None a'tall."

"What personal things were wrong between you?"

"Personal means personal. It means you don't go discussin them with your minister, or with your doctor, or even with your lawyer either."

"Were they matters that *could've* been discussed with a minister or a doctor?"

"They were *personal*, Mr. Hope, an' that's that, so let's juss forget it."

"Okay, let's talk about your service overseas. You were with the military police, is that right?"

"Uh-huh."

"Were you unusually cruel to anyone you took into custody?"

"Nossir."

"Did you use your club on drunks?"

"Nossir."

"Never beat up any soldiers who'd . . ."

"Never."

"I'm getting conflicting stories, Mr. Harper."

"From who?"

"From you, and Sally Owen, and Lloyd Davis. The only thing everybody seems to agree on is that you were in Miami on the morning of Sunday the fifteenth. Aside from that . . ."

"Thass *juss* where I was."

"But aside from that . . ."

"I don't know why anybody would want to lie about me an' Michelle, or whut kinda person *she* was, or whut kinda person *I* am. Wun't nothin wrong with our marriage, we loved each other, we respected each other, an' anybody says it wun't that way is a plain and simple liar. Now whut *I* want to know, Mr. Hope, is why they ain't lettin me out of here. Thass why I been tryin to reach you all day long while you was in Miami with people who tole you nothin but lies about me an' Michelle. I want to know whut you doin to get me *out* of here. That sum'bitch jailer told me this wun't be comin to trial till maybe January sometime, am I spose to sit here all that time? Why'd you send that peachfuzz kid to the judge with me this mornin? I coulda told you beforehand no judge'd let a kid like that talk him into settin bail for me. When you gonna get me *out*, man, *thass* whut I want to know."

"There's nothing I can do about getting you out," I said. "Nothing in the law obligates the court to grant bail. Bail was denied in your case because the court considers the crime a particularly brutal one. That's why they can put you in the electric chair, Mr. Harper, the fact that the crime was 'especially heinous, atrocious, or cruel.' I'm quoting directly from the statutes, the aggravating circumstances of the crime are what make it a capital offense. Which is why I'd like you to reconsider everything you just said to me, and if any of it wasn't the truth . . ."

"All of it was the truth."

"Then everybody *else* is lying. Do you know a man named Luther Jackson?"

"Nossir."

"He says he saw you on the beach with Michelle the night she was murdered."

"He's mistaken."

"Another liar, right? Sally Owen's lying, Lloyd Davis is lying, Luther . . ."

"Maybe they juss ain't rememberin correctly. Anyway,

Sally never *did* like me, an' Lloyd's somebody I mostly do business with. Which reminds me, Mr. Hope. How *much*, ezzactly, is all this gonna coss me?"

"I haven't had a chance to discuss it fully with my partner," I said. "I've already told you . . ."

"Well, I wish you'd do that soon," Harper said. "Won't be no sense 'scapin the chair and then havin to work the ress of my life to pay off a bunch of lawyers."

"Mr. Harper," I said, "let's take first things first, okay?"

"Far as I'm concerned, that *is* the fust thing. An' I want it put in writin, hear? When you comes to a fee, I want you to put it for me in writin. I don't want you to go changin it later on."

"I'll put it in writing," I said, and sighed deeply.

"Okay," Harper said, and nodded.

It occurred to me that a man worring about legal fees rather than the possible loss of his life was surely a man who was as innocent as the day is long. In which case, why did his version of events differ so strongly from what Lloyd Davis and Sally Owen had—

"You said Sally never liked you. What's she got against you?"

"Her husband's a friend of mine. Her *ex*-husband. When the divorce come about, I took his side. She ain't never forgive me for it. Never will."

"Where is he now? Her former husband?"

"Right here in Calusa. Owns a liquor store on Vine and Second, I think it is. Second or Third."

"Andrew, is it?" I said, trying to remember. "Is his first name Andrew?"

"Andrew Owen, correct."

"What's the N in *your* name stand for?"

"Whut?"

"The N. Your middle initial."

"Nat. I was named for Nat Turner. Whut's *that* got to do with anythin?"

"I hate mysteries," I said.

94

It was close to 5:00 P.M. when I got to the liquor store owned and operated by Andrew Owen. He was standing at the cash register when I came in, the drawer open, the shelves behind him lined with rows and rows of whiskey in differing shades of brown. His own shade of brown was a deep mahogany. He was almost as tall as I was, but much heftier, a burly man with huge hands that deftly transferred the cash from the drawer to the countertop, stacking the money there in neat little piles of singles, fives, tens, and occasional twenties. At last, he looked up.

"What'll it be?" he said. "I'm about to close."

"My name is Matthew Hope," I said. "I'm representing . . ."

"Hope," he said, and looked at me more closely, and nodded, and came around the counter. He went to the front door, locked it, and then turned a sign hanging there so that the word *Closed* faced the plate-glass inset. Over his shoulder he said, "I remember you. You're the lawyer who got Sally that big settlement."

"Well, not so big," I said. I was thinking of what my *own* wife had managed to get from *me*, under the guidance of that mealymouthed shyster, Eliot McLaughlin.

"The house and three hundred bucks a month is plenty big where *I* come from," Owen said, walking back to the counter. "So what's it this time? Is she starting up again? I make my payments each and every month, right on the dot. What's she . . . ?"

"This has nothing to do with the divorce settlement."

"Then what?"

"Your friend George Harper has been accused of murdering his wife. I'm the attorney . . ."

"Yeah, I saw that on television," Owen said.

"I'm representing him."

"I suppose he could do worse. After what you got for Sally, maybe you won't do so bad by George."

"He *is* a friend of yours, isn't he?"

"I guess you might call him that."

"What would *you* call him?"

"A friend, sure."

"How good a friend?"

"So-so. We used to go fishing a lot together. He was nice to me when all that shit with Sally started. Is that a good friend? I guess. Who knows? We sort of lost touch lately, but I guess we used to be good friends."

"What happened to change the friendship?"

"Nothing. Who says it changed? He's *still* my friend, okay? It's just that people drift, man, they drift."

"What kind of support did he give you during the divorce?"

"Shoulder to cry on," Owen said.

They were the exact words his former wife had used in describing her relationship with Michelle.

"Can you go into that?"

"Sure, why not? I wish you'd asked me this at the time of the divorce, though, I might've come out of it with something more than the shirt on my back. I loved Sally a lot. She wanted the divorce, I didn't. I cried to George about it, and George listened. He was a good listener, George. A friend in need."

"This was when?"

"Almost a year ago to the day. You handled the divorce for her, don't *you* remember when it was?"

"I was trying to . . . she'd have been friends with Michelle by then, isn't that so?"

"Oh, sure."

"Good friends?"

"I suppose."

"Good enough for Michelle to have confided in?"

"Man, I had troubles enough of my own without wondering whether Michelle was confiding in my wife."

Someone rattled the front doorknob.

"We're closed!" Owen shouted. "Read the sign! It says closed!" He shook his head, and said, "Damn winos wait till the last minute to get what they need. The sign says closed, what's he shaking the doorknob for?" He looked to the front door again, and again shouted, "We're closed! Go home! Get lost!" He shook his head again, said, "Damn winos" under his breath, and then said, "Anyway, that's the story."

"Did Harper ever discuss Michelle with you?"

"No."

"Did he seem like a jealous person to you?"

"No."

"How'd she behave when other men were around?"

"Fine."

"Ever flirt with any of them?"

"No."

"Ever see them argue in public?"

"No."

"Ever come home and find her in tears in your house? Talking to your wife?"

"No."

"What'd Harper talk about on those fishing trips?"

"They weren't trips. We'd go over to the bridge and fish from there."

"At night?"

"At night, usually. Sometimes on weekends. Wouldn't be a bridge, would it, unless half a dozen niggers were fishing from it."

He waited for my reaction, and seemed disappointed when my face registered nothing.

"So what'd you talk about while you were fishing?"

"Is this before the divorce started or afterward?"

"Before."

"Everything under the sun. Most talkative guy I ever met in my life, George. He'd bend my ear all night long. Army stories, stories about his business, things that happened when he was growing up in Miami, everything. Nonstop talker."

"That wasn't your wife's impression of him."

"Well, that's what he was. Mr. Big-Mouth himself. Listen, Sally is the most fucked-up woman in the universe, her impressions of things aren't always too accurate, you follow me?

The only thing that interests Sally is her own little self and the two inches of vertical real estate between her legs. George Harper could've conducted a four-day filibuster in the Senate and Sally wouldn't have noticed. All Sally cares about is *Sally*, period."

"Yet she seemed to be concerned enough about Michelle to have listened to her whenever she came to the house with . . ."

"The black woman's burden," Owen said, and again studied my face for a reaction.

"Well, it *must* have been difficult for Michelle, don't you think?" I said. "A foreigner. A white woman married to a black man. She couldn't have had too many friends in Calusa . . ."

"I never heard anything about any difficulties Michelle was having. I don't know what bullshit Sally gave you, but I wouldn't trust anything she said. Did she come on with you?"

"No. Not that I was aware of."

"Didn't cross her legs so her skirt rode halfway up her ass?"

"No."

"Didn't shake her tits in your face?"

"No."

"She must be getting old," Owen said.

"What's your impression of Lloyd Davis?" I asked.

"Who's Lloyd Davis?"

"I thought you might've met him. He was best man at Harper's wedding . . ."

"I wasn't there."

"And apparently he saw the Harpers socially on several occasions."

"Oh, yeah, Davis. Big black nigger like me, right?"

I said nothing.

"I remember him now," Owen said, and smiled as though he had won some sort of secret victory.

"Tell me a little more about Harper," I said.

"What do you want to know?" Owen said, and sighed. "It's been a long day, man, I want to get home."

"Does he seem like a violent person to you?"

"No. Just the opposite. Gentle as can be. Used to bother him to have to take a hook from a fish's mouth. Used to say fish had feelings, same as us."

"Do *you* think he killed his wife?"

"Never in a million years."

My partner Frank was still in the office when I got there at a little past six. He had not liked the deal I'd made with Willoughby, and he *still* didn't like it.

"We're supposed to be partners," he said. "You had no right to go to him behind my back."

"I had no intention of deceiving you," I said.

"No? But without consulting me, you go to a little prick whose vendetta complex is well known in Calusa, and you make a deal with him that requires *you* to do all the shit work while *he* sits back and takes all the glory *if* he manages to win this case, which I doubt even *he* can do for a man as guilty as Harper seems to be."

"I'm not convinced of his guilt."

"Who's supposed to absorb our loss, Matthew?"

"What loss?"

"The loss we'll incur while you run all over town doing Willoughby's work for him. The loss of your *time*, Matthew, the loss we've *already* incurred while you were off in Miami today, out of the office all day long with the phones going like sixty. To quote Abraham Lincoln, 'A lawyer's time and advice are his stock in trade.' Our *time* is what we sell here at Summerville and Hope, Matthew, your time and my time, that is what we get *paid* for here. Now if you can explain to me how the loss of the revenue your time would normally generate if you hadn't become obsessed with . . ."

"I'm not obsessed, Frank."

"What do you call it then?"

"Look," I said, "I don't want to talk about this, okay? If

it's bothering you so much. I'll waive my draw for however long it takes to . . ."

"And that's not obsession, huh?"

"What*ever* the fuck it is, let's not talk about it anymore, okay?"

"Okay, fine," Frank said. "I'm going home. Will you grace us with your presence tomorrow morning, or are there other pressing matters that will necessitate your being away?"

"I plan to be here," I said.

"I feel honored. If you have a moment, you might take a look at the stack of messages Cynthia piled on your desk. Good night, Matthew," he said.

It occurred to me as he went out that in all the years we'd been practicing together we had never before that moment had an argument of any real substance. I went into my own office and found the promised stack of messages Cynthia had left on my desk. I pulled my briefcase out from under the kneehole and unceremoniously dumped all the messages into it. They would wait till I got home; tomorrow was another day. But there was one thing I wanted to check before I left.

In the cabinets lining Cynthia's receptionist cubbyhole, I located the file I wanted, and then carried it back into my own office. It was beginning to get very dark. I snapped on the desk lamp, and then opened the bottom drawer and pulled out the whiskey bottle I kept there on reserve for clients who became overly distraught, as some clients were wont to do while pouring out their complaints to me. Rarely did I ever touch a drop of whiskey in the law offices of Summerville and Hope, preferring instead to imbibe on my own time, leisurely and hardly ever to excess, although my former wife Susan's constant complaint had been that Beefeater martinis made me "fuzzy and furry and slurry" (her exact words) whenever I had more than one of them. In fact, and with all due respect for Susan's judgment, it was Susan *herself* who'd made me fuzzy and furry and slurry. From the bottom drawer, I pulled out one of the clean glasses Cynthia always kept in readiness for impending hysterical outbursts, poured myself two fingers of Scotch, and then opened Sally Owen's divorce file.

She had come to us in October last year, complaining that her husband, Andrew N. Owen (another N, I thought; what is it *this* time—Nicholas, Norris, Newton, Nathaniel?), had deserted her and had taken up residence with a woman named Kitty Reynolds, who at the time was living in an apartment on Lucy's Key, over the boutique she ran in the exclusive Lucy's Circle shopping complex. The woman Sally claimed had stolen her husband was described as a white thirty-five-year-old blonde.

I closed the file.

I felt suddenly weary.

6

I did not get to see Kitty Reynolds, the woman named in Sally's divorce action, until four o'clock on Wednesday afternoon. Guilt kept me chained to my office desk. Guilt and Frank's dark scowl. Guilt and a pressing number of duties that had to be performed for a varied number of clients before a deadline defined by the holiday tomorrow and my imminent departure on Friday for the nine-day vacation that would end the following Saturday, but that would nonetheless keep me out of the office till Monday, December 7.

My first call that morning was from a client named Mark Portieri.

"Mark," I said into the phone, "how are you?"

"Lousy," he said.

"What's wrong?"

"I want a new will."

"*Another* one?" I said, surprised. "Why?"

"To make sure she doesn't get a nickel."

"Who?" I said.

"Janie," he said.

Janie was his former wife. The firm of Summerville and Hope had handled the divorce for Mark only six months ago, and had since drawn a new will for him that excluded his former wife from the list of beneficiaries.

"But she's no longer named in the will," I said.

"I know that. Still, I want a specific provision saying she won't get a penny when I die."

"You don't need such a provision," I said. "If she isn't named . . ."

"I want it *in* there."

"Mark," I said, "you're under no obligation to leave anything to your former wife. If the will doesn't name her, she has no possible claim . . ."

"When the will is read out loud," he said, "when everybody gathers to hear it read out loud, I want the words in there. I want it to say, 'And to my former wife Jane Portieri, I leave nothing at *all*!' "

"Okay," I said, and sighed. He was thinking about one of those Hollywood scenes where the entire family congregates in some dusty office to hear an ancient lawyer read a will aloud. In real life, the beneficiaries of a will are normally informed by telephone or mail that they're about to inherit a large sum of money or a house in Bermuda or a goldfish in a tank. "But think over what I just said, okay? I hate to put you to unnecessary legal expense when, really, you're adequately . . ."

"I want that will *changed*, Matthew!" he shouted, and hung up.

Cynthia buzzed again to say that a man named Abner Fieldston—whose name I remembered from yesterday's telephone messages—was outside and wondered if he could have a moment of my time. I asked her to show him in. The wall clock read 9:30.

Fieldston was a black man in his mid-seventies, who told me he'd been born in a small town in Mississippi at a time when the authorities weren't keeping vital statistics records on blacks. He told me he didn't have a birth certificate. "I'm getting on in years," he said, "and I doan even have a certificate of my own *birth*. Can you get me a birth certificate?"

"Not if one doesn't exist," I said.

"Then what am I spose to do?"

"Well, there are other ways of establishing your birth and obtaining the equivalent of a birth certificate."

"You mean it?" he said, and broke into a wide toothless grin.

"Are your mother or father still alive?"

"No," he said, and the grin dropped from his face.

"Do you have any older brothers or sisters who are aware of the date and . . . ?"

"I'm an only child," he said.

"How about any aunts or uncles who might know when and where you were born?"

"Aunt Mercy was there at the actual birthing," he said. "She was midwife to my mother."

"Is she still alive?"

"Oh, yes."

"How old is she, Mr. Fieldston?"

"Ninety-eight," he said.

"Still of sound mind?"

"Sharp as a needle," he said.

"Let me have her name and address," I said. "I'll arrange for an affidavit to be mailed to her."

"Will that make me legal?" he asked, and grinned again.

"You've been legal all along," I said, and returned his smile.

At a quarter to ten, I began returning some of the calls that had piled up the day before. The first call I made was to a client named Hal Ashton, né Harold Ashkenazy, who was an Equity actor appearing in a production of *The Time of Your Life* at the Candlelight Club, one of Calusa's dinner-theaters. In the dark, during the curtain calls two nights ago, he had tripped on one of the set's barstools and broken his collarbone. He wanted to know if he could sue the owner of the place.

"Which place?" I said. "The Candlelight Club, or Nick's Pacific Street Saloon?"

"Hey, how come you know the name of the *bar*?" he asked, pleased. "Did you come see the show?"

"I was *in* it," I said.

"What? What do you mean?"

"In college."

"You're kidding!"

"Would one old actor kid another?"

"Who'd you play?"

"Blick. The vice-squad cop."

"He's the *heavy*!" Hal said.

"Somebody has to play the heavies," I said.

"So can I sue or not?" he asked, dismissing my past, brief, illustrious acting career.

"This sounds like a worker's compensation matter," I said. "Have you got a pencil?"

"Shoot."

"Give this man a call," I said, "tell him I referred you. He's an attorney who specializes in such claims."

"Worker's compensation, huh?" Hal said, disappointed, and then took down the name I gave him.

Cynthia buzzed the moment I hung up.

"Your daughter's on five," she said.

I stabbed at the button in the base of the phone.

"Hi, sweetie," I said.

"Dad, I have to make this fast because I'm in study hall. Mom wants to know should I pack *before* I come to your house tomorrow, or should I pack later on in the day?"

"What do you mean, later on in the day?"

"I promised her I'd come home for a little while, after the turkey, I mean. Would that be okay? 'Cause I'll be going to Mexico, and I won't be seeing her for a whole nine days."

"Sure, that's fine. But you'd better pack *before*, okay? What time did you tell her you'd be back?"

"I said after dinner sometime, is that okay?"

"Fine."

"Okay, Pops," she said, and hung up.

She rarely called me "Pops." I looked at the receiver in wonder, pressed the receiver-rest button for a dial tone, and then—reminded of tomorrow's festivities by my daughter—placed a call to Dale O'Brien at the law offices of Blackstone, Harris, Gerstein, Garfield, and Pollock.

"Blackstone, Harris, Gerstein, Garfield, and Pollock," the telephone receptionist said.

"Dale O'Brien, please," I said.

"May I say who's calling?"

"Matthew Hope."

I waited.

"Hello, Mr. Hope?" a woman's voice said. "This is Cathy, Ms. O'Brien's secretary. I'm sorry, she's in a meeting just now, can I have her get back to you?"

I looked up at the wall clock. It was only ten minutes past ten.

"I'll be leaving here at about noon," I said. "Ask her to call me before then, would you?"

"Yes, sir."

"Thank you," I said, and hung up.

Dale called back twenty minutes later.

"Hi," she said, "how's it going?"

"Miserably."

"Poor baby," she said. "Wait'll you see the turkey I bought."

Dale and my daughter had insisted, against my desire to liberate them from any kitchen chores tomorrow, on preparing an "old-fashioned" Thanksgiving dinner, complete with turkey and stuffing, roasted sweet potatoes, homemade cranberry sauce ("What's the matter with the canned variety?" I'd asked), green beans, and deep-dish strawberry shortcake, not to mention the celery, olives, home-baked bread, and other assorted goodies that would precede or accompany the main course. I had told them we could do just as well in a restaurant, especially when there were such minor matters as packing to worry about. They had informed me, in something close to high dudgeon, that they would both be packed long before they began preparing the meal, and this was something they *wanted* to do, and I had better endure it because God knew *what* we'd be eating in Mexico. What we'd be eating in Mexico had been one of our major concerns. I had visited Jamie Phelps, my family doctor, a man for whom I'd once handled what had turned out to be my initial brush with a homicide case, and he'd prescribed for us a drug named Vibramycin, to be taken every morning as a preventative, and another drug named Lomotil, to be taken only if and when Montezuma's Revenge struck any one of us. We were still a bit apprehensive. Reminded of dire illness, I suddenly thought of Dale's cat.

"How's Sassafras?" I asked.

"Fine," Dale said. "She doesn't have worms, they checked, and her fever's completely gone. One of life's little mysteries. What time will I be seeing you tonight?"

"Had you planned on staying over, or what?"

"Yes."

"Then why don't you come by straight from work?"

"No, I want to pack first. Let's say eight-ish, okay?"

"I'll see you then."

Cynthia buzzed the moment I put down the phone.

"Honest Abe on five," she said.

I picked up the phone again.

"Hello, Abe," I said. "Why don't we just put in a tie-line?"

Abe Pollock was one of the partners in Blackstone, Harris, Gerstein, Garfield, and Pollock, the firm with the longest name in town. He had no idea that I'd just finished a conversation with Dale, and was understandably baffled by my opening remark.

"Have we talked already today?" he asked.

"Inside joke," I said.

"Don't give me with inside jokes before lunch," he said. "What's this with your cockamamie client?"

"Which one?"

"The one who hired Okay Contracting to stucco his house."

"Okay *ain't* so okay," I said.

"Meaning?"

"He hired them six months ago, Abe. Some of the work isn't completed yet, and even what's done has been done poorly. So now your man wants payment, and I'll be damned if I'll approve it until . . ."

"Have a heart, Matthew," Abe said. "All Schultz is asking for is half what's due."

"Is he related to that *other* legendary gangster?"

"What? Who?"

"Dutch Schultz," I said.

"Never heard of him."

"Big Chicago gangster," I said.

"You're an even *bigger* Chicago gangster," Abe said. "Tell your client to give him the half, willya? Get Schultz off my back for a while."

"Not a penny, Abe. Not till the job is completed and the remedial work done to my client's satisfaction."

"Have a heart, Matthew," Abe said.

"I'll hold the balance of payment in escrow till then, how does that sound?"

"You don't know Conrad Schultz."

"I know his work, though."

"Let *me* hold it in escrow, okay? He'll feel safer that way."

"Fine."

"What?"

"I said fine, *you* can hold it in escrow."

"Will wonders never?" Abe said.

"I'll be out of the office next week, but I'll make sure the check is sent to you."

"Where you going?" Abe asked.

"Mexico."

"Looks like every lawyer in Calusa is going to be in Mexico next week," Abe said, and I could swear he was leering.

"Only two of us," I said.

"Well, have a nice time," he said. "And please don't trouble yourself for even a minute about those of us in the legal profession who'll be minding the store while you're off frolicking in the sun."

"I won't," I said.

"Is that a promise? I wouldn't want your vacation spoiled by undue guilt or remorse."

"I promise. Abe, it's been nice talking to you, but . . ."

"Send the check," he said, and hung up.

My lunch date that afternoon was with three Calusa investors represented by our firm. Together, they owned a parcel of Sabal Key land on which they had planned to build 170 condominium units. The owner of the parcel next door to theirs planned to build 110 units on his land. But because of the vagaries of the zoning ordinance, if my clients and the man next door *combined* their two parcels, they'd be able to build—within the zoning restrictions and within the law—300 units as opposed to the 280 if they'd proceeded separately. In unity, there is strength; there is also the two million bucks those additional twenty units, at a hundred thousand a throw, would bring into a combined entity. My three investor-clients wanted to form a joint venture with the man next door, and they wanted me to arrange a meeting with him and his attorney.

They were the dourest of men, these three, singularly intent on making money, determined to amass fortunes for themselves even if it meant manufacturing plastic vomit. ("There are the Vomit-Makers and the Dream-Makers," my partner Frank is fond of saying, apropos of nothing.) It never once occurred to any of them that crowding an additional twenty units onto the parcels they and their neighbor owned, while within the law if they could pull off their merger, might contribute to the wall-to-wall condominium look Calusa was so desperately trying to avoid. Money was the be-all and the end-all, poor Sabal Key's natural beauty be damned. They were grim and humorless men for the most part, and it was with some surprise that I listened to (and actually enjoyed) a joke one of them told, "a story a lawyer like you ought to appreciate," he said before telling it.

It seemed that one of the recreation parks up Tampa way had recently put in a tank with two male porpoises in it, these to supplement the other wildlife roaming free over the park's vast acreage. But it turned out that the porpoises had developed, of all things, an obscene letch for tender, young seagulls. In order to satisfy their yearning—and incidentally to keep them happy so they'd perform their little *non*sexual stunts for the thousands of paying visitors who came to the park each day—the owner of the park had taken to secreting nubile seagulls into the tank each night, the better for the porpoises to indulge their appetites for youthful birds.

Well, on a moonless night several weeks back the owner was sneaking onto the grounds a young and beautiful plump female seagull, carrying her in his hands up the path that led to the tank where the panting porpoises awaited their connubial sacrifice. (One was not supposed to ask, I gathered, how a pair of porpoises could *possibly* mate with a seagull.) As he moved stealthily forward, the owner of the park was startled by the sight of a lion sleeping across the only path that led to the tank. What to do? Hoping he would not awaken the lion, the owner stepped across his prone body, still carrying the young seagull in his arms, and a policeman came out of the bushes, brandishing a revolver and placing the man under arrest.

"Do you know what the charge was?" my client asked.

"What?"

"Carrying an Underage Gull Across a Sedate Lion for Immoral Porpoises," he said, and burst out laughing.

I did not get back to the office until almost three o'clock. I returned all the calls that had accumulated while I was out, and then buzzed Karl Jennings and asked him if he could come in for a minute.

Karl was twenty-seven years old, a recent—well, two years ago—graduate of Harvard Law who had decided to begin practice in the South, where the living was easy and the cotton was high. As the youngest member of our firm, he often brought to any difficult case a fresh point of view sometimes sadly absent in middle-aged men like Frank and me. Middle-aged, yes. Or perhaps, if one wishes to stretch a point, already over the hill. I am thirty-eight years old, and I figure my life expectancy to be somewhere between seventy and seventy-five. Thirty-eight is half of seventy-*six*, so there you are: already over the hill. Karl always dressed for work as though he were about to attend a funeral, a sartorial legacy inherited from his banker father in Boston. He had also inherited from the *pater familias* a head of wiry blond hair, an unfortunate eagle's beak, and very weak brown eyes magnified behind thick-lensed tortoise-framed eyeglasses. His voice was tinged with the unmistakable regional dialect one usually associated with members of the Kennedy clan. Cynthia cheerfully referred to him as "The Chairman of the Board."

I told Karl about the conversation I'd had with Abe Pollock, and asked him to make certain our client wrote a check to Abe, as attorney for Okay Contracting, for transfer to Abe's escrow account. Karl said he'd do that first thing Monday morning, when he got back to the office after the long holiday weekend. I then told him there was a man I wanted him to talk to while I was gone, a Mr. Harry Loomis at A&M Exxon on Wingdale and Pine. I wanted him to find out from Loomis everything he remembered about the morning George Harper went there to have his truck filled with gas, and especially what he remembered about selling him a five-gallon gasoline can and filling *that* for him as well.

"I'm specifically interested in learning why his fingerprints weren't on that can," I said. "Harper thinks he wasn't wearing gloves, and he can't remember whether or not Loomis wiped off the can. Find out."

"Okay," Karl said. "Anything else?"

"I've given Cynthia a Puerto Vallarta number where I can be reached. That's until Monday night. On Tuesday we'll be in Mexico City, at the Camino Real—Cynthia has that number, too."

"Okay," Karl said.

"That's it," I said.

"Have a nice time," Karl said, and went out.

I picked up the phone and called Kitty Reynolds at work, telling her I was representing a man accused of murder, and asking if I might see her sometime that afternoon. She told me to come right over, and I was in Lucy's Circle not twenty minutes later. It took me another ten minutes to find a parking space, however, and it was not until four that I paused on the sidewalk outside Miss Reynolds's boutique, and looked up at the sign over the brimming front window.

The Circle, as it is familiarly known to Calusa's residents and visitors, was indeed that—a wheel the hub of which was a fair-sized park, the rim of which was lined by restaurants, jewelry stores, souvenir shops, a photography shop, a florist, an optical shop, a post office, several shops selling antiques, three art galleries, a cheese shop, two shoe stores for men, five shoe stores for women, a half-dozen women's clothing stores, a barbershop, several luncheonettes, three men's clothing stores, a chocolate shop, an ice-cream shop, a store selling modern furniture, a pharmacy, a five-and-dime, a greeting-card shop, a shop selling oranges and grapefruits you could ship home to less fortunate people in Minnesota or Toronto, a luggage shop, a store selling furniture fashioned from redwood trees, a shop selling only earrings, and a discothèque that on Wednesday nights featured an act called "The Body Machine" (the rage of Calusa at the moment), wherein several male dancers performed a mild striptease to which only women were admitted.

The sign over the front plate-glass window of the boutique read KITTY CORNER. I decided at once that it had been inappropriately named. It was, to begin with, *not* on a corner—although there were some corners in the Circle, being fed as it was by sidestreets funneling into it—but was instead in the middle of the block, sandwiched between a shoe store and an art gallery. It was, secondly, and judging from the array of sexy lingerie, minuscule bikinis, and slinky dresses in the front window, not the sort of place selling anything even remotely warranting the adjective "kittenish." And lastly, the name Kitty Corner seemed to suggest what the owner of a cat might have called the place under a stove where nestled a box full of torn paper scraps or the packaged, deodorized litter one could buy in any supermarket.

There was only one person in the shop when I entered it and closed the door behind me. She was, to be sure, a blonde who appeared to be in her mid-thirties, five feet six or thereabouts, weighing a well-curved 120, and wearing one of the more spectacular creations displayed in her front window, a satiny concoction slit to the thigh on one leg, and cut low over resplendent breasts that threatened the skin-tight fabric. I felt for a moment as though I'd wandered into Calusa's Club Alyce, where ladies in scanty costumes danced at any male patron's table, thrusting aggresssive crotches into willing faces, for the price of a few dollar bills stuffed into their G-strings.

"Miss Reynolds?" I said.

"Yes?"

"I'm Matthew Hope. I phoned a little while . . ."

"Yes, how do you do, Mr. Hope?" she said, and walked toward me, her hand extended, a smile on her face, every curve of her body insinuating itself against the sleek shiny fabric of the dress she was almost wearing.

The dress was a pastel blue, a shade lighter than the color of her eyes. She was wearing a smoky gray eye shadow and a string of baroque pearls that lustrously echoed it. Her lipstick was the color of a pomegranate's skin, glossily spread on bee-stung lips still parted in a smile. She took my hand in a delicate clasp; her palm was slightly moist. There was about her the lingering scent of a musky perfume.

"You said on the phone . . ."

"Yes, that I'm representing a man accused of murder, and I would appreciate your assistance."

"But how?" she said, and released my hand.

"The man's name is George Harper."

"Yes?"

"He's a friend of Andrew Owen."

"Yes?" she said again.

I had the distinct impression that neither of the names meant anything at all to her. I had not expected her to know Harper. But after what I'd read in Sally Owen's file—

"Andrew Owen," I said again.

"Am I supposed to know either of these people?" she said.

"I thought you might have known Mr. Owen."

"I'm sorry, I don't."

"He's a black man who runs a liquor store on Third and Vine."

"I'm sorry, but . . ."

"Miss Reynolds, last year I handled a divorce case for a woman named Sally Owen. At the time, she was Mr. Owen's wife." I paused. Not the slightest flicker of recognition showed on her face. "Mrs. Owen named you as a witness in her action."

"Me?" she said, her eyes opening wide.

"You *are* Kitty Reynolds, aren't you?"

"I am."

"And you *do* live in an apartment over this store, don't you?"

"No, I don't. I live on Flamingo Key."

"Did you *ever* live in an apartment over this store?"

"Not for the past six months."

"Did you live here a year ago?"

"I did."

"That's when the divorce action started, in October last year."

"And you say I was named by Mrs. Owen as . . ."

"She said Mr. Owen had deserted her and was living here with you."

"That's absurd."

"It's what she told us."

"Then why wasn't I . . . ? I mean, if there was a trial or a hearing or whatever you call it, then why wasn't I called as a witness or whatever?"

"We reached a settlement before it ever got to court. There was no need to . . ."

"Well, anyway, this is absurd. Who *is* this woman? How could she *say* such things about me? Living with a black man? The only black man I *know* is my gardener!"

"I take it you're single, Miss Reynolds? Were you . . . ?"

"Yes, I've been divorced for the past six years."

"Then you were single last year, when Mrs. Owen alleged . . ."

"That doesn't mean I knew her husband! I never even *heard* of him till you mentioned his name."

"Then he wasn't living here with you?"

"Of course not! Besides, what's any of this got to do with me—"

She cut herself short.

The abruptness with which she'd interrupted her own question, the way she'd left the sentence dangling with only the word "me" at the end of it, was somehow jarring to the ear. Had she been about to add something more to the "me," a person's name, perhaps, making it "me and Andrew"? or "me and whoever"? And then it occurred to me that perhaps the "me" wasn't a word at all, perhaps the "me" was only *part* of a word, part of a name, in fact—part of the name "Michelle."

"What were you about to say?"

"I said what I had to say."

"No, you stopped yourself."

"You told me you were representing . . ."

"Yes?"

"Someone named George Harper."

"Yes."

"So what's any of this got to do with . . . with . . . with whatever it is that happened?"

"What happened is that his wife was murdered."

"Yes, so what has that got to do with these questions about . . . what . . . whatever his name is?"

"Andrew Owen. Miss Reynolds, what were you about to say?"

"I told you, I said what . . ."

"I think you were about to say the name 'Michelle' ".

"I don't know anyone named Michelle.

"But that's what you were about to say, isn't it? You were about to say, 'What's any of this got to do with Michelle?' "

"Well, really, I can't imagine how you can possibly know what I was about to say. Are you a mind reader, Mr. Hope?"

"*Did* you know Michelle Harper?"

"No."

"You're sure about that?"

"Positive."

"Do you know *George* Harper?"

"No."

"Let's get back to Andrew Owen for a minute."

"No, let's not get back to anyone. Let's find the door and get out of here, okay, Mr. Hope?"

"Miss Reynolds . . ."

"Before I call the police," she said.

"Sure," I said, and left.

I had the sudden feeling that everyone in the entire world—including my own client—was lying.

And I wondered why.

7

In the year 1621, Governor William Bradford of Massachusetts decreed that December 13 be set aside as a day of feasting and prayer to express the gratitude of the colonists for the bounty of the first corn harvest they'd had since landing at Plymouth Rock. The Indians invited to the feast brought gifts of venison and wild turkey, which the women served together with the fish, geese, and ducks the men of the colony had provided. There was cornmeal bread in abundance, of course, and journeycake and succotash and nuts and pumpkin stewed in maple sap. The colonists and their Indian guests spent three days in prayer, singing, and feasting. That was America's first Thanksgiving.

In this part of Florida, the Calusa and Timucua tribes of Indians weren't faring quite as well as their neighbors far to the north. The first white man they had ever seen was the Spanish conquistador Juan Ponce de León, who came to the Gulf Coast in 1513, fresh from his exploration on the Atlantic side, where he had given Florida its name and claimed for

Spain all the land upon which he'd set foot. Here on the western side, he met with fierce resistance from the Indians, and was forced to sail back to Puerto Rico without the gold he was seeking. He did not keep his promise to return until eight years later, in 1521, only to be welcomed by a poisoned Indian arrow that ended his life and his dreams of glittering riches and eternal youth. (If he'd still been alive today, he'd probably have joined my three investor-clients in their intended conquistadorial plundering of the natural riches of Sabal Key.)

But de León wasn't to be the last of the Spaniards who came to Florida's shores. In 1539, his countryman Hernando de Soto landed on what is now known as Stone Crab Key, looking for the same gold that had eluded his predecessor, a treasure the Indians seemed not to know existed. The fighting was fierce and bloody, causing a Spanish defeat so monumental that Spain thereafter called off any future gold-seeking Gulf Coast expeditions. Other white men, however, could not be dissuaded from coming to Florida again and again, bringing with them a delightful array of civilized treasures like smallpox and syphilis (the Spanish disease, the French disease, the English disease, depending on where you came from) and taking back with them a commodity more valuable than the elusive gold they constantly sought—the able young bodies of Calusan and Timucuan braves.

By 1621, when those Massachusetts white men and Indians were celebrating together at their outdoor tables laden with food and drink, the Calusans and Timucuans were well on their way to extinction. By the turn of the century, there were scarcely more than three hundred of them left on the coastline they had inhabited for two thousand years. To the north, in Georgia and Alabama, the formidable Creeks were having troubles of their own, with the British, who were desperately trying to free their territories of Indian claims. Forced to move southward (where they became known as the Seminole, alternately meaning "seceders" and "runaways" in their native Muskogean language) the tribe met little resistance from the decimated Calusan-Timucuan inhabitants. Indian met Indian on Indian ground and Indian triumphed. The Calusa and the Timucua were no more—but the days of the Seminole were equally numbered.

Florida did not become an American territory until the year 1822, after the United States government purchased it from Spain. Fourteen years after that, at the insistence of impatient homesteaders, the government began its War of Indian Removal, a "final solution" to rival that undertaken in yet another civilized country a century later. The Seminole Indian War, as it was more familiarly called, did not end until 1842—three years before Florida was admitted to the Union as its twenty-seventh state. By then, those of the Seminoles who had not been butchered had been sent off for relocation on reservations in Oklahoma, where perhaps their descendants were today celebrating Thanksgiving (the fourth Thursday in November, ever since a 1941 Congressional ruling) with the *rest* of us true "Americans."

My partner Frank insists that one day the archaeologists will unearth a fossil proving without question that the first human beings on American soil were Russians who had crossed over from Siberia to Alaska when the Bering Strait was still a land bridge. This monumental discovery, Frank says, will cause the Soviet Union to make immediate claim to all the territory encompassed by the United States, thereby triggering a legal tangle that will last for centuries and provide gainful employment for every lawyer on either side of the Iron Curtain. As a by-product, the archaeological find will end all possibility of nuclear attack, the Russians then being loath to destroy a land that is theirs by birthright. Maybe Frank is right. Or maybe he should tell it to the Seminoles.

Thanksgiving Day was cold and bleak and gray—perfect for three people who planned to leave for Mexico's sunshine early the next morning. Susan dropped off my daughter at 10:00 A.M., by which time Dale and I had already breakfasted, cleared the kitchen table, and begun taking from the refrigerator the raw materials she and Joanna planned to transform into our midafternoon feast. Joanna was carrying a suitcase designed for a month in Europe rather than the nine days we planned to spend south of the border. When I asked her why it was so heavy, she shrugged and said, "I always carry a traveling iron whenever I travel." Susan, catching a glimpse of Dale in the kitchen—where she was simultaneously poring over a cookbook and pulling pinfeathers from the naked turkey—surprised me by saying, "She's quite beautiful, Matthew," and then walked swiftly to where her Mercedes-Benz (part of the divorce settlement) was parked at the curb. Dale hugged Joanna, and Joanna hugged her back, and then both of them shooed me out of the kitchen with the admonition that too many cooks spoiled the broth.

I went into the small room I had furnished as a study and placed a call to Jim Willoughby at his home on Stone Crab. When I reported what I'd learned (or rather *failed* to learn), and told him I thought everyone had been lying to me, he immediately asked what had given me such an impression.

"Well," I said, "their stories seem contradictory."

"That doesn't necessarily mean they're lying," Willoughby said. "Besides, Matthew, I want you to remember something very important. The neophyte criminal lawyer will often fall into the trap of seeking a *true* murderer to replace his client, whom he believes has been wrongfully accused. That's not our job. Our job is to show that our man is innocent of the crime, period. We don't *care* who actually did it, Matthew. That's a job for the cops once we get our man acquitted—let *them* find the maniac loose in the streets, do you see?"

"I don't see that the two are mutually exclusive," I said.

"Don't go looking for a murderer," Willoughby said more firmly. "Instead, go looking for people we can put on that witness stand to rebut the prosecution's contention that our man is guilty beyond a reasonable doubt. That's what we're looking for—a parade of witnesses who'll raise the question of reasonable doubt. That's *all* we're looking for. We want to know where Harper was and what he was doing while his wife was getting herself killed. I don't know why you bothered going into all that shit about how he met her and when and where they got married, I really don't see how that's any concern of ours, Matthew. If you'll stick to . . ."

"I thought if we could show how much he loved her . . ."

"A man can adore his wife in the morning and slit her throat in the afternoon. That's a sad fact of life."

"Why are these people lying to me, Jim?"

"*If* they're lying, which of course you don't know for a fact. Perhaps their memories are faulty—as well they might be if you're asking questions about events that occurred a year ago, two years ago, which you shouldn't be asking in the first place. Or perhaps they've got their *own* skeletons in the closet and they're . . ."

"That's just what I'm beginning to think," I said.

"It's not our job to rattle anybody else's bones," Willoughby said. "I don't *care* if Owen Harris . . ."

"Davis."

"Davis, was fucking Kitty Foyle and . . ."

"Reynolds."

"And a dozen Chinese girls in Calusa's only opium den, which to my knowledge does not exist. I'm interested in where the hell George Harper spent all day Sunday and Monday while his wife was first getting her brains beat out and then getting put to the torch. That's what I'm interested in learning. If you can find me one person, male or female, who can testify that he or she actually *saw* George Harper in Miami at eleven forty-five on Sunday night, then he couldn't have been here in Calusa beating his wife black and blue. And that'll take care of the *first* part of the prosecution's case, the alleged beating which they'll attempt to tie in to the subsequent murder. And if we can find somebody who'll say he was with George Harper on Monday night, why then the prosecution can *shove* its case, Matthew, and I don't care *how* many of Harper's gasoline cans they found at the scene, or *how* many of his fingerprints were all over them. A man can't be in two places at the same time, that's Newton's Law or somebody's. If we can prove where Harper was—and I hope to God it wasn't here in Calusa—then we're home free. So, Matthew, please concentrate on what we're trying to prove here, and stop looking for skeletons in the closet, okay?"

"If there *are* skeletons, we should know about them," I said.

"Why?"

"Because the state's attorney is going to have a crack at any witness we put on the stand, and if those skeletons have something to do with George Harper, I sure as hell don't want to be surprised by them."

"Let me handle that when the time comes, okay?"

"No, Jim," I said, "*not* okay. I don't want any surprises."

"What kind of surprises are you expecting?"

"I don't know. But when people start lying to me . . ."

"I've already told you, that may only be . . ."

"And it may not."

"Matthew, this is Thanksgiving Day, my brother and his wife are coming down from Tampa for the big turkey dinner, and that's enough trouble for one day without you starting to sound like amateur night in Dixie."

"I *am* amateur night in Dixie," I said.

"Then change your act," Willoughby said. "Unless you want our man to be the *next* turkey who gets roasted."

"You know I don't want that."

"So trust me. I've had a lot of experience in such matters."

Whenever anyone asks me to "trust" him, I usually run to hide the family silver. I listened now while Willoughby emphasized once again the *sole* matter that should concern me upon my return from Mexico—namely *where* and *how* George Harper had spent his time on the Sunday and Monday he claimed to have been in Miami.

"Okay," I said.

"Okay?"

"Okay."

"You're doing a good job so far, Matthew," he said. "Just don't lose sight of the forest for the trees."

"To coin a phrase," I said.

"Huh?" he said.

"*Nada,*" I said. "I'll talk to you when I get back."

"Yes, do that," he said. "Have a nice time, Matthew."

One of the things I like most about Dale is her unpredictability.

Another is her spontaneity.

We had made love the night before (lengthily and satisfactorily, I'd thought) and had finally fallen asleep at two in the morning after promising ourselves similar and frequent passionate excursions during our nine days in Mexico. It was now 4:00 P.M. on Thanksgiving Day, scarcely fourteen hours later. We had consumed a meal that surely could have fed the entire population of Kansas. I had washed and dried all the pots and pans, stacked the dishes in the dishwasher, bagged and carried out the garbage, and taken Joanna to her mother's house, where I'd exacted from Susan the promise that she would have her back to me by nine. I was still feeling logy and a bit drowsy as I pulled the car into my driveway, wanting nothing more than a little nap before I started packing. The sun had broken through at noon, and the temperature had reluctantly climbed to a shade above sixty-five, not quite warm enough to be lounging by the side of a pool in a string bikini—but that's where Dale was, and that's what she was wearing.

"Hi," she said.

"Hi."

"Get her home okay?"

"Yep."

"When will she be coming back?"

"Nine."

"Nine," Dale repeated.

I should have detected a warning, or perhaps a promise, in the way she echoed that single word. Instead, I remained blithely unaware.

"What would you like to do now?" she asked.

"Take a nap," I said. "How about you?"

"I'd like to practice," she said.

"Practice?"

"For the beach in Mexico."

She was wearing her hair tied at the back of her head with a green ribbon. I could not see her eyes behind the prescription sunglasses that shielded them from the sun. She lay quite still on her back, her body entirely relaxed and superbly tanned, a smooth even bronze against the white of the bikini. A pair of white, high-heeled sandals were on the terrace floor beside the chair.

"What's there to practice for the beach in Mexico?" I asked, puzzled.

"What the ladies do here on North Sabal," she said. I still could not see her eyes. There was a faint smile on her mouth.

"You do that in Mexico, you'll end up in jail," I said.

"I thought Puerto Vallarta was very chic and continental," she said.

"It's also very Catholic."

"So are France and Italy. The ladies in France and Italy take off their tops, Matthew."

"If you take off your top in Mexico, they won't consider you a lady."

"Didn't Liz Taylor take off her top in Mexico?"

"I doubt it."

"Mm," Dale said. She was quiet for several moments. Then she said, "I'll have to practice for *here* then. For when we get *back* from Mexico."

I looked at her.

"Why don't you sit down?" she said. "Sit down, Matthew."

I took the chair opposite hers. Watching me, the smile still on her face, she sat up, and then reached for the sandals, and put on first one and then the other, and then rose suddenly, uncoiling the long length of her body, the high heels adding two inches to her already spectacular height. She reached up to loosen the ribbon in her hair, pulling it free like the ripcord on a parachute, unfurling a cascade of auburn hair that fell loose to just below her shoulders. She shook out the hair. She took off the sunglasses and placed them on the chair behind her. I saw her eyes.

"Tell me if I'm doing it right," she said.

She turned abruptly then, and walked away from me to the far side of the pool, where low-growing mangroves and taller Australian pines shielded the house from the bayou beyond. There were people living on either side of us, but the owner from whom I was renting was known in the neighborhood as "Sheena, Queen of the Jungle," a sobriquet applied after she had planted more trees, bushes, shrubs, and vines on her property than could be found on the entire six acres of Calusa's Agnes Lorrimer Memorial Gardens. Whatever Dale planned to do, she'd be afforded a privacy she could never find on any beach in Calusa. I suddenly found myself very wide awake.

At the far end of the pool, she turned and put her hands on her hips. "I thought I'd walk sort of innocently," she said, "like this," she said, "so no one'll suspect what's coming," she said, and began undulating toward me as innocently as Delilah must have approached Samson, hands still on her hips, high-heeled sandals clicking on the baked clay tiles surrounding the pool, her breasts, captured in the flimsy string top of the bikini, bobbing ever so gently with each long-legged stride she took. I felt a vague, distinctly adolescent stirring in my jeans.

"And then, you know," she said, "I'll just sort of reach up behind me," she said, "casually, no big deal, Matthew, just reach up behind me," she said, still moving slowly and inexorably toward me, high heels clicking, belly gently rounded above the patch of white that shielded the contradictorily blond hair of her crotch, arms going up behind her, bent at the elbows, "and just give the string here a little tug, you know, and let them just sort of . . . ooooh!" she said, and glanced down at her own breasts in mock surprise as they virtually exploded free of the scanty top. "Am I doing it right?" she asked.

She stopped stock still some ten feet away from me, approximately half a pool-length away from me, and put her hands on her hips again, one hip jutting. Her breasts, where the sun had not touched them, were a pale white, the nipples surprisingly erect. She stood that way for what seemed a long time, motionless, and then began walking toward me again in that same slow, tantalizing strut, her eyes never leaving my face, her hands moving lower on her hips, her thumbs hooking into the tight band of the bikini bottom.

"And then," she said, "if I can find the courage," she said, "and if I can quell my natural fear of the police, why then I might just, you know, slowly lower the bottom part, Matthew, just to where" (and she began lowering it) "the blond hair begins to show, you know, just about to here, Matthew" (and she lowered it to just about there) "where you can see the, you know, the beginning of my . . ."

The telephone rang.

"Shit," Dale said.

The phone kept ringing.

She stood there with her thumbs still hooked into the waistband of the bikini, her long fingers pointed downward in a triangle that framed the triangle of the string patch, the uppermost side of it exposing the faintest hint of the crisper blond patch beneath it.

"Don't answer it," she whispered.

"It might be Joanna," I said.

"No, it's your fucking friend Bloom," she said.

It was my fucking friend Bloom.

"Matthew," he said, "something terrible has happened, I hope you're sitting down."

"What is it?" I said.

"Your man's out."

"What?"

"Harper. He's broken out of jail."

"What?"

"Stole a sheriff's car parked out back, knocked the officer flat on his ass, Christ knows *where* he is now, Matthew. I've put out an all-points bulletin—excuse me, BOLO, I'll *never* get used to what they call it down here. That's a 'Be on the Lookout For,' it means every law enforcement officer in the state'll be looking for him, not that I think he'll hang on to that sheriff's car any longer than he has to. Matthew? Do you hear me?"

"I hear you," I said.

It was raining when we got to Puerto Vallarta, the kind of torrential downpour that one expected in Calusa during the summer months; when we'd left Calusa that morning the sun had been shining brightly. My partner Frank claims to like rain; he also claims to like snow. He says that the sameness of the weather in Calusa can drive a man to distraction, this despite the fact that he has lived through many a hurricane season there. Frank would have enjoyed the wind and the water that swept in through the sides of the windowless Jeep as Sam Thorn drove us from the airport.

Sam was wearing a yellow hat and rainslicker better suited to a Cape Cod fisherman than a retired Circuit Court judge, but he obviously knew his environment and he was the only one properly dressed for the wild ride to his villa. The rest of us were wearing what we'd worn in sunny Calusa that morning; none of us had expected to step off the plane into a goddamn typhoon. Dale had on blue jeans and a green T-shirt that matched her eyes; her long auburn hair flailed wildly in the wind, her face was wet, her glasses flecked with raindrops. Joanna had dressed identically in emulation and adoration—blue jeans, green shirt, even a locket that looked identical to the one Dale had around her neck. Her blond hair was caught in a pony tail. She kept squinting her eyes into the wind and the rain. I, too, was wearing jeans with a causual sports shirt open at the throat, the sleeves rolled up over my wrists. The shirt was soaked through even before we'd driven out of the airport and onto the road that hugged the shoreline, where the wind blowing in off the Pacific was much fiercer.

Sam explained that this was unusual for Puerto Vallarta in

the month of November. Sam said that the precipitation in November was supposed to average something less than a third of an inch, and the temperature was supposed to average seventy-eight degrees Fahrenheit, twenty-six on the Celsius scale. For the past few days, he said, it had been rainy and cold. Very unusual, he said. Sam was a man in his mid-sixties, tall and slender, with a nose like a hatchet, and bright intelligent blue eyes, and a shock of white hair that somehow made him look younger than his actual years. He spoke with the precision one might expect from a former judge, weighing his words as carefully as if he were charging a jury, measuring them out as surely as justice itself.

The villa he had purchased (or rather leased for ninety-nine years: in Mexico, foreigners are not allowed to own real estate) was located six windy, rainy, shitty miles south of the center of town, perched high on a hilltop overlooking Mismaloya Beach. It took us fifteen minutes to get there, but it seemed more like an hour. "Here it is," Sam said at last, and we stepped down out of the Jeep and passed through a wrought-iron gate to the right of which was a tile set into the wall and lettered with the words CASA ESPINA.

"*Espina* means 'thorn' in Spanish," Sam said, and then shouted at the top of his lungs, "Carlos! *Ven acá!*"

Carlos was one-half of the live-in couple Sam had only recently hired and whom, he confided in a whisper, he would fire as soon as he could find a pair more suited to the job. Carlos did not speak a word of English. He came clambering up the stone steps that wound down the side of the villa for the height of its full three stories, almost slipping on the uppermost step and catching his balance in time to avoid what I was sure would be a fatal plunge to the highway far below and the beach on the other side of it. The villa had been built almost at the very top of the mountain, approached only by a winding dirt road that had been all but washed away during the last few days' torrential rains, Sam explained, but affording him the privacy and solitude he wanted in his retirement. Carlos scrambled into the Jeep and began piling our luggage onto the tiled entryway outside the wrought-iron gate. In the pouring rain, we started our precarious way down the stone steps that led to the entrance door on the uppermost level of the house.

"The door is two centuries old," Sam said, "almost as old as I am."

We followed Sam into a room—and a view beyond—that caused me to catch my breath. We were on the dining level of the house—what Sam called *"el comedor,"* a spacious, open, terraced area that included the dining room itself and *"la cocina"* off to the left. The floor was covered with tiles glazed a green as deep as Dale's eyes, somewhat imperfectly cast so that they created an illusion of a swelling sea enclosed by a waist-high wrought-iron railing that defined the terrace and provided a sense of security against the rugged terrain dropping off below the room and the *real* sea far below that. The view was spectacular. To the left was the wide sandy arc of the beach with its fishing dinghies bellyside up against the rain, and its thatched *palapas,* and the jutting peninsula where (Sam explained) the company shooting *Night of the Iguana* had built a functional set later destroyed by fire for a scene in the film. "This is where it all started," Sam said. "You can thank Elizabeth Taylor and Richard Burton for what Puerto Vallarta is today."

The highway curved past the ruins of the *Iguana* set and disappeared into jungle-fringed mountains that seemed to roll endlessly into the distance, each lush succeeding peak a fainter echo of the one before it. To the right of the beach and the highway that ran above it was the Pacific itself, roiling and tempestuous today, stretching as far as the eye could see, presumably to China itself, punctuated by a pair of huge boulders closer inshore, identified by Sam as *"Los Arcos,"* so called because of the natural arches that ran through them and under them. And there—suddenly on the horizon—a rainbow!

"Daddy, look," Joanna whispered beside me, and took my hand.

"You brought the good weather," Sam said, and grinned. "Let's all have a drink. Toni should be back from town any minute."

Toni was a nineteen-year-old Swedish girl, almost as tall as Sam, blonder than my daughter, braless in T-shirt and string-tie baggy white pants, and obviously Sam's live-in *au pair*, judging from the way she embraced him after she'd swept into the villa and put down the armful of packages she was carrying. She shook our hands energetically when she was introduced and then excused herself ("For just one minute, yes?") and, her arms full of the purchases she'd made in town, hurried down the stone steps leading to the master bedroom below the living room, on the same level as the guest wing, and similarly opening onto the poolside terrace.

"You should see our bed," Sam said like the good judge he used to be, leaving nothing open to interpretation. "It's round, like the one that *Playboy* guy has in Chicago."

We were on the living-room terrace, sipping margaritas prepared by Maria and served by Carlos, who seemed to be ideal servants, causing me to wonder why Sam wanted to fire them.

"Toni speaks six languages," Sam said.

The six languages she spoke were Swedish (of course), English, French, Italian, Spanish, and a little bit of Portuguese. When she joined us, she was wearing one of the dresses she'd picked up in town, a white lace concoction with peek-a-boo eyelets that did nothing to discourage the notion that she was completely naked under it. She was barefoot ("It's better so not to slip on the tiles," she explained) and carrying in her hand the low-heeled sandals she expected to wear to dinner in town that night. "I have already made a reservation for nine o'clock," she told Sam, who accepted the information with a judgelike noncommittal nod. It was obvious—at a little past four in the afternoon—that Toni's "minute" in the master bedroom had included a shower, a shampoo, a careful makeup job, and the donning of what she called her "wedding dress." She explained, rather mysteriously, that there was an errand she had to attend to, but that she'd be back before seven, and perhaps we would all like to drive into town together then, to walk around a little or perhaps to shop ("I adore the shopping here!" she said, and rolled her big blue eyes) before we had dinner at La Concha, which, she assured us, and Sam affirmed, was the best restaurant in town. She kissed Sam briefly on the cheek, said, "See you later then, okay?" and whisked off up the tiled steps to the main level, her sandals dangling in one hand, her long legs flashing briefly before she passed out of view above. A moment later, we heard a car starting outside.

"I love her to death," Sam said, and I thought of George Harper saying almost those identical words during his interrogation, and felt a sudden pang of guilt.

There were two spiders, each the size of a fifty-peso coin, on our bathroom ceiling. I wanted to spray them dead, but Dale informed me that they'd been there before us and were entitled to their space. She named them Ike and Mike. Everytime I went into the bathroom, I checked to see that they were where they were supposed to be. They seemed never to move. Neither did they have webs. They simply *sat* there. I wondered how they survived.

On our first morning at Casa Espina, I began to understand why Sam planned to fire his live-in couple. We were all awake and bustling by seven-thirty, but Carlos and Maria did not come into the kitchen to prepare breakfast until almost nine, Maria explaining that she had misunderstood (although Toni had given her instructions in impeccable Spanish) what time we planned to have our first meal. The meal itself was worth waiting for—freshly squeezed orange juice, sliced papaya, eggs served with bacon unlike any I'd ever tasted before, crisp and only faintly salty, rich dark coffee brimming in pottery cups Sam had bought on his last trip to Guadalajara. Sam asked us if the people who manufactured the decaffeinated coffee Brim were still broadcasting their asinine television commercials, the ones in which the tagline "Fill it to the rim—with Brim" provoked gales of hysterical laughter, as though the actors had just heard the wittiest comment of the century. I told him I didn't watch much television.

There were no television sets at Casa Espina. Neither was there a telephone. Sam had told me, when he'd invited us, that we could be reached at the Garza Blanca Hotel—perhaps a mile or two away on the road to town—where of course there were telephones, and where the hotel manager would be happy to send a runner to the house with a message. I had left the number with Cynthia, but I did not expect her to call except in an emergency. Sam told us now that he *could* have a phone installed, but he preferred not to.

"The thing I like best about being here is the utter sense of serenity," he said. "Nothing disturbs it, unless you want to call the flock of green parrots that flies past the terrace at precisely nine each morning a disturbance. I can remember being back in Calusa, Matthew, that damn phone ringing every ten minutes. I'm happy to be away from it all. I'll never go back."

I, too, was happy to be away from it all. But, unlike Sam, I had to go back on the fifth of December.

On Sunday morning Sam awakened us at 7:00 with the announcement that we would have an early breakfast and then take a boat to Yalapa—a beach accessible *only* by boat—some two hours away. We boarded the boat—a ferry, really—at 9:00 A.M. and were in Yalapa before lunch, which we ate at a beachside restaurant called Rogelio's, where a wandering peddler tried to sell Dale the identical abalone barrette she had bought in Puerto Vallarta for forty pesos less. On the beach after lunch, I met a man who suddenly reminded me again of what was waiting for me back in Calusa.

He and his wife came wandering up the beach, and spread a blanket beside us. She was the thinnest woman I'd ever seen in my life, with contradictorily enormous breasts swelling in the top of a brown bikini almost as dark as her tanned skin. Her hair was black. She smiled as she made herself comfortable on the blanket. Her husband smiled, too, and soon we were chatting. He told me he had worked for an advertising agency in New York before coming to Mexico eight years ago. He told me he had been accused of killing his wife in a fit of rage one night, and had been acquitted of the crime after a trial that had lasted almost two months. He told me he had quit his job soon afterward, selling all his worldly possessions, and moving down here to Yalapa with his former secretary—the wife who now lay smiling beside him on the blanket, her enormous breasts bulging in the scanty top of the bikini—where together they had found a happiness they had never known before. As he told all this to me, his eyes were twitching, and his mouth was twitching, and I sensed in him a loneliness so deep and so pathetic that it almost caused me to weep. We shook hands when the ferry blasted the signal for departure. I waded into the water beside Dale and my daughter, and as we boarded the waiting motor dinghy I thought of George Harper, who had broken jail and stolen a sheriff's car, and I wondered what sort of loneliness *he* might be feeling just then.

The ferry left at 4:30 P.M. and we were back in Puerto Vallarta by 7:00. We ate dinner at a restaurant in town, and during the meal Joanna informed us that tomorrow was the big day, tomorrow she would wear her bikini for the first time anywhere in public, and she exacted from all of us the promise that we wouldn't laugh. When we got back to the villa, all the womenfolk, as Sam called them, went promptly to bed, leaving both of us in the living room with cognacs and our chess pieces. Sam was white, I was black. Within ten minutes, he had me checkmated.

"What's troubling you?" he asked.

I told him all about the Harper case. I told him about my conversations with Lloyd Davis and his wife, and Sally Owen and her former husband; I told him about having talked to Harper's mother and the woman who lived next door to her;

I told him about my unsatisfying conversation with Kitty Reynolds and my conviction that almost everyone I'd spoken to had been lying to me.

"Nobody lies unless there's something to hide," Sam said.

"But *everybody*? Does *everybody* have something to hide?"

"In a conspiracy, yes."

"Come on, Sam, what the hell kind of conspiracy?"

"Dope?" Sam asked.

"No, no."

"Florida's second biggest industry next to tourism. You say some of these people live in Miami?"

"Yes."

"The local drug trade there is estimated at seven billion dollars annually," Sam said. "Seventy percent of the cocaine, eighty percent of the marijuana, and ninety percent of the counterfeit Quaaludes coming into the United States pass through the port of Miami from South America."

"I don't think Harper or his wife were involved in dope traffic."

"How about their friends?"

"I didn't get any indication of that, Sam."

"Then why are they lying?"

"I don't know."

"Okay, what else?"

I told him I'd asked Karl Jennings to track down the garage attendant who'd sold Harper the gasoline can and then filled it with five gallons of gas, told him I'd asked Karl to find out why Loomis's prints weren't on that can, and then admitted I was concerned over the fact that Karl hadn't yet called to let me know what he'd found out.

"Did you leave the number at the Garza Blanca?"

"Yes."

"Well, this is Sunday," Sam said. "Thursday was Thanksgiving Day, and your office was probably closed on Friday . . ."

"It was."

"You can't expect him to have worked over the weekend, Matthew. Besides, he knows you'll be back on the fifth, so even when he *does* have the information you requested-which, by the way, is sound prepar—"

"It wasn't my idea," I said. "Jim Willoughby put me onto it."

"Is he the lawyer you're working with?"

"Yes."

"A good man, but a bit on the paranoid side. Skye Bannister's the best state's attorney Calusa ever had, and I've seen plenty of them, believe me. The way Willoughby badmouths him, you'd think . . ." Sam shook his head. "Anyway," he said, "you'll have the information on that can when you get home, I'm sure of it."

"Yeah," I said. "I suppose."

"What would you do with it if you had it here?"

"Well—nothing."

"Exactly. Relax, Matthew. Enjoy being here, enjoy Mexico City when you get there. You'll be back in the Calusa salt mines soon enough."

"Am I handling it right so far?" I asked.

"Your approach cannot be flawed," Sam said, and grinned.

We finished our drinks. Sam rose and yawned, and said we might as well sleep late tomorrow since nothing was planned but a leisurely day of flopping on the Mismaloya Beach. Dale was still awake when I got to our room.

"What's going on here?" she asked.

"What do you mean?"

"Why is Toni tiptoeing around like a spy?"

"I didn't notice her tiptoeing around."

"You haven't noticed all those secret whispered conversations in Spanish with Carlos and Maria?"

"No."

"What's going on?" Dale asked again.

We did not find out what was going on till Monday night at eight o'clock. Sam, Toni, Dale, and I—Joanna had finally got back from the beach and was downstairs frantically packing—were sitting in the living room drinking the piña coladas Carlos had made for us, when suddenly we heard the sound of several automobiles outside, car doors slamming, voices calling to each other, laughter, and—all at once—music. Toni was grinning from ear to ear as a dozen or more people, followed by a mariachi band, came down the steps from the main level and into the living room, all of them singing "Happy Birthday to You" at the top of their lungs, while the band played a distinctly Mexican accompaniment behind them.

"I'll be a son of a gun," Sam said, and embraced first Toni and then Dale and me, and then all the guests Toni had invited to celebrate Sam's sixty-fifth birthday. Carlos and Maria—in on the secret, of course—had informed us earlier that dinner would not be served till nine o'clock, and they now paraded down from the dining level carrying pitchers of margaritas and piña coladas, followed by Maria's sister Blanca, hired especially for the occasion and carrying a platterful of hors d'oeuvres. The mariachi band consisted of two guitarists, a trumpet player, a violinist, and a man shaking maracas, all of them wearing ruffled white shirts with blue silk scarves tied at the throat, sombreros large enough to float the owl and the pussycat out to sea, and shiny black suits, the trousers of which were decorated with tiny silver bells along each outside leg. They set up shop near the fireplace, and—encouraged by the margaritas Carlos served them and the general high spirits of the guests—launched into a medley of Mexican hits they knew far better than "Happy Birthday to You."

"Was it a surprise? Did I surprise you?" Toni asked Sam.

"You are *constantly* surprising me, my dear," Sam said, and hugged her close again.

Four of the invited guests lived there on the hill—a retired schoolteacher and his wife from Michigan, and a homosexual couple who had just built a $250,000 house as a retreat from the perilous climate of Connecticut, where they ran a motor lodge. The other guests lived in town, all of them along Gringo Gulch, some of them ninety-nine-year property owners, the rest renters. The couples broke down unevenly into seven Mexicans and five Americans; the odd man out (or *woman* as the case happened to be) accounting for the uneven breakdown was a Mexican married to a retired dairy farmer from Pennsylvania. She looked a lot like Carmen Miranda; he looked a lot like the man holding the pitchfork in the Grant Wood painting.

I was deep in conversation with him—I had never met a dairy farmer, retired or otherwise, in my entire life—when another car pulled up to the main gate of the villa. I thought at first that more guests were arriving. But Carlos came down the steps into the living room, and held a hurried conversation in Spanish with Toni, and then Toni came to me and said under the sound of the trumpet playing an old Mexican favorite even I recognized, "Matthew, it's a runner from the Garza Blanca. There's been a telephone call for you!"

The runner was actually a driver. The vehicle he maneuvered down the curving hillside road was a Jeep not unlike the one Sam himself was renting, except that it was brand-new and painted white and decorated on its side panels with the hotel's distinctive colophon. The runner did not speak a word of English. When we reached the bottom of the hill and he made the turn onto the highway, I could still hear above us the sound of the mariachi band playing another chorus of "Cielito Lindo." He drove a bit more recklessly than Sam did; we were at the hotel in seven minutes. A young Mexican woman wearing a long gown slit up the leg to the thigh turned to look at me as I approached the main desk where she was standing talking to the room clerk. I interrupted their conversation ("The Ugly American," I could hear her thinking) and told the clerk I was Matthew Hope.

"Ah, yes, Mr. Hope," he said, "would you call this number, please? You can use the booth on the left there. It is better to make it collect or to use your credit card."

The number he'd scrawled on a piece of hotel stationery was Morris Bloom's at the Public Safety Building in Calusa.

"Morrie," I said, "it's Matthew."

"Hello, Matthew," he said, "I'm sorry to break in on your trip this way, but this is important."

"What is it?"

"I called your partner at home, he gave me this number I could reach you at in an emergency. I hope it's okay, my calling . . ."

"Yes," I said, "it's fine. What is it?"

"I hate to be the one giving you this news, but I thought I'd better get to you right away. Your man's still loose out there, we haven't been able to find him, and now it looks like he's killed another person."

"What?"

"Sally Owen's been murdered."

"What?"

"Lady who lives next door found her at . . . what time is it there, anyway? How many hours difference is there?"

"It's eight-thirty," I said.

"Only an hour behind us, huh?"

"Morrie, tell me what . . ."

"Lady who lives next door went over there about seven o'clock our time, to return a pie dish, nice lady, walked in on bloody murder. She was lying on the floor near the sink. Her head was crushed, Matthew. With a hammer."

"How do you know it was a hammer?"

"Found it on the floor next to the body."

"What makes you think Harper . . . ?"

"His initials are on the hammer, Matthew. Burned into the handle. G.N.H. for George N. Harper."

"Anyone could have burned those initials into . . ."

"Well, I know that. But if it really *is* his hammer, the way we think it is, then this is another one, Matthew, this is the second one. And I was thinking if you could make some kind of personal appeal to him, talk to him personally, then maybe we could get him to come in before he hurts somebody else." Bloom paused. "Before he kills somebody else, Matthew."

"How can I talk to him if I don't know where he is?"

"I thought you could go on television or something."

"How can I do that, Morrie?"

He didn't answer me.

"Morrie, I'm here in Mexico," I said. "How can I go on television when I'm here in Mexico?"

He still didn't answer me.

"Morrie," I said, "the answer is no."

"I was hoping . . ."

"The answer is no."

"Before he does it again, Matthew."

This time, I didn't answer.

"Well, think it over," Bloom said. "How's the weather down there?"

"Fine," I said.

"Think it over," he said, and hung up.

8

I did not arrive in Calusa—via Houston—until two o'clock the next day, Tuesday, December 1. I went directly to the office, talked briefly with my partner Frank (who told me the worst move I'd ever made in my life was to start any sort of relationship with Detective Morris Bloom), and then buzzed Cynthia and asked her if I could see Karl Jennings for a minute.

I had still not called Susan to tell her that Joanna had gone on to Mexico City alone with Dale; I wasn't sure I planned to tell her at all. But Calusa was a small town, and if I ran into her in a restaurant or a supermarket, she'd surely want to know what I was doing back here and where the hell our daughter was, and I would only have to explain *then* how it had been *my* idea for Joanna and Dale to continue the vacation without me. Better to do it on the telephone. But not just yet.

Karl Jennings was ready to report.

"Not that it's going to make much difference," he said. "Now that he's killed another person."

"That's only the police allegation," I said.

"It's also the line the papers and television stations are taking," Karl said. "You should've seen this morning's headlines. Made it sound like we've got our own Jack the Ripper down here. Anyway, I talked to this guy Harry Loomis yesterday, got there at the crack of dawn—are you aware that Frank doesn't appreciate the way our firm is spending nonproductive time on . . . ?"

"Yes, I'm aware of it. What'd Loomis have to say?"

"He showed me this little room where they sell automobile accessories, you know? Windshield wipers, jacks, those little ashtrays with the beanbags under them, key rings with the emblem of your car on a little leather fob—*and* five-gallon gasoline cans. Half a dozen of them still on the shelf there, all of them exactly the same."

"Like the one he sold Harper?"

"Identical to the one he sold Harper. The brand name is Reddi-Jiff, the can is manufactured by a company in Ohio. I have the name here if you need it."

"Okay, go ahead. What happened on the morning Harper went in?"

"Loomis was filling Harper's tank when Harper said, 'Think I could use a gas can. You got any gas cans?' or words to that effect. Loomis took him back to this little room, and said, 'Pick one out, man,' or words to *that* effect."

"Pick one out."

"Right."

"Were those his *exact* words?"

"More or less. The point is he left Harper alone in there to make his own selection while he went out to get the reading on the pump."

"Then it was Harper himself who took the can from the shelf, is that it?"

"That's what Loomis says. Harper personally took the can from the shelf and carried it out to where Loomis was at the gas pump."

"Then what?"

"Harper asked him to fill it for him."

"And?"

"Loomis unscrewed the cap and . . ."

"Loomis did?"

"Yeah."

"Then what?"

"He filled the can," Karl said, and shrugged.

"Who screwed the cap back on?"

"Loomis."

"Did he touch the handle?"

"No, just the cap."

"Who picked up the can when it was full?"

"Harper, and put it in the back of the truck."

"Which means Loomis's prints were *still* on the cap."

"No."

"No? If he screwed the cap back on . . ."

"Yes, but his hands were greasy, he'd just been changing some spark plugs when Harper came in. He noticed he'd got the cap all greasy, and he wiped it off with a rag."

"Harper told me he didn't remember Loomis wiping off that can."

"Harper was in the cab of the truck already—starting it up, in fact. Loomis yelled for him to hold it a minute. He wiped off the cap, said, 'Okay, that's got it,' or words to that effect, and waved him off."

"Good," I said. "That accounts for Loomis's missing prints. If whoever murdered Michelle was wearing gloves . . ."

"Well, gloves, yeah," Karl said dubiously.

"Then only Harper's prints would be on the can."

"The hammer, too," Karl said.

"What?"

"They found Harper's prints on the hammer, too. His and his alone. It was in the papers this morning." Karl hesitated. "Matthew," he said, "this may be out of line, I'm low man on the totem pole here. But it looks to me as if Harper really *did* do it. *Twice.*" He hesitated again. "Maybe when they find him, you ought to start considering a plea of guilty."

I called Bloom the moment Karl left my office.

"I'm here," I said.

"I figured you would be," Bloom said. "I appreciate it, Matthew. This is getting to look worse and worse for Harper. I hope you'll agree to go on . . ."

"Worse and worse how?"

"Well, there doesn't seem to be any doubt now that the hammer's actually his. Guy who lives next door to Harper, bright young guy who knew him well . . ."

"What's his name?" I asked, and pulled a pad into position before me.

"Roger Hawkes, 1126 Wingdale Way."

"White or black?"

"Black. You can talk to him, Matthew, but he'll only tell you what he told us."

"And what's that?"

"He recognized the hammer as the same one he borrowed from Harper a couple of weeks ago. Had some work to do around the house, knew Harper had good tools, went over to borrow the hammer from him. Same hammer, he's identified it for us. G.N.H. on the handle, burned into the wood."

"When did he return it to Harper?"

"Same afternoon."

"Okay," I said.

"That's not all of it, I told you it's getting worse and worse."

"How much worse *can* it get?" I said.

"Harper's garage has a good lock on it, no Mickey Mouse stuff. Front door, too. No way to get into that garage except through the garage door itself or through a door leading from the house into the garage. The place is locked up tight, Matthew, and there are no signs of forcible entry."

"Meaning what?"

"Meaning Harper went into his own garage and took his own hammer from . . ."

"Or anyone *else* who had a key," I said.

"Well, who else *would* have a key, Matthew? Michelle's dead . . ."

"Did Harper stop to pick up his personal possessions when he broke jail?"

"Well, no, but . . ."

"Don't you normally confiscate a man's wallet, and his keys, and his . . ."

"Well, yes."

"If Harper didn't *have* his keys, how could he have unlocked either the garage door or the . . . ?"

"People sometimes leave a spare outside. In one of those little magnetic cases you hide under something."

"An invitation to burglars, am I right?"

"Well, yes, Matthew, but . . ."

"Even if there *was* a spare someplace outside the house, *anyone* could have found it, isn't that true?"

"Yes, but . . ."

"So it wasn't necessarily *Harper* who . . ."

"Matthew, this isn't a court of law. I'm only trying to tell you how this thing looks to *us*, okay? I admit I hadn't thought of him not having a key, a man breaks out of jail, he doesn't have his house keys with him, that's true, Matthew. But if there *was* a spare key someplace outside the house, and if Harper *did* use it to get into his own garage, then that would explain his fingerprints on the hammer we found next to the body of the dead woman. Now that is an incontrovertible fact, Matthew, the fact that Harper's fingerprints are on the murder weapon—*both* murder weapons, in fact. The gasoline can *and* the hammer. What I'm asking you to do is go on television tonight. I've already called the local station here in Calusa and the one in Tampa that covers a wider area. They've agreed to put you on if you *want* to go on. It's up to you. I've got to tell you something else that may influence your decision, Matthew."

"What's that?"

"We found the sheriff's car Harper swiped when he broke out. Located it near the Chickasee River Lookout. There used to be a shotgun on the back shelf of that car, Matthew. There isn't anymore. Harper took it with him when he ditched the car. That means the BOLO now reads 'armed and dangerous.' Are you following me, Matthew?"

"I'm following you."

"We've got a list of all the cars reported stolen in the area since Harper broke jail last Thursday. Sizable list; you wouldn't think there was so much auto theft in a nice place like Calusa, would you? Oh, well. Anyway, we've tacked that list to the BOLO, too, just in case Harper decided to swipe himself *another* car after he ditched the sheriff's. So what we've got now is a fugitive from justice, charged with first-degree murder, possibly driving a stolen vehicle, and armed with a shotgun. Are you beginning to get the picture, Matthew?"

"Yes, Morrie."

"I'll spell it out, anyway. Some of the redneck law enforcement officers in this state aren't going to ask polite questions if they spot a coal-black 'nigra' who maybe committed two murders in a row and is now armed with a loaded shotgun. I'm trying to tell you the knife cuts both ways. *I* want Harper to come in before he hurts somebody else. *You* should want him to come in before somebody hurts *him*."

"Okay," I said, "arrange the television stuff."

"Thank you," Bloom said.

"Couple of things *I'd* like," I said.

"Name them."

"I'd like to take a look at the scene."

"Which one?"

"Sally Owen's house."

"We've still got a man posted at the door there. I'll pass your name on, and he'll let you in. My men and the lab techs are finished inside and out, there's nothing you can foul up for us."

"And I want to see Harper's garage."

"I'll see if I can get his keys from the county jail."

"Will you call me back?"

"Soon as I can," Bloom said. "I'll check with the television people, they'll probably want to put you on live here in Calusa for the six o'clock news, and tape you in Tampa for the eleven o'clock segment there. I'll get somebody to drive you up there, if you like. I know it's going to be a long day for you."

"I'd appreciate it."

"I'll get back to you," Bloom said, and hung up.

Susan was her usual sweet charming self when I called.

"What do you *mean*, she went on to Mexico City with Dale?" she shouted.

"Yes," I said. "At my suggestion. I had to come back here, but I saw no sense in Joanna cutting her vacation short just because I had to."

"Without consulting *me*, right?" Susan said.

"I was not aware that consultation was necessary," I said.

"You'd better read our separation agreement, Buster," Susan said.

She had never in all the time I'd known her called me "Buster."

"I am familiar with the terms of our agreement," I said calmly. "It does not call for consultation with you while Joanna is enjoying visitation privileges with her own god-damn *father*!" I said, not so calmly.

"I'm going to call Eliot McLaughlin," Susan said.

"What for? Do you want him to extradite Joanna from Mexico? For Christ's sake, Susan, she'll be home on Saturday, that's only four *days* from now. I can assure you Dale . . ."

"I don't want to hear about Dale," Susan said.

"I can assure you she's a responsible adult," I said, calmly again, "who will be taking excellent care of Joanna for the remaining length of their stay in Mexico."

"Where they fertilize their crops with human *excrement*!" Susan shouted.

"Dale is not a farmer," I said.

"If anything happens to my daughter . . ."

"*Our* daughter," I suggested.

"A fine father *you* are," Susan said, "leaving her alone with a stranger . . ."

"Dale isn't a stranger."

"Oh, I'm sure of *that*," Susan said.

"Susan," I said, my voice rising, "I called to tell you that I'm home and Joanna is still in Mexico. She'll be back this Saturday, and that's all I have to say to you."

"That's not all *Eliot* will have to say to *you*."

"I welcome a call from that mealymouthed shit," I said, and hung up, trembling.

There are people in Calusa who are quick to remind anyone that the blacks here have it much better than the blacks living in big cities like New York and Detroit. They will point out with pride that many of the houses in New Town are in the forty-to-fifty-thousand-dollar price range, the equivalent of what a lower-middle-class white might own in any big-city suburb. They do not notice, perhaps, that at Count Basie's recent personal appearance at the Helen Gottlieb Memorial Auditorium, a hall that seats two thousand people, there were only eight blacks in the audience. I notice such things. So does my partner Frank.

I had not slept much the night before in Puerto Vallarta; Bloom's call, the knowledge that I would have to begin coping with a travel agent in the morning, and the mariachi band blasting till 2:00 A.M. had combined to render me limp by the time Sam dropped me off at the airport. Neither had the two hours I'd spent on the ground in Houston, or the subsequent bad news from Bloom, or the unsatisfying conversation I'd had with Susan helped much to lift my spirits. As I started up the walk to Sally Owen's house, three doors up from the Harper house, I was feeling an odd blend of irritability and lightheadedness, rather like what a pugnacious drunk might feel while picking an argument with a benign bartender and simultaneously giggling at his own aggressiveness.

The house was a white clapboard building surrounded by a white picket fence. The police officer standing at the door was also white. Big, burly man wearing a blue uniform, a .357 Magnum holstered at his waist, sweat-stained armpits, fat red face sprinkled with freckles, red hair showing at the sideburns and tufting onto his forehead from under his peaked cap. He watched me suspiciously as I came up the front walk. A Crime Scene sign was tacked to the front door, and a huge padlock hung from a hasp undoubtedly fastened to the door and frame by the police.

"Off limits, buddy," the cop said, waving me off with his stick.

"I'm Matthew Hope," I said. "Detective Bloom promised he'd . . ."

"Oh, yeah, right," the cop said. "You want to look the place over, right?"

"Right."

"You from the State's Attorney's Office?"

"No, I'm not."

"Then what?"

I didn't feel like presenting credentials; I sidestepped the question. "Bloom called, didn't he?"

"Radioed it to the motor patrolman on the beat."

"Then it's okay to go in," I said.

"Sure," the cop said, and fished a key from his pocket and unlocked the padlock. "Better not touch anything, though."

I did not bother mentioning that Bloom had told me the police were already finished here, inside and out. For some odd reason, the man's presence rankled, perhaps because Bloom had said there were redneck law enforcement officers out there who would as soon shoot a black man dead as give him the right time of day.

I felt the presence of death in that house the moment I stepped through the front door. Something terrible had happened here; the sense of it hung on the pale afternoon light that filtered into the hallway through a small arched window at the far end of it. There was a standing grandfather's clock in the entry hall, but it had stopped ticking. There was un-opened mail on the entry-hall floor, dropped through the door slot by a letter carrier making his appointed rounds come snow, come sleet, come hail—come murder. Through the open kitchen doorway, I could see chalk outlines on the linoleum floor covering. The unmistakable outline of a body. A smaller outline that was clearly meant to represent a hammer, some three feet from the other outline and in a red chalk as opposed to the white that had outlined Sally Owen's body as she lay in death.

I went into the kitchen, stepping carefully around both outlines.

I tried to visualize George Harper entering this house, surprising Sally as she stood at the kitchen sink, raising the hammer above his head, bringing it down repeatedly on her skull, crushing her skull, and then dropping the hammer before he fled into the night. Why? I wondered. Why kill her? Why leave behind the murder weapon with his initials burned into it and his fingerprints all over it? *People panic*, Bloom had told me. *Even the pros panic.* Harper wasn't a pro, although according to the police he was well on the way to becoming one, two murders in as many weeks, practice makes perfect. And apparently he had panicked *twice*, leaving behind a gasoline can with his prints on it the first time around, and then a similarly incriminating hammer after the commission of the second murder. Why? I wondered. Had it been panic or sheer stupidity? Was the man careless? Reckless? Suicidal? All three of the above? None of the above?

I moved out of the kitchen and into the entry hall again.

The mail, a dozen envelopes or so, still lay on the floor, touched by a slanting beam of sunlight swimming with dust motes. I moved down the hallway and into a small living room on the left. A sofa and two easy chairs. A green carpet. The drapes open to let in more sunlight than had been in the hallway, the same silent dust motes. Over the sofa, a framed oil painting of a pair of Scottish terriers like the ones in the Black & White whiskey ads, heads cocked, quizzical looks on their alert little faces. I leaned over the sofa and looked for a signature. None. The painting looked like the sort of badly executed representational art one could buy for five dollars or so at any of Calusa's street fairs during the months of March and April, when the tourists were thickest and the suckers were born one to the minute. Had Sally Owen been an art lover with poor taste? An animal lover who favored dogs? An animal *hater* who preferred even a lousy representational painting to the real live objects scurrying underfoot and shitting around the house? Or was she a Scotch drinker, and did the painting of the two adorable mutts, one white, one black, serve to remind her that Happy Hour came to Calusa at four-thirty each and every afternoon, rain or shine?

The bedroom was just across the hall.

An unmade water bed. At the foot of the bed, a mattress covered with a rumpled sheet. On the walls, more paintings, undoubtedly by the same untalented artist in the same distinctive style. All of them unsigned. Some of them unframed. Canvases varying in size from what appeared to be three-foot squares to several smaller and several larger rectangles, all of them oils. The subject matter was as banal as the style. Hanging over the water bed was an unframed canvas I estimated to be some four feet wide by six feet long and depicting, of all things, a salt shaker and a pepper shaker standing side by side and magnified a hundred times life-size. To the left of the window on the wall adjacent to the bed was a smaller painting of a pair of chess pieces, one white, one black, intended as the king and queen, if the badly executed crowns were any clue. To the right of the window was another masterpiece by the same artist, this one showing a pair of penguins on an ice floe. On the wall opposite the water bed was another painting executed in the same larger-than-life style as the salt and pepper shakers, this one depicting a pair of dice standing side by side and blown up to some three feet in height. Several unframed canvases were leaning against the wall just inside the entrance door. The top one showed a pair of birds, one presumably a crow, the other a dove. The one under that was a badly rendered painting of a pair of zebras. Over the dresser on that same wall, there was a mirror in a black frame and—just alongside it—a framed and glass-covered copy of the front page of the Calusa *Herald-Tribune*, the bold headline announcing BLACK BUSINESSMAN SLAIN. I leaned over the dresser and read the story under the headline.

Early in August last year, a cruising Calusa cop had noticed a car parked on the access road to the airport. The time was 6:00 A.M. The cop made a pass at the car, noting the license-plate number, and then radioed in for a check with Tampa. The message came back to him that the car was a stolen one. He drove around past the airport and then back onto the access road again, where the reportedly stolen car was still parked, the driver slumped over the wheel, his head on his folded arms. The cop drew his gun, rapped on the window, and asked the driver for his license and identification. The driver rolled down the window, said, "Leave me alone," and then—as an apparent afterthought—reached over to thumb open the glove compartment. The cop shot him twice in the head.

The *rest* of the story, as it was later revealed—and as I recalled it now because the subsequent hearing caused quite a stir in Calusa's legal community—was that the slain man was the owner of a carpet-cleaning business on U.S. 41, and that he'd been informed the night before of his sister's death. The sister lived in Chicago; he was driving to the airport to catch an early-morning flight out. But, apparently grief-stricken, he had pulled over to the side of the airport access road, and was weeping, slumped over the wheel, when the cop approached. The stolen-car report from Tampa had been erroneous; the car belonged to the man driving it. But the cop, believing he was dealing with a criminal, automatically assumed the man was reaching into the glove compartment for a weapon. The story had an unhappy ending: the cop was exonerated of all charges against him. But the front page of a sixteen-month-old newspaper was framed and hanging behind glass on Sally Owen's bedroom wall, together with her priceless collection of representational art.

I did not know what I'd expected to find here. Perhaps proof that George Harper couldn't possibly have killed her. It seemed to me that I hadn't found very much. The cop outside was smoking a cigarette when I came out of the house. Apparently, he still believed I was from the State's Attorney's Office; he ground out the butt the moment he saw me.

"Get what you need?" he asked.

"Thanks," I said.

Bloom was waiting for me at the Harper house down the street, sitting in a Calusa Police Department car, a white Calusa cop at the wheel. He opened the door on the curb side as he saw me coming down the street, and then extended his hand as I approached.

"See the house?" he asked.

"Yes," I said, "thanks."

"What'd you make of the paintings?"

"Lousy," I said.

"For sure. Sally did them herself."

"How do you know?"

"Didn't you go in the garage?"

"No."

"Easel set up in there, unfinished painting on it, long table with tubes of paint and a palette. Neighbor on the left—the woman who found the body—says Sally was all the time painting up a storm."

"What'd the painting in the garage look like?"

"Same as the others. Terrible."

"I mean the subject matter."

"A pair of Dalmatians. The dogs you see around all the firehouses. Had her inspiration on the worktable, a photograph clipped from a newspaper. By the way, what'd you think of that newspaper on her bedroom wall?"

"I don't know. I guess the incident meant a lot to her."

"Oh, sure. Son of a bitch shoots and kills a guy headed for a funeral, if *I* was a black man in this town I'd have burned down the police station. Had it framed, huh?" Bloom said.

"Nice piece of glass over it. To remind her, I guess. Everything there in black-and-white where she could read it whenever she put on her lipstick. Why do you suppose she kept that mattress on the floor?"

"Why are you asking me all these questions?"

"Thought you might have some insights."

"Not a one."

"King-sized water bed could sleep the Russian army. So why did she need a mattress on the floor?"

"I have no idea."

"Me neither. Things like that bother me. Don't they bother you?"

"What bothers me is that black businessman who was killed by a trigger-happy cop. *That's* what bothers me."

"Bothered her, too, apparently."

"Sally Owen didn't have a client on the run out there."

"Well, maybe that'll change after you go on television. I set it all up, by the way. You have to be at WSWF at five-thirty, you know where it is?"

WSWF was Calusa's own Channel 36, the "SWF" in the call letters standing for Southwest Florida. I did not know where the station was; I told Bloom I did not know where it was. I was still feeling rotten, only now the lightheadedness had dissipated and only the crankiness remained.

"Two miles east of Spinnaker, on Old Redford," Bloom said. "Immediately on your left, you'll see a white building with a dish antenna on top of it. You'll be going to Tampa right after you do your number here, so maybe I ought to have somebody drive you *both* places, wait for you outside, is that all right with you?"

"That's fine," I said.

"You seem very perturbed today," Bloom said.

"I am."

"So am I. There's a lot I don't like about this case, Matthew, I'll be honest with you. That's one of the reasons I'm eager to get Harper back in, few more questions I'd like to ask him. Like, for example, how could he have been so fucking *stupid*? I mean, *once* okay, I can accept that. You kill somebody, you forget to wipe your fingerprints off the murder weapon, okay. But *twice*? Even a trained *flea* knows enough to wipe off his fingerprints. Doesn't that bother you, Matthew?"

"It bothers me."

"Me, too."

"We're on opposite sides of this one, Morrie."

"Who says? I want to make sure we've got the right customer. I don't like shooting fish in a barrel, and I don't like frying innocent people in the electric chair, either."

"So now you think he's innocent, huh?"

"I'm not saying that. On the evidence, we had to arrest him and charge him. But he's not guilty until a jury *says* he is. That's the way it works, right, Matthew?"

"That's the way it's *supposed* to work."

"That's the way I'd *like* it to work," Bloom said. "Otherwise I picked the wrong job. I'm not eager to pin a rose on your man unless he actually killed those two people. There are things that bother me, like I said. I want some answers from him. Do your best tonight, will you? Convince him to come in."

"I'll try."

"Okay. You want to see this garage, or not?"

We walked up toward the Harper house. It was similar to Sally Owen's house down the street, obviously built by the same contractor, but it was painted gray rather than white and there was no fence around it, a low line of shrubs defining the property instead. Bloom pulled a key ring from his pocket. "Had to sign a receipt for these, can you imagine? A police officer," he said, and shook his head. "I had to take the whole ring 'cause I don't know which of these is for the house. Guy's got more keys than a jailer." He tried several keys on the garage-door lock, finally found the one that fit, unlocked the door, and then reached down to yank on the handle. The door rattled up over our heads.

The garage, in contrast to Lloyd Davis's in Miami, and considering the fact that he and Harper were in virtually the same business, was a model of neatness. Here, too, every inch of floor and wall space was covered with merchandise Harper presumably hoped to sell, but whereas Davis's garage and its adjacent lawn and driveway areas had been a cluttered, jumbled mess, Harper's garage gave the impression of a carefully catalogued storeroom. Radios were with radios, picture frames with picture frames, plumbing fixtures with plumbing fixtures, everything with its mate or mates, a veritable Noah's ark of organization. Alongside one wall was a rack hung with women's dresses and topcoats on wire hangers. Adjacent to it, on the same wall, was a rack bearing men's suits and sports jackets. Used books were arranged in alphabetical order, by title, in a corner bookcase. Old magazines were stored in cardboard cartons onto which Harper had hand-lettered (and often misspelled) their different names: NEW YORKER, NATIONAL GRAPHIC, LADY'S HOME JOURNAL, HARPER'S BAZAR, TIME, PLAYBOY. Even Harper's personal workbench was backed by a large piece of pegboard fastened to the wall and painted with the outline of each tool hanging on it, undoubtedly his personal possessions and not for sale. Conspicuously absent was the hammer that should have been hanging over the painted outline on the board.

"Neat person," Bloom said.

"Yes," I said.

"So why does he go around leaving his fingerprints all over the place?"

On a shelf over the workbench was an assortment of lidded jars in various sizes, separately containing nails of different weights, screws of different lengths, washers, nuts, bolts, latches, and hinges. A second shelf contained a can of turpentine, several cans of paint and varnish—and an empty space that could have accommodated a five-gallon can of gasoline. A power lawn mower, looking oiled and spotlessly clean, not a blade of grass clinging to its cutting edges, stood against the wall near the workbench. And alongside that, a tarpaulin covered something angled in against the wall. Bloom lifted the tarpaulin.

We were looking at a stack of oil paintings. The one in the

forefront of the stack was a Sally Owen original, unmistakable in style. The content, however, was somewhat startling. The painting depicted a black man and a white woman in passionate embrace. Bloom and I looked at each other. The unframed canvas behind it was another oil, a crude portrait copied from Rembrandt's *The Man with the Golden Helmet*. Behind that was a painting of a fishing skiff. And behind that what was supposed to be a glorious sunset. Only the first canvas seemed to have been painted by Sally; the others were in varying, equally lousy styles, but definitely not hers, not from her distinctive hand.

"Think it's supposed to be Harper and his wife?" Bloom asked.

"Doesn't look much like them."

"Doesn't look much like *anyone*," Bloom said. "Just a black guy kissing a white woman."

"Maybe he bought it for her," I said.

"Or maybe it was a gift from the *artist*," Bloom said, emphasizing the word so that it became a critical judgment.

He replaced the tarpaulin, and we went out of the garage and into the backyard. Lumber piled in orderly stacks, by length and width. Three chairs painted green, standing side by side against the back wall of the garage. A pair of stripped-down chairs beside them. Four ladders leaning against the wall, one against the other. A bathtub, and alongside it a ceramic washbasin in a matching shade of blue.

"You sometimes get these big guys," Bloom said, "they're very neat people. Like fat guys who are light on their feet, you know? My uncle Max, may he rest in peace, he must've weighed three hundred pounds, but he was as delicate as a butterfly, I mean it. Organized? Like a clock. A place for everything, and everything in its place. Gentle, too. A very gentle person."

"Harper's been described that way to me."

"By who?"

"A friend of his. Sally's former husband."

"Oh?"

"Said it would pain Harper to take a hook out of a fish's mouth."

"But not to set fire to somebody, huh? Or to bash in somebody else's skull."

"You're changing your tune again," I said.

"I'm only trying to understand it," Bloom said gently. "Are we finished here?"

"One thing," I said.

"What's that?"

"Will you have your people look for a spare key outside the house someplace?"

"First thing in the morning," Bloom said.

A police car picked me up at the office at a quarter past five, and we drove over to Channel 36, Calusa's own WSWF. The news-team's anchorman told me I would have to be made up before I went on. I told him I had once read an interview with Alfred Hitchcock in which the master, in talking about actors, had said something like, "How can anyone respect a person who makes a living by putting makeup on his face?" The anchorman did not find this amusing or informative. He said I would *have* to wear makeup because if *I* didn't then the rest of the team would, by comparison, look as if they *were* wearing makeup. I failed to understand his logic, but I followed him nonetheless into a small room where a rotund little lady wearing a smeared blue smock was standing behind a seated blonde, whom I recognized as WSWF's Weather Lady, brushing out her hair.

"Are you the guest?" she asked me.

"Yes," I said.

"You'll need a little touch-up around the eyes and beardline," she said, judging me from where she stood.

I had not shaved since seven that morning, Puerto Vallarta time. In the mirror lined with small electric light bulbs, I looked like Richard Nixon about to face the nation.

"Okay, dearie," the makeup woman said to the blonde,

who leaned forward closer to the mirror, touched her fore-finger to the corner of her mouth, delicately dabbed at something invisible there, and then got out of the chair. She smiled at me as she went out of the room; I guessed there would be blue skies tomorrow. I took her vacant chair.

"This is pancake," the makeup lady said. "It'll wash right off later."

I went on the air at 6:21 P.M. after the Weather Lady reported that tomorrow would be rainy and cold, and before the sportscaster, waiting in the wings, gave the news on Calusa's local teams. The anchorman introduced me. I looked directly into the camera and said, "I'm addressing this to George Harper. George, this is Matthew Hope. If you're watching this somewhere, I want you to listen very carefully. I still believe strongly in your innocence, and I'll do everything I possibly can to prove that to a jury when the time comes. I want you to call me, George. I'm in the Calusa phone book, call me either at home or at my office, that's Summerville and Hope on Heron Street. I want to talk to you, George. It's important that we talk. Please call me. Thank you."

I felt like a horse's ass.

I did not get home from Tampa, where I'd taped essentially the same message for a potentially wider audience, until almost 10:00 P.M. I was exhausted. I mixed myself a very strong Beefeater martini, dropped two olives into the glass, and walked into the study, where I turned on my answering machine. The first message was from Jim Willoughby.

"Matthew," he said, "I don't know why the hell you went on television, but I hope the state's attorney doesn't ask for a change of venue after hearing you proclaim Harper's innocence to any listening prospective juror. That was a dumb thing to do, Matthew. You'd better call me as soon as you can. Anyway, I thought you were in Mexico."

The next dozen messages were from lunatics.

"Mr. Hope," the first caller said, "I caught your little speech on television, Mr. Hope, and I'd like you to know just how I feel about your defendin that murderin nigger. Serve him right if he gets the chair. And *you*, too!"

The man hung up. There was a hum on the tape, and then the next caller, a woman, said, "*I* know where he is, Mr. Hope. He's in Niggertown is where he is, gettin drunk enough so's he can go out and kill somebody else. You should be ashamed of yourself."

A click. Another hum. Then another woman's voice:

"You looked cute on TV, Mr. Hope. Anytime you feel like partyin, you just give me a call, hear? Ask for Lucille, but call me at work, 'cause I'm married and all. I'm a waitress at the Loftside Restaurant, down on the South Trail. Or maybe you can just drop in sometime, look over the goods 'fore you commit yourself. You're awful cute, honey."

A click. A hum. A man's voice on the tape:

"I wish that Harper nigger not only *calls* you but actually comes to *see* you, Mr. Hope. 'Cause I'll be parked outside your house with a sawed-off shotgun, an' I'll blow that fucker's brains out the minute I see him. Sleep tight, Mr. Hope."

The next voice, a man's, said only, "God will strike you dead, Mr. Hope, for taking up with niggers."

And then a woman: "Hope is the thing with feathers."

Click.

Another woman: "If God intended niggers to be masters, then Harper'd be defendin *you* 'stead of the other way around. He's already raised his hand against *one* white person, an' I hope he comes to see you an' uses the same hammer on you that he used on that nigger trash he killed next. Good riddance to her and you, too, Mr. Hope. Say hello to the devil for me."

A man: "Well, Mr. Hope, you got yourself a real good one this time, dinn you? You do your best on this one, Mr. Hope, and every nigger in town'll be runnin over to your office so's you can get him offa whatever he done—be it murder, be it armed robbery, be it rapin white women. Congratulations, Mr. Hope, you're a real credit to the community."

And a woman: "I told my husband you're the scum of the earth. He said you should be shot in public."

Another woman: "Why don't you move to Africa, Mr. Hope? Plenty of people there who'd love you to death, maybe even make you chief of they tribe, so's you can get to wear beads and paint and all. Think it over."

A man: "I'm calling on behalf of the CCAC, Mr. Hope. I don't know if you're familiar with our organization, the letters stand for Concerned Citizens Against Crime. We've been working hard to see that people like your client Mr. Harper are punished adequately for the crimes they commit against our community. I want you to know, Mr. Hope, that we're adding your name to the list of people we feel are working *against* that goal. I doubt you'll see too many honest and law-abiding clients in your office after that little speech you made tonight. I hope you know how to shine shoes, Mr. Hope. Or maybe cleaning toilets is more in your style."

And lastly: "Mr. Hope, this is Lucille again. You might like to know I'm five feet eight inches tall, and I weigh a very curvy hundred and fifteen pounds. A lot of people think I look like Jacqueline Bisset, if you're familiar with her. You may have seen her wearing that wet T-shirt in *The Deep*, the movie *The Deep*. My husband calls me 'Bullets,' if you take my meaning. Call me or come see me, hear?"

After Lucille's voice, there was only a long hum on the tape. I switched off the machine, and went back into the living room, stunned. I had not until that moment fully believed the accounts I'd read of crank calls and letters from the public in cases involving any major crime. And whereas I knew that black-white relations were as strained in Calusa as they were anyplace else in the nation, I had until now entertained the perhaps naïve hope that things could only get better; now I knew exactly how deep the hatred ran. I sat sipping at my martini and wondering if I should call Bloom. A man had threatened to park outside my house with a sawed-off shotgun, hadn't he? Should I ask for police protection? Should I have my telephone number—

The phone rang.

I suddenly regretted having turned off the answering machine. I did not want to talk personally with anyone spouting abuse or making threats. The phone kept ringing. I put down the martini glass, and went to answer it.

"Hello?" I said.

"Mr. Hope?"

"Yes?"

"This is Kitty Reynolds."

"Yes, Miss Reynolds?"

"I'm sorry to be bothering you so late at night, but I wonder if . . . Mr. Hope, do you think you could come here for a few minutes. There's . . . something I'd like to discuss with you."

"What is it, Miss Reynolds?"

"Well, not on the phone. I'm on Flamingo Key, the address is 204 Crane Way, just past the yacht club and over the bridge. I know it's late, but if you could come here, I'd appreciate it."

I looked at my watch. It was ten minutes to eleven.

"Give me twenty minutes," I said.

9

I did not get to Flamingo Key until almost midnight because a northbound trailer truck had jackknifed across U.S. 41 and the resultant traffic tie-up was a Fellini version of Hell. I-75, the new Calusa bypass, was scheduled to open in May (promises, promises!), a four-lane highway that would connect Travers to the north with Venice to the south and eliminate (we hoped) much of the tourist traffic that clogged Sarasota's and Calusa's main artery. In the meantime, I sat for forty minutes behind a long line of irritable motorists, listening to what Frank called Calusa's "Old-Fart Network," a radio station that played shlock arrangements of all the Golden Oldies of the forties, introduced by a dove-throated announcer who dropped lyric bits of poetry such as, "We walked the beach alone that day, you and I, picking up sand dollars like street urchins beseeching travelers. We've journeyed long and far since then, my love, but the treasure is still ours alone, to share." I found the man amusing; Frank kept saying he was no William B. Williams, who I gathered was a New York City disc jockey.

Frank calls Flamingo Key "Fandango Key," this because of the largely Spanish style of architecture favored by the residents there. If there is a Gold Coast in Calusa (and there truly isn't), then Flamingo Key qualifies, I guess; the homes there are all in the $500,000-and-over class, and the canals are lined with sailboats and motor cruisers that in some instances are even more expensive than the houses. Each of the houses on Flamingo is on what is known as "waterfront acreage," be it Calusa Bay itself or one of the many waterways winding through the immaculately landscaped development. Frank says that the lawns on Flamingo always look as if they'd recently been clipped by a U.S. Marine Corps barber on Parris Island. Frank does have his prejudices.

The security guard at the main gate stepped out of the booth as I braked the Karmann Ghia to a stop. It was a few minutes to midnight, a bit late in the day for callers. I told him Miss Reynolds was expecting me, and he said, "Just a moment, please, sir," and stepped back into the booth, where he consulted a sheet of paper attached to a clipboard. He picked up the receiver of a hanging wall phone, dialed a number, and while he waited for it to ring, said, "Your name, please?"

"Matthew Hope," I said.

He turned back to the phone. "Miss Reynolds," he said, "a Mr. Hope to see you." He listened, said, "Thank you," and then hung up. "First street on your right," he said, "it's 204 Crane Way, the second house in."

I put the Ghia in gear, drove to the corner, made the first right, and found the mailbox for 204 in front of a Spanish hacienda next door to another Spanish hacienda with the number 206 on its mailbox. I pulled into the driveway, turned off the ignition, and walked up the path to the front door. There were lights burning all over the house. Kitty Reynolds opened the door the moment after I took my finger off the bell button.

"I was afraid you weren't coming," she said. "Come in, please."

She was wearing another of the creations she undoubtedly

sold at Kitty Corner, a blue nylon peignoir slit high on the left leg and slashed low over her breasts. Her long blond hair was hanging loose to the shoulders. She wore no makeup. Her eyes, an echo of the pale blue peignoir, shifted suddenly from my face, glanced out beyond my shoulder, swept the lawn outside. I almost turned to look.

"Come in," she said again, and stepped aside to let me pass, and then closed and locked the door behind her.

"I'm sorry I'm late," I said. "There was an accident on Forty-one."

"I'm usually up till all hours, anyway," she said. "Would you care for something to drink? I was just about to pour myself a cognac."

"Cognac would be fine," I said.

She led me into a living room furnished almost entirely in blue—pale blue carpeting, darker blue upholstery, diaphanous blue drapes, a Syd Solomon painting in various shades of blue on the white stucco wall over the fireplace. Blue was the lady's color, no question about it. She'd been wearing blue when I'd called on her in her shop, and she was wearing blue now in a room predominantly blue. Even her high-heeled satin mules were blue. I watched as she poured cognac into a pair of snifters. She carried both glasses back to where I was sitting on one of the modular sofas arranged before the fireplace hearth.

"Do we need a fire?" she asked, handing me one of the snifters. "It's a little chilly, isn't it? Would you mind making one? I'm an idiot when it comes to fires."

I tore two sheets of newspaper into narrow strips and placed them under the grate. I put a small bundle of kindling onto the grate, and placed two logs on top of it. I struck a match and held it to the paper. The kindling caught, the logs—a fat pine and an oak—began crackling at once.

"Thank you," she said.

"So," I said, and rose from where I was crouched, and pulled the firescreen across the hearth, and then sat again, facing her.

"I want to apologize for my behavior last week," she said.

"That's okay," I said.

"It's just . . . you were raking over the past, and right then I preferred forgetting it. Is the cognac all right?"

"Fine," I said. "Miss Reynolds, why'd you want to see me?"

"Because I'm scared."

"Of what?"

"These murders . . ."

"Yes?"

"They frighten me."

"Why?"

"Because I'm a woman living alone, and . . ."

"That's not why you called me, though, is it?"

"No."

"If you wanted protection or reassurance, you'd have called the police, isn't that true?"

"Yes."

"So why *am* I here, Miss Reynolds?"

"All right, I knew Andrew, all right?"

"Andrew Owen, do you mean?"

"Yes. And now his wife, his *ex*-wife, has been killed, and maybe it's connected somehow to me . . ."

She cut herself short.

"Michelle?" I said.

"Michelle, yes."

"Then you knew Michelle, too, is that right?"

"Yes, I knew her."

"Why don't we start at the beginning?" I said.

"That was more than a year ago," she said, and sighed.

"When, exactly?"

"Well, it was August when Jerry got shot . . ."

"Jerry?"

"Tolliver. Gerald, actually. And this is December already . . . today's the first, isn't it?"

"The *second* already," I said, and looked at my watch.

"So that would make it . . . August, September, October, November," ticking off the months on her fingers, "that's

165

four full months, this would've been sixteen months ago."

The name suddenly rang a bell.

"Is Jerry Tolliver the man who got shot by a cop—"

"Killed, actually. Yes, he's the one. He owned a carpet-cleaning place on the South Trail. He was on his way to his sister's funeral when a police officer . . ."

"Okay," I said, nodding. "What about him? Did you know *him*, too?"

"No."

"Then what . . . ?"

"Well, I was coming to that. *Some* of the people on the committee knew him—or *had* known him, actually—but not me. I joined the committee only because it seemed so unfair. A man gets murdered and they just let the police officer go *free*? That's why I joined it. Because I thought we could *do* something about it."

"What committee is that, Miss Reynolds?"

The committee, as she explained it, was a relatively small group of blacks and whites who believed justice had been circumvented, if not aborted, in the Jerry Tolliver case. It was started by a black woman married to a white doctor out on Fatback Key, and at first it consisted only of herself and a handful of whites like her husband, most of them residents of Fatback, but then it expanded to include two or three dozen people from all over Calusa and elsewhere in Florida, whites and blacks both, some of them well-to-do, some of them poor as dirt. The first meeting Kitty attended was out on Fatback—this was maybe a week after the committee was formed—and that was where she'd met Michelle and George Harper.

"Because what this doctor and his wife were trying to do," Kitty said, "was get some *other* mixed couples like themselves on the committee. There aren't too many of *those* in Calusa, I guess you know."

"I wouldn't think so."

"Well, take it from me," Kitty said. "All told, by the time the committee got off the ground—well, it never *did* get off the ground, actually, that cop's still out there free as a bird. But what I'm saying, the only mixed couples she came up with—the doctor's wife, I forget her name just now—were herself and her husband, and Michelle and George, and a couple from Venice, which isn't Calusa at all. The rest of the people weren't married—I mean, there were blacks married to blacks and whites married to whites but no other salt-and-pepper couples, do you know?"

I suddenly thought of the painting of the salt and pepper shakers hanging over Sally Owen's water bed. I said nothing.

"The committee broke up three weeks after the first meeting. Meetings day and night, but you know *this* town, you never *can* get anything done in this town. Everybody went back home to cry in his beer. Fatback lady and her rich doctor husband—I remember her name now, it was Naomi Morris—went back to growing orchids, rest of us went back to doing our own things. Except . . ."

She hesitated.

"Yes?" I said.

"Well, some of us got to know each other pretty well during all those committee meetings. So we kept seeing each other socially."

"Were Andrew and Sally Owen at any of those meetings?"

"Well, yes, they were on the committee."

"Is that where you met Andrew? At one of the meetings?"

"Yes," she said. Her voice was very low. She sipped at the cognac. In the fireplace, one of the logs suddenly crackled and spit. Out on the bay, I heard the distant sound of a speedboat.

"And, you know," she said, "I was a divorced woman with a successful boutique on the Circle, but there wasn't much else to my life just then, which is maybe why I joined the committee to begin with, to feel that I was doing something *meaningful*, you know, something *important*. Divorce is rough," she said.

"Yes, I know."

"You've been the route, huh?"

"I've been the route."

"Well," she said, and sighed again. "Andrew was attentive to me, Andrew was attractive, Andrew and I . . . well, you know."

"When was this?"

"September last year? October? The fall sometime."

"And Sally found out."

"I guess."

"You guess?"

"Well, yes, she found out."

"And immediately sued for divorce."

"Well, yes."

"Well, she *did*, didn't she?"

"Yes, she did."

"Why were you so reluctant to tell me this the last time we talked?"

"Well, it was personal."

"It's *still* personal, isn't it?"

"Yes, but Sally wasn't dead then."

"Michelle *was*."

"I hadn't been involved with Michelle's husband."

"Are you saying you think Sally's death . . . ?"

"No, no."

". . . had something to do with your involvement with her husband?"

"No, of course not."

"Then how has her death changed anything? You didn't want to discuss any of this a week ago, but now you seem . . ."

"It just started me thinking, that's all. First Michelle, then Sally, almost as if *all* the women in the oar . . ."

She cut herself short. She had a habit of cutting herself short. She had interrupted herself earlier when she'd been about to say the name "Michelle," and now she had just said the word *oar* and then closed her mouth on it as effectively as a shark on a fisherman's paddle.

I looked at her.

She lowered her eyes and said, "It's just that, well, in a

social group like ours, after the committee broke up, I mean, it wasn't considered . . . well, you weren't *supposed* to fall in love the way Andrew and I did, to make waves the way we did."

"But that would apply to *any* group in which there were married . . ."

"Well, sure, but Sally's reaction . . . she sort of went off the deep end, do you know what I mean? She was a very vain person, you know, and . . . well, she just got *furious*. Made it clear to both of us that we'd be outcasts from then on, told us that none of the oar . . . none of our friends would have anything to do with us ever again. Which is why she asked for the divorce and named me in the action. To make sure we were out for good, do you understand? *Out.* Excommunicated."

"This 'oar' you keep mentioning . . ."

"What?"

"You keep saying the word *oar*."

"You must be mistaken."

"I thought that's what I was hearing."

"Really? No," she said. "Would you care for some more cognac?"

"No, thank you. So, as I understand it, you lost touch with most of the people you'd been socializing with . . ."

"Yes, because that's the way Sally wanted it."

"People here in Calusa?"

"Yes. Well, from all over, actually. The case attracted a lot of attention, you know. There was the couple from Venice, you know, and people from Tampa, Miami, Sarasota . . . well, wherever anyone was concerned about the injustice of what had happened."

"Who from Miami?" I asked.

"Well, I really can't remember. This was all so long ago."

"Would it have been someone named Lloyd Davis?"

"I don't remember all the names, really."

"He was in the army with Harper, I just thought . . ."

"Mm, well . . ."

"If Harper and his wife were on the committee, as you say they were . . ."

"Yes, they were."

"Then possibly he contacted Davis, tried to interest him in . . ."

"Well, I guess, now that you mention it, there might have been someone named Davis at one of the meetings."

"Lloyd Davis?"

"I guess."

"And his wife?"

"Yes, I think so."

"Leona, would it have been?"

"I really don't remember."

"Where was this?"

"At one of the meetings. Andrew's house, I think. This was a year ago, more than a year ago. I think that's where it was. People used to just, you know, come to the meetings. I don't know if Sally and Andrew actually *knew* him, or whether someone else brought him. There were a lot of people, you see."

"Two or three dozen, you said."

"Sometimes more. In the beginning, anyway. Before the committee started breaking up."

"Uh-huh." I looked at my watch. "Well, Miss Reynolds," I said, "I'm still not . . ."

"Kitty," she said.

"I'm still not sure why you asked me to come here tonight."

She hesitated for a long time. Then she said, "Because you're George's lawyer."

"And?"

"And I heard what you said to him tonight on television, and I thought, if he *does* call you . . ."

"Yes?"

"You could tell him I had nothing to do with it."

"With what, Miss Reynolds?"

"With starting it."

"Starting what?"

"Well, you just tell him. *Whatever* he's thinking . . ."

"What do you *think* he's thinking?"

"I think he found out, and he's . . ." She shook her head. "Forget it," she said.

"Found out what?"

"Nothing. Just tell him. If he's out to get *all* of us, I don't want to be the next one."

"Who do you mean by all of us?"

"The women."

"What women?"

"In the . . . our friends, do you know?"

"No, I don't. What friends?"

"Those of us who were friends. Before the divorce. Before Sally and Andrew split up."

"And you think George . . . or *whoever* killed Sally and Michelle . . ."

"It was George," she said.

"How do you know that?"

"Who else could it be?"

"You think *George*, then, might be after all the friends you and Andrew Owen used to have?"

"Well . . . yes."

"That doesn't make sense to me. Why would he . . . ?"

"If you don't understand what I'm trying to tell you . . ."

"I don't."

"Then forget it, okay?"

"Why don't you just *tell* me?" I said. "What*ever* the hell it is, just come out and *say* it."

"I've said enough."

"You really *are* frightened, aren't you?" I said.

"Yes." She was staring into the wide bowl of the snifter. Her voice was very small.

"Maybe you'd *better* call the police."

"No," she said, looking up sharply. "In *this* town? After what happened to Jerry? No, sir, no damn police."

"Well," I said, and sighed, and got up from where I was

sitting. "If there's anything else you want to tell me, you know where to reach me. If not . . ."

"Just tell George, okay? When you talk to him."

"*If* I talk to him."

"I'll let you out," she said, and rose suddenly, the peignoir parting over her legs. She pulled the flap closed, walked swiftly to the door, unlocked it, and said, "Good night, Mr. Hope. Thanks for coming here."

"Good night," I said, and stepped out into the first of the Weather Lady's promised rain, a light drizzle sifting gently from the black sky overhead. Behind me, I heard the lock tumblers falling with a small oiled click.

It was a quarter past one when I got home.

I put the Ghia in the garage, rolled the door down behind me, opened the door leading from the garage into the kitchen, turned out the garage lights behind me, turned on the kitchen lights ahead of me, and then closed and locked the kitchen-garage door. I didn't know whether I wanted another martini or a glass of milk. I opted for the milk. I went to the refrigerator, took out the bottle, poured myself a glassful, returned the bottle to the refrigerator, and was starting into the living room with the glass in my hand when I got the fright of my life.

George Harper was sitting in the dark there.

"*Jesus!*" I said, and snapped on the light.

"How you doin, Mr. Hope?" he said.

His huge hands were clasped in his lap; he sat as still as death in a wingback chair near the fire, facing the arched entry to the kitchen where I stood with the glass of milk in my hand. My hand was shaking.

"How'd you get in here?" I said.

"Back door was open," he said.

"No, it wasn't."

"Well, then, I guess I forced it open," he said.

"You scared the hell out of me. Where have you been?"

"Miami."

"Doing what?"

"Went t'see my mama."

"Broke jail to go see your 'mama,' huh?"

"Thass right, Mr. Hope. Missed her somethin terrible."

"Do you know Sally Owen's been murdered?"

"Yessir, I heard about it."

"Did you kill her?"

"Nossir."

"Do you know your hammer was found at the scene?"

"Yessir."

"With your fingerprints on it?"

"So I unnerstan."

"Got any idea how it got there?"

"Nossir."

"Anybody but you and Michelle have a key to your house?"

"Not that I know of."

"Was there a spare key outside?"

"Nossir."

"Then how'd that hammer get out of the garage?"

"I can't say, Mr. Hope."

"Do you know what kind of trouble you're in?"

"I reckon so."

"Why'd you do a damn fool thing like breaking jail?"

"Tole you. Had to see my mama."

"What about?"

"Business."

"What kind of business?"

"Personal, Mr. Hope."

"Listen to me, Mr. Harper. You'd better get off this goddamn *personal* shit, you hear me? If you want me to help you, then nothing's *personal* anymore. Everything's out in the open, we're *partners*, understand?"

"Never did like the idea of bein partners with anybody," Harper said.

"No, huh? How do you like the idea of the electric chair? Does *that* appeal to you?"

"Not much. But whut's gotta be's gotta be."

"Nothing's *got* to be, Mr. Harper. Not if we don't *want* it to be."

"Well, *some* things just *gotta* be," he said.

"You broke jail last Thursday," I said. "Have you been in Miami all this time?"

"Yessir. Got back to Calusa tonight, thought I'd better come see you."

"Where were you when you heard me on television?"

"Whut?"

"Aren't you here because . . . ?"

"Whut?" he said again.

"Didn't you hear me on television?"

"Nossir."

"Then why'd you come here?"

"You're my lawyer, ain't you? Thought I'd find out how the case was comin along."

"Oh, the case is coming along just dandy. Every cop in the state is ready to shoot you on sight. They think you killed two people, they know you've broken jail, they know you've got a shotgun in your—have you still got that shotgun?"

"Yessir."

"Where is it?"

"In the car."

"What car?"

"Car I picked up."

"A car you stole?"

"Yessir."

"Terrific," I said.

"Needed a car," Harper said, and shrugged.

"Where is it?"

"Parked up the street. Dinn want t'block your driveway, figgered you'd have to get in your garage."

"Thank you, that was very considerate."

Harper said nothing.

"I want you to turn yourself in," I said.

"Nossir, I ain't about to do that."

"If you didn't kill your wife . . ."

"I din't."

"If you didn't kill Sally Owen . . ."

"Her neither."

"Then why the hell are you running?"

"Ain't runnin, Mr. Hope."

"Then what *are* you doing?"

He did not answer.

"Mr. Harper," I said, "can you give me one good reason why your wife would have come to me on Monday morning, November sixteenth, claiming that you had brutally beaten her the night before, and asking that . . ."

"Can't think of a single one," Harper said.

"You were in Miami that Sunday, right?"

"Right."

"Where you went to see Lloyd Davis and then your mother . . ."

"Right, but they wun't there, neither of them."

"So you called an old army buddy . . ."

"Yessir. Ronnie Palmer."

"A recruiting sergeant in Miami."

"Yessir."

"And then you drove up to Pompano and Vero Beach."

"Yessir."

"Why?"

"Tole you. Sightseein. Lookin."

"Where were you on Monday night? The night she was killed."

"Back in Miami. Tole you that, too."

"Why'd you go back to Miami?"

"Thought Lloyd might be comin back."

"Mr. Harper," I said, "you're beginning to give me a pain in the ass."

"I'm sorry 'bout that," he said, "but they's things you don't know."

"Then why don't you tell them to me?"

"Can't," he said.

"What'd you find out, Mr. Harper?"

He did not answer me.

"Kitty Reynolds thinks you found out something. *What*, Mr. Harper?"

He sat as still as a stone in the chair, staring at me.

"Mr. Harper," I said. "I want you to come with me to the police. I want you to turn yourself in voluntarily before somebody out there blows off your head. If you didn't commit these murders, you've got nothing to hide. What do you say? Will you come with me?"

He sat in the chair thinking this over for what seemed like a full minute.

He nodded.

He lumbered to his feet.

And then the son of a bitch hit me full in the face with his huge bunched fist.

10

The phone was ringing.

The weather outside was rainy, windy, and cold.

It was nine o'clock on Wednesday morning, December 2, a little less than eight hours since George Harper had knocked me unconscious and fled into the night. I had come to about twenty minutes later. My watch had read 1:46. It's a digital watch. Nobody says, "It's a quarter to two" anymore. It's always either 1:44 or 1:46. I had debated calling Bloom, and had gone to bed instead. He was on the phone now.

"I didn't wake you, did I?" he asked.

"No, I was up."

"Any word from Harper?"

I hesitated. Then I said, "No."

"Well, sometimes it takes a little while for somebody to make up his mind," Bloom said. "Maybe he'll show at the funeral today."

"What funeral?"

"Sally Owen's. I have to tell you, Matthew, we're covering

it like it's a presidential visit, just in case Harper *does* decide to drop in. Half the cops in the city'll be there, good day to rob a bank downtown, huh?"

"Good day for a funeral, too."

"Yes, wonderful," Bloom said dryly. "You going?"

"What for?"

"*If* Harper shows, he's going to need his lawyer again."

"I doubt if he'll show, Morrie."

"Oh?" Bloom said, and there was a long pause on the line. "What makes you think that?"

"If *you'd* killed her, would *you* go to her funeral?"

"Lots of people who kill people do crazy things later on. I once had a guy on Long Island, he stabbed his wife with a butcher knife, you know? So the very next day, half of Nassau County looking for him, he takes the knife in to have it sharpened, can you imagine? Like locking the barn door after the horse is gone, right? Brings in a knife with blood on the handle, around those little rivets in the handle, you know? So the grinder takes the knife to the back of the store, and he calls us, and when we arrest the guy, all he says is 'The knife was dull.' People do crazy things, Matthew."

"Yeah," I said.

"Well, anyway, it's at eleven o'clock, Floral Park Cemetery, if you feel like dropping in."

"Don't expect me," I said.

"You sound grumpy this morning," he said.

"I've got a toothache."

"Ah, too bad. Do you have a good dentist?"

"Yes, thanks, Morrie."

"Let me know if you hear from Harper, okay?" he said, and hung up.

I don't know why I went to the funeral; funerals depress me, even when it *isn't* raining. I certainly didn't expect to see Harper there; you do not sock your own lawyer on the jaw the night before and then walk into the arms of the police the next day. Besides, I really *did* have a toothache; *two* toothaches or perhaps teethaches, where Harper had hit me. Moreover, the entire left side of my face was swollen and discolored, and my lower gum had begun bleeding when I'd brushed my teeth that morning. I had not liked getting hit on the jaw. The last time I'd been hit on the jaw (or anyplace else) was when I was fourteen years old and got into a fistfight with an eighteen-year-old football player over a girl on the cheerleading squad. The girl's name was Bunny, and she had allowed me to fondle her breasts one night, thereby granting me (it seemed in my adolescent fantasy) priority, privilege, and longevity. The football player, whose name was Hank, thought otherwise, perhaps because he'd been laying her steadily (Everybody but me, I thought, I *love* you, Bunny!) since the start of the season. He told me to keep away from her. I told him he was a moronic turd. He blackened both my eyes, dislocated my jaw, and knocked out one of my molars. I still have in my mouth the restoration Dr. Mordecai Simon put in for me in Chicago. It reminds me never to start up with football players, or with practically anyone else, for that matter. But who expects a *client* to hit him? From now on, I would expect clients to hit me. I would expect priests to hit me. I would expect little babies in their buggies to slam me with their bottles. Frank's extension of Murphy's Law: If you expect the worst, it will nonetheless surprise you when it comes.

The only surprise at Sally Owen's funeral was the appearance of her former husband, Andrew Owen. He arrived late, holding an umbrella over his head, catching the last of the minister's words just before the coffin was lowered into the ground. He kept watching the descending coffin. As the mourners began to disperse, he stood looking into the open grave. Bloom was standing some distance off, talking to a uniformed police captain. The cops assigned to the job—I guessed there were three dozen in all—stood like specters in the rain, black rainslickers glistening wet, eyes roaming the rain-soaked perimeter of the cemetery, hands hovering close to the protruding butts of their revolvers. I suddenly wished Harper would not be foolish enough to show up here today. I walked to where Owen was still staring into the open grave, the umbrella over his bent head.

"How are you?" I said.

He looked up, turned to face me. "Hell of a thing," he said.

"I'm surprised to see you here."

"We were married once," he said. "I loved her once," he said, and shrugged, and then sighed and began walking up toward where the cars were parked in a muddy open space at the top of the grassy rise. The rain kept pouring down. *Let it come down,* I thought. First Murderer, *Macbeth,* Act III, Scene 3. I had played Macduff in our college production during my sophomore year at Northwestern. The critic for the school newspaper wrote of my performance, "Lay *off,* Macduff! *Out,* damned Hope!" Our umbrellas, Owen's and mine, nudged each other like spies exchanging secrets.

"Any idea who might have done it?" I asked.

"No."

"Do you think it was George Harper?"

"Not a chance. He may be stupid, but he's not crazy."

"Have the police questioned you?"

"Naturally. Ex-husband? Bitter divorce? Sure."

"And?"

"From what they asked about where I was at what time, I figured they already knew she'd been killed sometime between two and four o'clock in the afternoon. Well, I was at the store all day Monday, from eight in the morning till I closed at seven o'clock. Monday's my busiest day—well, Mondays and Saturdays, actually. By Monday, all the alkies have guzzled down their weekend stash, they come flocking by the store in *droves,* man. Cops didn't get to me till almost midnight. By then, I'd already seen on television that the body was found at seven o'clock, that's when the lady next door—Jennie Pierce, I know her, nice lady—went over to bring Sally a pie dish or something. I told the cops that at seven o'clock I was just locking up my store, and I had only a million and a half witnesses who'd swear on a case of Chivas Regal that I was *in* that store all day long, right behind the counter where I was supposed to be. The cops thanked me for my time, this was now one o'clock in the morning, and went on their way. 'Keep your nose clean,' they told me. Keep my nose clean. I've been an honest businessman in this town for the past ten years, ever since I got back from Nam, never even got a *parking* ticket in this fucking town, but they tell me to keep my nose clean. All they forgot to add was 'nigger.' "

He had stopped at his car now, a blue Pontiac wagon, and was fishing in his pocket for his keys. Bloom and the police captain, still in deep conversation, were trudging up the slope toward the parking lot.

"I spoke to Kitty Reynolds last night," I said.

Owen looked up from where he was inserting his key into the door lock. "Oh?" he said.

"Yes." I paused. Then I said, "Are you still seeing her?"

"Nope."

"How come?"

"Things end, man, people drift."

"When did it end?"

"Almost before it began. Minute Sally sued for divorce, it began to pall. All our old friends, you know, people we used to be with all the time . . . well, they just stopped seeing us. Gets kind of lonely out there if you don't have any friends."

"Harper, too?"

"What?"

"Did *he* stop seeing you?"

"No, not George. But he didn't know . . ."

Owen cut himself short. Maybe it was contagious. Maybe when you spend enough time in bed with another person, you pick up her habits. Kitty Reynolds was an expert at interrupting her own sentences. Owen had just now swallowed the tail end of whatever he'd been about to say, and was busying himself with the door lock again.

"Didn't know what?" I asked.

"Don't know what you mean, man."

"You were about to say . . ."

"I was about to say good-bye, Mr. Hope."

"Just one second, okay?"

He had unlocked the door and opened it. He closed it again when he noticed that the front seat was getting rained on.

"What is it?" he said, and sighed.

"The first time we talked, you had trouble remembering Lloyd Davis."

"So?"

"Kitty Reynolds says she met him at your house."

"She did, huh?"

"At one of the meetings there."

"Really? What meetings?"

"She told me a woman out on Fatback Key formed a committee . . ."

"Oh, yeah, that bullshit committee."

"To do something about the Jerry Tolliver case."

"Yeah, uh-huh."

"And that she'd met you—*and* Lloyd Davis—at one of those meetings. At your house."

"Then I guess she must be right, huh?"

"And yet you had trouble remembering him."

"People came and went all the time at those meetings," Owen said, and shrugged.

"I was at your house yesterday," I said.

"Yeah?"

"Was that front page on your bedroom wall while you were still married to Sally?"

"What front page?"

"On the Tolliver killing."

"Oh. Yeah, I guess so."

"How about the paintings?"

"Sally's paintings? Yeah, she used to hang them all over the house."

"Ever see a painting of a white woman and a black man in embrace?"

"Who remembers? She was painting all the time."

"Any idea how that *particular* painting ended up in George Harper's garage?"

"No idea at all."

"You don't remember Sally *giving* it to him, do you? Or *selling* it to him?"

"Sally didn't get along with George, I already told you that."

"Would she have given the painting to *Michelle*?"

"She handed them out all over the place."

"She did? To whom?"

"Anybody who'd take them. You saw the paintings, you know how lousy they were."

"Who'd she hand them out to?"

"I told you. Anybody. Everybody. I have to go, Mr. Hope. I've lost half a day already, I have to go open the store."

"One last question," I said.

"Okay, but . . ."

"What is it that Harper didn't know? What is it that Harper found out?"

"That's *two* questions. And I don't know the answers to either one of them."

He furled his umbrella, threw it over the back of the seat, and got in behind the wheel. I watched as he slipped his key into the ignition and started the car, and then I stepped back as he pulled off into the rain. Bloom was just behind me, peering out from under his umbrella as the car negotiated the turn at the top of the hill and drove out of sight around it.

"Who was that?" he asked.

"Andrew Owen," I said.

"Clean as a whistle," Bloom said. "Alibi a mile long." He peered at me through the falling rain. "What happened to your face, Matthew?"

"Ran into a door last night."

"Yeah?"

"Yeah, when I got up to pee."

"You ought to be more careful," Bloom said.

The last shuttle from Calusa to Miami left at 2:50 P.M. and arrived there at 4:20. It was a little windy on the east coast, but the sun was shining, and the cab driver who drove me to Mrs. Harper's house kept turning over his shoulder to look at my umbrella as though it were a broadsword clutched in the fist of a medieval knight. Mrs. Harper was bent over a bed of gardenias in her front yard when the taxi pulled up to the curb. She looked up as I got out of the taxi, and continued watching me as I paid the driver and started up the front walk. A tangle of weeds was in her left hand; in her right hand she held a trowel.

"Hello, Mrs. Harper," I said.

"Mr. Hope," she said, and nodded curtly.

"I tried reaching you by phone," I said, "but . . ."

"Had it disconnected. Too many reporters calling."

"I hope I can have a minute of your time."

"All's anybody wants these days is a minute of my time. Used to was I wouldn't see nobody for days on end. Now they bangin down my door."

"It's about your son," I said.

"Thass whut *all* of them's about."

"You know he broke out of jail last Thursday, don't you?"

"So I unnerstan."

"And you know someone else has been killed, a woman named Sally Owen."

"Yes, I know that too."

"When your son came to see you last Thursday . . ."

"Ony wisht he had," Mrs. Harper said.

I looked at her.

"Musta figgered this'd be the fust place they'd come lookin for him, though. Fust place they *did* come, matter of fact. Miami police was here that very night, astin did I know where my boy was. I tole 'em my boy was in jail. So they camped on my doorstep waitin for him to show up. I tell you, Mr. Hope, I wisht he hadda. He shunta broke out of jail like he done. Ony makes it look bad for him, ain't that right?"

"He told me he came here to see you."

"No, he never did."

"Said he had some personal business with you."

"Can't think of no personal business he mighta had with me. Nor why he'da said he was here when he wasn't."

I had flown to Miami hoping she might be able to tell me what she and her son had talked about last week, hoping he might have revealed to her what he'd refused to reveal to me, hoping *she* might have been the one to whom he'd confided whatever the hell it was he'd learned. It was now 5:12 P.M. by my wonderful Japanese digital watch. It had taken me two and a half hours, door to door, to get here, and it would take me another two and a half hours—if I was lucky—to get back. There was no way I could catch Sunwing's 5:30 shuttle that would have got me into Calusa at a little before 7:00. Eastern had a flight going out at 6:10, with a change of planes in Tampa, arriving in Calusa at 8:15. I was debating whether to try getting a seat on *that* one or, instead, to have dinner at the airport here and then catch Sunwing's last shuttle back at 7:30, when Mrs. Harper—bless her heart—said, "Maybe he went to see Lloyd. Maybe he figgered he could hide out at Lloyd's."

The taxi I called from a corner phone booth deposited me in front of Lloyd Davis's house five minutes later. It was almost 5:30 when I started up the junk-flanked front walk. The sun was almost gone, the shadows were very long. A record player was going inside the house; I could hear the scratchy strains of Billie Holiday's "Strange Fruit." I knocked on the screen door. No answer. I knocked again.

"Yes?"

A woman's voice.

"Mrs. Davis?" I said.

"Yes?"

"It's Matthew Hope. May I come in?"

"Sure, come ahead." she said.

I opened the screen door and stepped into the house.

She was sitting in the living room, the last of the evening's light coming feebly through a window behind her easy chair, a battered relic that must have been salvaged from her husband's garage. She was wearing a floral-printed Japanese kimono belted at the waist with a bright red sash. She did not turn to look at me as I came into the room, the screen door clattering shut behind me. She kept staring at the turntable where the Billie Holiday record was spinning, as though trying to absorb sound through her eyes.

On the end table alongside her chair was a torn glassine packet, and beside that a spoon with a blackened bowl. On the floor at her feet was a hypodermic syringe. The record spun to its end. Now there was only the empty click of the needle caught in the retaining grooves. It seemed to alert her to my presence. She turned to look at me.

Her complexion was the color of unrefined sugar, the result of generations of racial admixture, her eyes as brown and as wet as sorghum molasses, sunken in a face with high cheekbones, a patrician nose, and a generous mouth. She must have been a beautiful woman at one time, but the body slumped in the chair seemed frail and brittle and the eyes studying me were dead.

"Well, hello," she said.

The light was almost gone now; the room was succumbing to the onslaught of dusk. She made no move to turn on the end-table lamp. The needle kept clicking at the record's end, the only sound in the room.

"I'm looking for your husband," I said.

"Ain't here," she said.

"Do you know where I can find him?"

"Nope."

"Mrs. Davis . . ."

"Would you turn that off, please?" she said, and raised her hand, and gestured limply toward the record player. I crossed the room and lifted the arm.

"*Who'd* you say you were?" she asked.

"Matthew Hope."

"Oh, yes, Hope."

"I was here last week . . ."

"Oh, yes, Hope," she said again.

"Are you all right?"

"Fine," she said.

"When will your husband be home, do you know?"

"Can't say for sure. Comes an' goes, you know."

"When did he leave?"

"Don't know. Comes an' goes," she said.

"Do you know where he went?"

"Army, most likely."

"Army? What do you mean?"

"Reserve, you know. Always off with the reserve some-place, who *cares*?" she said, and made a gesture of dismissal, impatiently swinging her arm, and then letting it fall. "Want to do me a favor?"

"Sure."

"That was *some* pow'ful shit, man."

"What is it you want?"

"*Some* pow'ful shit. Cost enough, but, man, it was *pow'ful*. Want to do me a favor?"

"Sure."

She nodded, and then—before she could tell me what the favor might be—closed her eyes, and lowered her chin, and drifted off into an atmosphere higher and thinner than any Sunwing had ever flown. I looked down at her. Her breathing was shallow but steady. The room was very dark now, I could scarcely see her in the gloom. I snapped on the end-table lamp, and just then the phone rang.

I turned toward the sound as sharply as if it were a gunshot. The ringing was coming from a room I could see through an open door, obviously a kitchen, the sink and re-frigerator vaguely illuminated by the light spilling over from the living room. The phone kept ringing.

"All right," she mumbled behind me.

The phone shrilled into the silence of the house.

"All right, all *right*," she said, and shook herself from her stupor, and started to rise from the chair, and then sank back into it again. "Wow," she said, "some pow'ful shit."

The phone rang again, and then stopped.

"Good," she said, and then looked at me as if discovering me for the first time. Her hands hung limply over the arms of the easy chair; her legs were stretched out in front of her; the kimono flap had fallen open to reveal the marks of her addiction on the insides of both thighs. "Hey, do me a favor, will you?" she said. "Get me a drink of water, I'm dying of thirst here."

I went out into the kitchen, found a clean glass on the drainboard, filled it with water, and carried it back to where she was sitting. She drank it down in virtually a single swallow, turned to place the glass on the end table, and let go of it before it had found solid purchase. I reached for the glass just as it tumbled to the floor and shattered.

"Ooops," she said, and grinned at me.

"You okay now?" I said.

"Comin through, man," she said. "Wow."

"Want to talk a little?"

"Want to *sleep*, man."

"Not yet," I said. "Mrs. Davis, can you remember exactly what you told George Harper on the Sunday he was here?"

"Long time ago, man."

"Not so long ago. Try to remember. He asked you where your husband was . . ."

"Uh-huh."

"And you told him he was off with the reserve."

"That's where he was."

"What else did you tell him?"

"That's all."

"Did you tell him *where* your husband was?"

"With the reserve."

"But *where* with the reserve?"

"Didn't *know* where."

"Where does he usually go?"

"Wherever the unit says."

"What unit is that? An MP unit?"

"No, no."

"Then what?"

"Artillery."

"Which one?"

"Who knows?"

"Did you tell George Harper . . . ?"

"Don't know *what* I told him," she said. "Man, you got to 'scuse me, I need some sleep."

"Mrs. Davis, if you can remember whether you told him . . ."

"Can't," she said, and grasped the arms of the chair with both hands, and shoved herself out of it. She noticed the syringe lying on the floor, knelt down to pick it up, carefully placed it on the end table beside the spoon, and started out of the room. The phone rang again as she was passing the kitchen. She glanced idly through the open door, and then continued down the corridor into what I supposed was her bedroom. The phone kept ringing insistently. I followed her down the hallway and stopped just outside the bedroom door. She was sitting on the edge of the bed, in the dark, taking off one of her slippers. She dropped it on the floor, and then took off the other one. The phone kept ringing.

"Don't you want to answer that?" I said.

"Never quits," she said. "Go home, mister, I got to get some sleep."

"In just a minute," I said. "Please try to remember whether . . ."

"Can't remember nothin."

The phone was still ringing.

"Mrs. Davis, did you tell George Harper that your husband was with the Artillery?"

"Maybe."

"Can you remember if you did for *sure*?"

"Go home," she mumbled.

I did not want her to flake off on me again. I reached for the switch just inside the door, and snapped on the light.

The first thing I saw in its harsh glare was a huge painting on the wall over the bed.

The painting was one of Sally Owen's.

The phone suddenly stopped ringing.

The house was silent again.

Leona Davis was lying full-length on the bed, on her back, blinking up at the overhead light, trying to shield her eyes with her hand. "Turn that off, will you?" she said.

I was staring at the painting.

Like the ones I'd seen hanging in Sally's bedroom and the one we'd found beneath the tarpaulin in Harper's garage, this too was an oil done entirely in blacks and whites. But this time around, Sally seemed to have gone straight to the heart of the matter.

According to Freud (as later interpreted by my daughter Joanna) an analysand's dreams about any given problem will at first be shrouded in symbolism. If the problem persists, however, the dreams will become more and more explicit until at last the true content will be revealed almost documentarily. The subject matter of Sally Owen's paintings seemed to have progressed from inanimate objects like chess pieces and salt and pepper shakers, to wildlife like penguins and zebras and crows and doves, to domesticated animals like Scotties and Dalmatians, and at last to humans as depicted in the painting we'd found in Harper's garage. But if it was true that any artistic endeavor was the end result of unconscious stirrings, then Sally Owen—like a dreamer awake—had allowed her unconscious to dictate an artistic expression that had moved inexorably from the symbolic to the absolutely explicit. The painting hanging over Leona Davis's bed left nothing to the erotic imagination.

The painting depicted a huge black phallus.

The painting further depicted a white woman engorging that phallus.

"Where'd you get that?" I said.

"Turn off the light."

"It's one of Sally Owen's paintings, isn't it?"

"Man, if you got to talk, turn off the damn *light!*" She sat up suddenly, and reached over to the bedside lamp. A splash of amber illumination spilled onto the bed. The bedside clock read 5:50. I was going to miss the Eastern flight. I snapped off the overhead light.

"*Is* it one of Sally's?" I said.

"From way back," she said, and nodded.

"How'd it get here?"

"Gave it to us."

"A gift?"

She nodded again. "From when we still had The Oreo."

"The what?"

"Oreo."

"What's that?"

"Never mind," she said.

"Oreo?" I said.

I suddenly remembered Kitty Reynolds cutting herself short each time she mentioned the word *oar*. Had she been about to say "Oreo"?

I looked at Leona.

"Tell me about The Oreo," I said.

"Nothin to tell. *Ain't* no more Oreo. Don't *exist* no more, man."

"What was it *when* it existed?"

"Nothin."

"Is it the *name* of something?"

"Man, I need to sleep," she said.

"Something called The Oreo?"

"Ain't got *time* for that shit no more," she said, and fell back wearily onto the pillow. "They's sweeter stuff, man. Sweeter than you know." She lifted one arm, gestured limply toward the painting over her head, and said, "That's Lloyd up there."

I looked at the painting again.

"And Michelle," she said, and nodded, and then drifted off again to wherever that sweeter stuff transported her.

11

At 9:00 sharp on Thursday morning, from my office in Calusa, I placed a call to the U.S. Army District Recruiting
Command on the South Dixie Highway in Miami. I had
tried to reach them the night before from the airport, before
I caught my Sunwing flight back, but I got only an answering
machine telling me the office was open daily from 9:00 A.M.
to 5:00 P.M., except on Saturdays when it closed for the weekend at noon. A woman named Corporal Dickinson answered
the phone now. I told her I hoped I was calling the right
place, I was trying to get in touch with a recruiting sergeant
named Ronnie Palmer, and she asked me to wait, please, sir.

"Sergeant Palmer," a man's voice said.

"Sergeant, my name is Matthew Hope, I'm an attorney
representing George Harper."

"Yes, sir?"

"Is this the Ronnie Palmer who knew Mr. Harper while he
was in the service?"

"Yes, sir?"

"I understand he called you while he was in Miami several

weeks back. That would've been on Sunday, November the fifteenth, do you remember him calling you?"

"Yes, sir, he called me at home."

"Do you remember what you talked about?"

"Sir?"

"Do you remember the gist of your conversation?"

"Well, it was just an ordinary conversation, sir. We knew each other in Germany, he wanted to know how I was, what I'd been doing, and so on."

"Would he have asked you any questions about the Artillery?"

"Well, yes he did. As a matter of fact, I found that puzzling at the time. I was George's ISR in Germany, you see . . ."

"His what?"

"In-Service Recruiter. Which is how I happened to be familiar with his particular commitment to the army. Do you know how this works, sir?"

"Not entirely."

"Well, when a man enlists, he normally commits to the army for six years, four on active duty, two in the reserve. In George's case—well, this gets a little complicated. To make it simple, when George's four years of active service were completed, he reenlisted for another three, and I was the one who helped him to pull *those* in Germany, too, instead of someplace where another shooting war could break out any minute. But, you see, when he came home from Germany, he was finished—that is, he didn't owe the army any reserve time. Which is what puzzled me."

"I'm not sure I understand, Sergeant."

"Well, he asked me whether a guy who'd been in the MP could end up in the artillery reserve."

"What'd you tell him?"

"I said it was entirely possible. We don't have any reserve MP units here in Miami. So someone who'd been with the MP would have had to request a new MOS, and assuming it . . ."

"MOS?"

"Military Occupational Specialty. And assuming his request was approved, he could then join one of the existing reserve units here in Miami. The field artillery is one of those units. The Seven/Nine Field Artillery Battalion."

"The Seventy-ninth?"

"No, sir the Seven-*Slash*-Nine. The Seven/Nine, sir."

"I see. And you told this to Harper?"

"Yes, sir. And then he asked me where somebody attached to the Seven/Nine would go for his monthly drills. I told him that depended on the battery. HHB is divided into . . ."

"HHB?"

"Headquarters and Headquarters Battery Battalion."

"Yes?"

"Is divided into Main Company, Service Battery, A-Battery, and B-Battery. The first two normally drill at Pompano . . ."

"Pompano, yes, go on."

"A-Battery drills at Vero Beach. B-Battery drills at Port Charlotte."

"Did you tell this to Harper?"

"Yes, sir, I did."

"Thank you very much," I said.

"Sir, do you have any idea why he *wanted* this information?"

"I think so, yes. I think he was trying to find someone. Sergeant, I wonder if you could do me one other favor. Could you check your records on a man named Lloyd Davis? He would have been with the Military Police, and I'm fairly certain he's now in a field-artillery reserve unit. Can you let me know what battery he's with?"

"I'd have to make some calls on that, sir."

"Could you? And get back to me, please?"

"Yes, sir," he said. "Be happy to."

"Thanks, Sergeant," I said.

He called me back ten minutes later to report that Corporal Lloyd C. Davis had begun his cross-training, or retraining, with the Seven/Nine in January almost two years ago, and that he would fulfill his obligation to the army *next* January, on the fourteenth. He further told me that Davis was with A-Battery of the Seven/Nine Field Artillery Battalion and that they had been drilling at Vero Beach on the weekend of November 14–November 15. The first sergeant of A-Battery had informed Palmer that Lloyd Davis had taken a phone call at about nine Sunday morning, November 15, and had come to him immediately afterward asking to be excused that weekend because there was an emergency at home. He promised he would make up for the missed session within the thirty days allowed by the army. The last his sergeant had seen of him, he was driving south in a red Thunderbird convertible.

I thanked Palmer again, and then hung up.

The call from Detective Morris Bloom did not come until almost the end of the day. I was, in fact, packing my briefcase and clearing my desk when Cynthia buzzed to say he was on the line.

"Matthew," he said, "we've got Harper. The Miami cops picked him up early this afternoon—he sure likes Miami, doesn't he? He was driving a car stolen here in Calusa, a Cadillac Seville, no less. He's here now; we're about to question him on Sally Owen's murder. I think you ought to come down."

I asked Bloom if I could have a few words with my client before they began the Q and A. A uniformed cop brought Harper into the empty office where I was waiting for him. He was manacled and chained. I had never before this moment seen a human being chained like an animal. The chain was wrapped around his waist and through the connecting links of the handcuffs that held his hands fastened behind his back, and then looped between his legs and through the connecting links of the leg irons on his ankles. There was blood caked on his face and both his eyes were swollen and discolored. Looking at him, battered and chained that way, I couldn't help remembering what Sally Owen had called him: King Kong.

"How are you?" I said.

"So-so," he said.

"Sit down."

"Ain't too comfortable, my hands locked behind my back this way."

He sat anyway, easing his huge body into a leather chair, shifting his weight so that he was resting on one hip.

"Why'd you hit me?" I asked.

"You was about to turn me in."

"No, I asked you to turn yourself in voluntarily."

"Same thing."

"Because I was afraid you might get hurt out there."

"Got hurt out there anyway, dinn I?"

"Who did it?"

"Don't actually know. Lots of cops 'tween Miami an' here, all of them with clubs."

"What were you doing in Miami again?"

"Sightseein. Lookin."

"For Lloyd Davis?"

He shifted his weight in the chair. His eyes avoided mine.

"Mr. Harper? Did you go to Miami looking for Lloyd Davis?"

He did not answer me.

"How about Pompano? You were there on the fifteenth, did you go there looking for Lloyd Davis?"

He still did not answer.

"Or Vero Beach? You went there that same day. Did you expect to find Lloyd Davis there?"

"Thass a lot of questions, Mr. Hope."

"But no answers so far. How about helping me?"

"Why would I go any of those places lookin for Lloyd?"

"Because his wife told you he was with an artillery reserve unit, and your former buddy Ronnie Palmer told you where all the Seven/Nine batteries drilled. You didn't know which battery he was with, so you had to start trying them all. Why were you looking for Lloyd Davis?"

"Thass personal, Mr. Hope."

"Not anymore, it isn't."

"I ain't sure I know what you mean by that."

"I think you found out about him and Michelle, Mr. Harper. I think that's why . . ."

He shoved himself out of the chair and lunged toward me. The chain between his legs and fastened to the leg irons caught him up short. He stood there shaking, straining at the chains, and I thought for a moment he might snap them as easily as King Kong had. And then suddenly, he began weeping the way he had the first time in this building, only this time he wasn't sitting, this time he stood there like a huge mountain erupting tears, his shoulders and his chest heaving, his entire body quaking, the tears streaming down his face like molten lava.

I went to him. I put my arm around his shoulders.

"It's all right," I said.

He shook his head.

"Sit down."

He shook his head again.

"Please. Sit down."

I helped him into the chair. He sat bent forward, his hands cuffed behind his back, his body still shaking, the tears still coming uncontrollably.

"How did you find out?" I asked.

"I found the paintin Sally Owen done."

"The one in your garage?"

"Yessir."

"What about it?"

"Found it in the closet, ast Michelle whut it was. Ast her whut it was spose to *be*. White woman kissin a black man, whut was it spose to *be*? She tole me it was her an' me, said it was spose to be her an' me. Said it was a present from Sally. I tole her the man in that pitcher dinn look nothin at *all* like me, an' if it was spose to be *us*, if it was a present from Sally spose to be *us*, then whut was she hidin it in the closet for? And then she . . . she tole me."

"When was this, Mr. Harper? When did you find that painting?"

"Saturday night, I been watchin television, musta been about one in the mornin' when I went in the bedroom. She'd been out on the beach all day, had herself too much sun, turned in early. Way I happened to spot the pitcher, I planned to do some fishin the next day, Sunday, and there was this ole pair of boots I kept in the back there, way back in the closet, an' thass where the pitcher was, face to the wall. So I wondered whut it was doin there, an' juss then she got up t'go to the bathroom an' I ast her. An' then it all come out."

"What did she tell you?"

"Said it was her an' Lloyd in that pitcher, said they'd begun seein each other reg'lar in Germany, right after that night they fust met. Said she . . . Mr. Hope, I can't tell you this, it hurts me to have to say this. Thass why I been keepin it all inside me, you unnerstan? Because of the *shame* of it."

"Tell me," I said.

"She . . . tole me she loved him, Mr. Hope. Said she'd . . . loved him from the start."

"What happened then?"

"I got dressed an' left for Miami."

"Why?"

"To go *fine* him," Harper said, and suddenly raised his head and looked directly into my eyes. "To *kill* him, Mr. Hope. Thass why I went to Pompano an' Vero Beach. Thass why I went back to Miami when I couldn't find him *either* of those places. To kill him. I planned to stay in Miami till hell froze over, waitin for him to come home from wherever he was. But then I heard the news about Michelle, an' I come right back here to Calusa. I busted outa jail to go lookin for him again, Mr. Hope. They's still business needs tendin to, Mr. Hope. Once I get outta here . . ."

"Let's worry about that later, okay? Right now, they're going to ask you about Sally Owen's murder. You're not to answer a single question, do you understand?"

"I dinn *plan* to anyway, Mr. Hope. I answered all they questions 'bout Michelle, an' I ended up in jail. I dinn kill Sally Owen neither, an' I don't plan to tell them nothin now but my name, rank, an' serial number."

"Name, rank, and serial number, right," I said, and smiled for the first time in three days.

I got home at a little after seven that night, mixed myself a martini, and then went directly into the study to play back the messages on the answering machine. There were only three crank calls; *sic transit gloria mundi.* One of the callers was my secret admirer, Lucille. "Still waiting for your call, honey," she said, and hung up. The other two calls were from men who described in detail what they would do to me if that nigger didn't get the electric chair. Castration was the gist.

The next call was from Jim Willoughby.

"Matthew," he said, "don't bother calling me back, okay? I simply want you to know I'm ending my association with you on this case. I don't like the way you've been handling it, I feel in fact that you've jeopardized any chance we might have had for an acquittal, and I want *out.* Good luck with it."

Mealymouthed Eliot McLaughlin was the next caller.

"Matthew, this is Eliot," he said. "I'd like you to call me back on this very serious matter of breaching the settlement agreement. I think you know what I'm referring to, Matthew. *Hasta la vista.*"

Stupid son of a bitch, I thought.

"Matthew," the next caller said, "this is Frank. Your partner, remember? I wanted to remind you that you've got a closing at Tricity tomorrow morning at nine. Our fee is close to twenty thousand dollars on this one, need I say more? Rumor in the trade has it that you're planning to open an office in Miami. Is that true?"

I smiled.

The machine hummed.

I snapped it off, and then picked up the receiver and dialed Kitty Reynolds's number. She answered on the fifth ring.

"Miss Reynolds," I said, "this is Matthew Hope."

"Oh," she said.

"I'd like to ask you some questions if I may. Will you be home for a while?"

"Well, actually . . ."

"Yes?"

"I was just on my way out to dinner."

"What time will you be back, Miss Reynolds?"

"I'm not sure."

"Would ten o'clock be convenient?"

"Well . . . can't this wait till morning?"

"I'd rather talk to you tonight, if that's all right with you."

"Well then . . . can you make it a bit later?"

"Ten-thirty?"

"Eleven?"

"I'll be there at eleven. Tell the security guard I'm expected, will you?"

I put the receiver back on the cradle, took off my jacket, and went out into the kitchen. In the freezer compartment of the refrigerator, I found a package of frozen chicken cacciatore, read the instructions on the back of the box, set a pot of water to boil, and then mixed myself a second martini. When the water was boiling, I dropped the plastic package into it, set the timer on my Japanese watch for twenty minutes, and then went into the living room and tried to make sense of the bits and pieces of information I now possessed.

There were still some questions that needed answering.

Why had Michelle Benois, for example—apparently enough in love with Lloyd Davis to have followed him to the States three months after he'd left Germany—settled for marriage with Harper instead?

Why had Michelle waited two weeks before coming to Calusa to find Harper?

Where had Lloyd Davis gone when he'd begged off drill at Vero Beach early Sunday morning, November 15, after receiving a phone call from—

Who?

Where had he been since?

Where was he now?

And what the hell was The Oreo?

Lots of questions.

The timer on my watch went off. I went out into the kitchen, spooned the plastic bag out of the boiling water, cut off one corner of it with a pair of scissors, spilled my chicken cacciatore out onto a plate, sat down at the kitchen table to eat, and hoped all through the meager meal that Kitty Reynolds would have the answer to at least *one* of those questions when I saw her at eleven o'clock.

I asked her flat out.

"What's The Oreo?"

She answered me flat out.

"I have no idea."

"What does that word mean to you?"

"Nothing. What does it mean to you?"

"It means a cookie. A layer of white icing between two chocolate wafers."

"Oh yes," she said, "of course. Oreo cookies."

We were sitting in her living room. She was dressed more sedately than I'd ever seen her, wearing a simple navy blue linen dress with muted horizontal stripes of a paler blue and pink, a checked sash in the same colors wrapped around her waist. A fire was going on the grate; apparently she'd learned how to make one since the last time I'd seen her.

"Does an Oreo cookie suggest anything to you?" I asked.

"What could it possibly suggest? Are you hungry?"

"No."

"Then why are you asking me about cookies?"

"Lloyd Davis's wife told me Sally Owen had given her

a painting—and I'm quoting now—'from when we still had The Oreo.' "

"Leona's a junkie," Kitty said, "I wouldn't trust anything she . . ."

"Oh? How do you happen to know that?"

"Well . . . it's common knowledge."

"Have you seen her recently?"

"No, but . . ."

"Have you seen *Lloyd* Davis recently?"

"Not since we had the committee."

"Was Leona a drug addict at the time?"

"I really don't know."

"Then how do you know she's an addict now?"

"Look, Mr. Hope, I'm not under oath here. I was kind enough to let you come here, but you can just walk right out again if this is going to turn into a third degree. I don't know anything about when Leona got to be an addict, I just know she *is* one, period. And I don't know anything about Sally's black-and-white paintings, either, or this Oreo you're . . ."

"How do you know they're black-and-white?"

"You *said* they were."

"No, I never mentioned that."

"I thought you did."

"But they *are* black-and-white, aren't they?"

"If you say so. Mr. Hope, you're beginning to irritate me. I just had a very boring dinner with a lingerie salesman from Tampa, so if you don't mind . . ."

"Miss Reynolds," I said, "I can subpoena you before trial, and take a deposition under oath . . ."

"Yes, well, you just do that," she said.

"I'd rather we talked quietly and sensibly here. Someone's murdered two people, do you realize . . . ?"

"Yes, George Harper."

"I don't think so," I said. "Have you ever seen any of Sally's paintings?"

"If I knew they were black-and-white, then I guess I'd seen them someplace, yes."

"Where?"

"At her house, I suppose. You *know* I was in her house for one of the meetings."

"Yes. Which is where you met Andrew, isn't that right?"

"That's right."

"*And* Lloyd Davis and his wife."

"Yes."

"Andrew had a little trouble remembering Davis."

"I'm not responsible for Andrew's memory."

"Doesn't it seem odd to you that Sally's paintings were black-and-white, and this committee you formed . . ."

"*I* didn't form it."

"The lady on Fatback then. This committee was composed of concerned black and white citizens . . ."

"Yes, we *were* concerned. Don't try to make it sound silly, Mr. Hope. We were actually *concerned* about what had happened. *Deeply* concerned."

"Was the committee called The Oreo?"

"No."

"Then what was?"

"I have no idea."

"Would it have been the group you socialized with after the committee broke up?"

"I don't know what it is, I already told you that."

"Have you ever seen the painting hanging in the bedroom of the Davis house?"

"I've never been to the Davis house."

"Have the Davises ever been *here*?"

"I wasn't even *living* here when The Oreo . . ."

She cut herself off.

"Yes, Miss Reynolds?"

"I wasn't living here."

"Uh-huh."

"I wasn't."

"Uh-huh."

"I had the apartment over the store."

"Uh-huh. What were you just about to say?"

"Nothing."

"About The Oreo, I mean."

"Nothing."

"The painting I saw in the Davis bedroom . . ."

"I think you'd better leave, Mr. Hope."

". . . depicted a white woman perfoming fellatio on a black man."

She looked at me and blinked.

"If you already *know* . . ." she said, and cut herself off again.

I said nothing.

"You're trying to get me in trouble, aren't you?" she said. "You're trying to involve *me* in what happened."

"No, I'm not."

"Then what difference does it make whether I was part of The Oreo or not?"

"*Were* you?"

"What the fuck *difference* does it make? Why don't you ask yourself why your precious client killed his wife, why don't you ask yourself *that*? I'll *tell* you why, Mr. Hope. Because he found out about Michelle, that's why. And Sally was the next one because that's where the whole thing started, with the three of them."

"Which three?"

"I thought you knew already. You saw the painting, I thought you . . ."

"No, I don't."

"Then forget it."

"You've come too far already, Miss Reynolds."

"I came too far the minute I let them talk me into . . ."

She stopped again.

"Go ahead."

"What do you want, a free show, Mr. Hope? Dirty movies? We had a little club, okay? It started with Michelle, Sally, and Lloyd, and then Andrew got involved, and one night they asked me if I'd like to party with them, so I did. Only five of us that first time, three on the bed, two of us—Lloyd and me—on the overflow mattress."

"The one on the floor?"

"Yes."

"Go ahead."

"That's all."

"There's more."

"All right, there's more," she said, and sighed. "Michelle and I were the only white women at first. But there were plenty of *other* whites on the committee, men and women both, and eventually—after the committee broke up—they dirfted into The Oreo."

"How many people?"

"In The Oreo? When it was in stride? A dozen, I guess."

"Leona was a part of this?"

"In the beginning. Before she got on heroin."

"Did George Harper ever attend any of these . . . ?"

"George? *That* ape? Don't be ridiculous! He never even knew what was going on. He was out peddling his junk while his wife was romping in the hay. Why do you think he killed her, Mr. Hope? Because he found *out*, that's why."

"What about those paintings?"

"Sally gave one of them to all of us in The Oreo. You saw the one at the Davis house, the one of Michelle and Lloyd? They posed for that one night, out on Fatback I think it was, Sally high on pot and sketching Michelle and Lloyd. Made the painting later. I've still got my *own* Oreo painting someplace. Mine has a panther on it. A black panther. Eating a white kitten."

I nodded.

"Got it all, Mr. Hope?" she said. "Any further questions, counselor?"

"Just one," I said, and paused. "*Why?*"

"Why? Well, I'll tell you, Mr. Hope. At first it was just a way of communicating. The committee had broken up, we'd failed to produce even a ripple, and this was a way of maintaining contact. Of proving that we *were* color-blind, proving it didn't *matter* to us who was white or who was black on those beds, it just didn't *matter*. And later . . ."

She shrugged.

She smiled wistfully.

"It was exciting," she said. "It was just so damn *exciting*."

It was Friday morning already—December 4, 12:06 A.M. by my digital watch—when I called Bloom at home. I had visions of interrupting a sex scene between him and his wife; turnabout is fair play. Instead, he answered the phone in a fuzzy voice that told me he'd been dead asleep.

"Morrie," I said, "this is Matthew."

"Who?" he said.

"Matthew Hope."

"Oh. Yeah," he said. I suspected he was looking at his bedside clock. Or perhaps his wristwatch. Did Bloom wear his wristwatch to bed? Was it a fine digital watch like mine, with a little button you could press to illuminate the dial?

"Morrie," I said, "I just had a very interesting talk with Kitty Reynolds."

"Kitty *who*?"

"Reynolds."

"Who the hell is that?"

"I thought you might have got to her by now."

"Matthew, it's midnight, *past* midnight, I was fast asleep. If you want to play games . . ."

"She and Andrew Owen were having a thing, Morrie. That's why Sally divorced him."

"Okay," he said. "So?"

"There's more."

"Let me hear it," he said.

I let him hear it. All of it. The committee, the paintings, The Oreo—*all* of it. He listened without uttering a word. All I could hear on the phone was his level breathing. When I finished my recitation, he was still silent. I thought perhaps he'd fallen asleep on me.

"Morrie?" I said.

"I'm here," he said.

"What do you think?"

"I think we ought to ask Lloyd Davis some questions," he said.

Friday is always the longest day of the week.

This Friday—while I waited for the police to locate Lloyd Davis—was the longest of any Friday I could remember. I did not get back to the office after the closing at Tricity until almost ten-thirty, to find a couple named Ralph and Agnes West waiting in the reception room. The Wests were the nephew and niece-by-marriage of an elderly client who had died without leaving any truly close relatives; they had called me several times since his death to ask if they might come to the office to collect their share of the estate. I had told them each time they called essentially what I told them now. On the phone each time, it had taken four or five minutes. It now took almost an hour because both Ralph and Agnes West were (a) dense and (b) blindly determined not to be cheated out of their rightful share of the estate.

"There are a number of matters that must be taken care of before the estate can be distributed," I repeated, by rote this time.

"What matters?" Ralph asked. He was a mean-looking man who had neglected to shave this morning. He sat with his knees pressed tightly together, as if he desperately needed to go to the bathroom. His wife, equally mean-looking, her blond hair pulled into a tight bun at the back of her head, sat beside him and nodded in affirmation.

"As I explained on the telephone," I said, "there are probate proceedings, and notices to other heirs, and notices to creditors, and tax matters to be cleared up before distribution can be made."

"That's what you told us two *weeks* ago," Ralph said, and Agnes nodded. "Uncle Jerry died on the thirteenth of November, Friday the thirteenth, this is already three weeks *later*, and we *still* ain't got our money."

"As I told you . . ."

"There's a big sum of money involved here," Ralph said, "and we aim to get it." Agnes nodded.

"There's ten thousand dollars in the estate," I said, "and you'll share it equally with the other heirs as soon as we can . . ."

"He shoulda left a will," Ralph said to Agnes.

Agnes nodded.

"But he didn't," I said.

"Stupid old bastard," Ralph said. "If he'da left a will, we wouldn't be havin all them other people comin out of the woodwork."

I was kind enough not to point out that Ralph and Agnes had themselves come out of the woodwork the moment they'd learned of dear Uncle Jerry's death.

"So how long is this gonna take?" Ralph asked.

"Four to six months," I said.

"What?" he said.

"What?" Agnes said.

"Four to six months," I said.

"Jesus!" Ralph said, and Agnes nodded. "What the hell can possibly take *that* long?"

So—once again—I went through the entire rigmarole of probate, and notices to other heirs and creditors, and taxes to be paid from the estate, point by point, ticking off each point on my fingers, laying out the details slowly enough for even pair of trained chimpanzees to have understood, and Ralph kept shaking his head and Agnes kept nodding and by the time I finally got them out of my office it was eleven-twenty and Cynthia buzzed to say that Attorney Hager was waiting on five.

Attorney Hager was a lawyer in Maine who had obtained a judgment there for $50,000 against a man who was now living in Calusa; he wanted my assistance in collecting. I told him to send me the papers so that I could file the judgment here, and I assured him I'd do my best to see that it was satisfied. I then took a call from a local author who had written a book chat had sold a modest twelve thousand copies and who had not received a penny beyond the minuscule advance from his publishers, a New York City firm that had ignored his numerous requests for accounting and further payment. I told him that as a preliminary move I would write to them demanding accounting and payment—well, what I actually said was, "Don't worry, I'll get on their asses."

Cynthia buzzed ten minutes later.

"There's a wandering gypsy lady on six," she said.

"What?"

"That's how she announced herself. A wandering gypsy lady. From Mexico City. She sounds a lot like your daughter Joanna."

I stabbed at the lighted button.

"Joanna?" I said. "Are you all right?"

"Who told you it was me?" Joanna said.

"Cynthia guessed. Is everything okay?"

"Yeah, but we miss you. Also, all the cab drivers in Mexico City are rip-off artists. And it was a feast day or something when we went to the museum—the big archaeological museum you're not supposed to miss, you know?—and there were no English-speaking guides and everything was in Spanish. I should be taking *Spanish* in school, Dad, and not *French* like you insisted."

"*As* I insisted."

"Yeah, as. We miss you to death, Dad, me and Dale."

I knew better than to correct the "me and Dale." There were young people with PhD.'s in comparative literature who still used the "me and" locution.

"How is she? Dale."

"Oh, fine, Dad, she's a real sweetie-pie. We had *such* a fun time at Xochimilco yesterday, that's where they have these little boats all decorated with flowers, you know? And you get rowed through these canals, well, *poled*, actually, the guys on the boats have these long poles they shove the boats through the water—Dad, guess *what*! One of the boats was *Joanna*! They all have names, you know, and *Joanna* was on one of the boats! Not Dale, though. I mean, not *her* name on any of the boats. She took a picture of the one with my name on it. Neat, huh?"

"Very neat," I said. "Is she there with you? Can I talk to her?"

"*May* I talk to her, Dad," she said, and I could swear she was grinning from ear to ear in grammatical triumph. "Just a sec."

I waited.

"Hi," Dale said.

"You okay?"

"I miss you."

"I miss you, too."

"The reason we're calling . . ."

"I thought it was because you were desperate for the sound of my voice."

"Oh, sure, *that*, too," Dale said. "But I *also* thought I'd remind you we're on Delta's flight two thirty-three tomorrow, arriving in Calusa at four-oh-five P.M."

"I've got it on my calendar," I said. "And also emblazoned on my forehead."

"I truly do miss you, Matthew," she said.

"Me, too," I said. "Dale, the phone's lighting up again. Hurry home."

"Delta number two thirty-three," Dale said.

It was already high noon on the longest day of my life.

Morrie Bloom did not call until eight o'clock that night. He caught me at home.

"Matthew," he said, "we've got Davis here in Calusa. What we did, we called him in Miami and said we were trying to nail down some points about Harper's alibi and would appreciate it if he could come here to help us. Said we'd pay his air fare, put him up in a motel here, the whole red-carpet routine. He fell for it—which is in itself suspicious, am I right? I mean, why didn't he tell us to come down *there* if we wanted to talk to him? Anyway, he's here now, at a place on the South Trail, and he'll be in tomorrow morning at eleven sharp. I asked him, incidentally, if he'd mind Harper's attorney sitting in on the questioning, and he said he'd be more than happy to confirm everything he told you in Miami. Now, Matthew, here's the problem. We can't charge him with anything, he's here as a voluntary witness, and besides we don't know if he *did* anything yet. At the same time, in case we hit pay dirt, I want a record of everything he tells us. I could wear a wire, be the easiest thing in the world to tape him that way. I don't think he'd suspect a bug, do you? But wire or not, the guy's not going to say anything incriminating unless we lead him down the garden, do you follow me, Matthew?"

"Not entirely," I said.

"Well, here's what I think. I think we're smarter than he is, and I think we can work out a Mutt-and-Jeff routine that'll get him to open up. Can you be here tomorrow morning at ten? To work it all out, I mean."

Davis greeted me warmly, and even apologized in advance for what he was about to confirm to the police, the fact that he had *not* seen his friend George Harper in Miami on the Sunday he'd claimed to have been there. I told him he had to speak the truth as he saw it, and I thanked him for coming to Calusa at Bloom's request. If Harper was *indeed* guilty, I said (lying like a professional Mutt), a guilty plea was often better advised than a stubborn claim of innocence. Bloom and I had worked out our strategy in detail, but I still felt we were about to perform a daring trapeze act without a net. One slip, and Davis would bound out of the tent.

"Well, why don't we begin then?" Bloom asked in the genial guise of Jeff.

"I think you should first read Mr. Davis his rights," I said.

"What for?" Bloom said.

"If you're going to use any of this at the trial . . ."

"Any of *what*? We're not even *taping* him, Matthew. All we're trying to find out is whether he can substantiate Harper's alibi."

"I still think he should be protected."

"Against *what*?" Bloom asked.

"Against the police later claiming Mr. Davis said something he might *not* have said. Look, it's up to Mr. Davis. If I were in his position, though, I'd ask you to read me my rights."

"Look, I'll read them, I know them by *heart*," Bloom said. "But I think it's a waste of time."

"Are you going to be taping what he says?"

"I just told you no."

I looked at him skeptically.

"Why?" Bloom said. "What's wrong with *that*?"

"There won't be any record, that's all."

"I don't *need* a record," Bloom said. "I just want to ask the man a few questions."

"What about *his* record?" I said.

"*His* record?"

"Doesn't *he* need a record of what he says here? In case he's later misquoted."

"We're not taking a deposition here," Bloom said. "The man's not under oath. Save all this crap for later, will you?"

"Look, do what you want to," I said. "I just thought I'd mention it, that's all."

Davis looked at me, and then he looked at Bloom.

"Maybe I *ought* to have a record of what I say here," he said.

"If you want us to tape it, we'll tape it," Bloom said, and sighed, and went to the door. "Charlie," he yelled, "bring in the Sony, will you?"

"And I think maybe you ought to read me my rights, too," Davis said.

"Whatever you say," Bloom said. "You know, Matthew, I did you a favor asking you here, I don't know why you're making such a big deal out of a few lousy questions."

"I just don't like to see anyone's rights violated," I said.

"Let's just get it over with, okay?" Bloom said, and shook his head.

Charlie—a cherubic-faced, uniformed cop—brought in the tape recorder and put it on the desk. Bloom turned it on, tested it, read Davis his rights from top to bottom, got his confirmation that he was willing to answer questions without an attorney present on his behalf, and then said to me, "Okay, counselor?"

"Fine," I said.

The trap was set.

"Mr. Davis," Bloom said, "George Harper claims he went to your home on Sunday morning, November fifteenth, looking for you. He further states that you were not there when he arrived, and that your wife told him you were off with the army reserve."

"That's what I understand she told him," Davis said.

"It's important that we pinpoint his whereabouts on that weekend because, as you know, his wife was murdered on Monday, the sixteenth."

"Yes."

"But you say you didn't see him that Sunday, is that right?"

"That's right."

"Where were you, Mr. Davis?"

"With the army. At Vero Beach."

"All day Sunday?"

"No, sir, not all day. I wasn't feeling good, so I asked if I could be excused for the rest of the weekend."

He had just made his first mistake. According to Palmer,

the sergeant at Miami recruiting, Davis had taken a phone call at 9:00 A.M. that Sunday, and had asked to be excused because of "an emergency at home."

"What time would that have been, Mr. Davis?" Bloom asked.

"Oh, I don't know. Nine, ten in the morning?"

"Is that when you left Vero Beach?"

"Yes, sir."

"How?"

"I had my car there."

"Where did you go from Vero Beach?"

"Home."

"To Miami?"

"Yes, sir."

"And got there at what time?"

"Oh, I don't know. Eleven? Eleven-thirty? I'm really not sure."

"Was your wife there when you got home?"

"Yes, she was."

"Did she tell you that Mr. Harper had been there?"

"Yes, she did."

"Did you see Mr. Harper at any time that Sunday?"

"No, sir."

"Mr. Harper claims he went looking for you in Pompano and later at Vero Beach. Did you see him at either of those places?"

"No, sir."

"Were you in Miami on Monday as well?"

"I was."

"Did you see Mr. Harper at any time Monday?"

"No, I did not."

"Because, you see, Mr. Harper says he was eager to see you, and that he spent all day Sunday and Monday looking for you. Claims he didn't come back to Calusa until Tuesday morning, after he'd heard news of his wife's murder."

"Well," Davis said, "if *I'd* beaten up *my* wife on Sunday and then killed her on Monday, I'd say *I* was nowhere near Calusa, too."

He had just make his second mistake. Not anywhere—not in the newspaper reports, not in the television or radio broadcasts—had there been the slightest mention of Michelle having been brutally beaten on the night before her murder. I caught the mistake, and I knew at once that *Bloom* had caught it as well; a slight lifting of just one eyebrow transmitted the intelligence to me.

"Where were you on Thanksgiving Day, Mr. Davis?" Bloom asked gently.

"Miami."

"That's the day Harper broke jail, you know."

"Uh-huh."

"He claims he went to Miami looking for you again."

"Can't understand why he couldn't find me. That's where I was."

"Until when?"

"Until last night, when you called and asked if I'd come up here to talk to you."

"In other words, you've been in Miami ever since you left Vero Beach on the fifteenth of November."

"Right there in Miami," Davis said, and nodded.

"And you never saw Mr. Harper there on any of the days he *claims* he was looking for you?"

"No sir, I never saw him."

"Well, that's that," Bloom said, and turned to me. "Your man claims he was trying to find him, and here's Mr. Davis telling us he was *there* all the time, so how come he *couldn't* find him?"

"Yeah, I guess so," I said, and sighed.

"You want to ask any questions?"

"I couldn't do that without Mr. Davis's permission."

"Stop worrying about his rights, will you please? I read him his rights, he can stop this thing anytime he wants to. Do you want to ask him any questions, or don't you?"

"If it's all right with you, Mr. Davis."

"Sure," Davis said.

"Okay, Morrie?"

"Be my guest."

"Mr. Davis, were you in Miami this past Wednesday?"

"Wednesday?"

"That would've been . . . what's today, Morrie?"

"The fifth," Bloom said.

"That would've been the second," I said. "Wednesday, the second."

"Yes, I was there," Davis said

"At home?"

"Working, yes."

"Out back in the garage? Where I spoke to you when . . ."

"That's my place of business, yes."

"And you were there this past Wednesday, you say?"

"Matthew," Bloom said, "the man just told us he's been in Miami ever since he got back from Vero Beach. He didn't leave Miami till last night, after I called him."

"I was just wondering—"

"I mean, if you're going to ask the man questions that cover ground we already went over—"

"From what time to what time were you there at the house, Mr. Davis?"

"All day," Davis said.

He had just made his third mistake. I'd been in Miami Wednesday, at Davis's house, talking to his wife Leona, and there hadn't been hide nor hair of him anywhere. I decided to pinpoint it.

"Were you there at five-thirty, six o'clock?"

"All day," he said again. "Well, wait, I went out for a sandwich at lunchtime."

"But other than that . . ."

"I was there all day."

"I must have missed you," I said.

"What?"

"I was there on Wednesday, talking to your wife at about five-thirty, just as the sun was going down. I didn't see you there, Mr. Davis."

He looked at me.

"Then you're right," he said, "you must've missed me."

"Did your wife tell you I'd been there?"

"No."

"That's strange, isn't it? If you were in Miami on Wednesday, and I missed you when I was at the house, wouldn't your wife have told you I was there?"

"Sometimes she tells me, sometimes she doesn't."

"But she told you *Harper* was there on Sunday the fifteenth, right? When you got back to the house after leaving Vero Beach."

"Yes, that's what she told me."

"And you've been in Miami all this time?"

"Until last night, when I got the call from Detective Bloom here."

"You didn't come to Calusa, did you, at any time during . . . ?"

"No, sir, I did not."

"Then how did you know Michelle Harper was brutally beaten on the night of Sunday the fifteenth?"

He hesitated, suddenly wary of me, and undecided as to whether he should brazen it out or simply shut up. He decided to risk a head-on collision. That was his final mistake.

"Sally told me," he said.

"Sally?"

"Owen. She called to talk to my wife, but Leona was out someplace, so she talked to me instead."

"When was that, Mr. Davis?"

"Monday sometime, I guess."

"The day Michelle was murdered?"

"I guess."

"Well, was it or wasn't it?"

"Who *remembers*? Listen, what *is* this, would you mind telling me? I come up here to lend a hand; and next thing I know . . ."

"He's right, Matthew," Bloom said. "I don't like this tack you're on. If I realized for a minute you were going to put the man through a third . . ."

"Thanks, Detective Bloom," Davis said, turning to him at

once, and nodding righteously. He still didn't know there were *two* of us tracking his spoor, still didn't know that Bloom was also waiting in the bushes to pounce.

"Would you like to call this off?" Bloom asked him.

"He can certainly stop answering questions if he wishes to," I said.

"That's right, Mr. Davis," Bloom said, picking up on it immediately. "Nobody's going to start thinking of you as a *suspect* here, instead of a friendly witness, if you decide to call off the questioning. That's your right, Mr. Davis. You can stop answering questions here anytime you like."

Bloom had just performed a triple somersault in midair and had caught the trapeze bar just before heading for a fall. According to the rules of Miranda-Escobedo, a police officer interrogating anyone isn't supposed to offer any advice (and *certainly* not threats) as to whether a person should seek counsel, or answer questions, or stop answering questions, or even blow his nose, for that matter. Bloom hadn't given Davis any advice at all, telling him only that he could stop answering questions whenever he wanted to, which was merely a repetition of the rights he'd earlier read to him. Nor had I openly suggested that a refusal to answer any further questions would constitute a presumption of guilt. All was innuendo in the sly little game of Mutt-and-Jeff we were playing. And try to prove innuendo on a played-back tape. But the seed had been planted.

"Shit," Davis said. "I came up here to answer questions about *Georgie*, and now—"

"Of course, you did," Bloom said.

"So what should I do?"

"About what?"

"Should I answer his questions?"

"I'm not permitted to give you advice on that," Bloom said, covering himself again, everything neat and clean, everything in accordance with the Supreme Court decision.

Davis looked me straight in the eye.

"Sally Owen called on the Monday Michelle was murdered, yes," he said.

"What time, would you remember?"

"Sometime in the morning."

"How early?"

"Not too early. Eight o'clock or thereabouts."

"And told you Michelle had been beaten up the night before?"

"Yes. Actually, she wanted to tell this to *Leona*, you understand, but Leona was out . . ."

"At eight in the morning?"

"Well . . . yes. We needed . . . orange juice. For breakfast. She ran out for some orange juice."

"Which is when Sally Owen called."

"Yes."

"And told you all about Michelle's beating."

"Yes."

"Did she tell you George Harper had been the one who'd beaten his wife?"

"Yes."

"How'd she know this?"

"Michelle told her."

"At eight in the morning?"

"I guess so. If Sally *called* at eight . . ."

"Then Michelle must have told her this *before* eight, isn't that right?"

"I suppose so."

He was lying like a used-car salesman. In my office that Monday morning, Michelle had told me she'd gone to see Sally Owen at nine o'clock. Sally *couldn't* have known about the beating by eight, and neither could Davis. Unless—

"How well did you know Sally Owen?"

"Not particularly well."

"But she chose to reveal this to you?"

"Well, she wanted to talk to *Leona*, actually."

"But she settled for you."

"Well, yes. Any port in a storm, right?" he said, and smiled.

"Did you know Sally well enough to have posed for her?"

"Posed for her?"

219

"For a painting she made?"

"A what?"

"In black-and-white?"

"I don't know what you . . ."

"A painting of Michelle Harper going down on you," Bloom said suddenly and flatly, and Davis realized in that moment that it had been a trap all along, even his friend and ally was in on the hunt, and the hounds were barking at his heels.

"What . . . what . . . makes you think Michelle would ever have . . . have . . . ?"

"A woman named Kitty Reynolds was there the night Sally made her sketch," Bloom said, no longer the friendly Jeff, hard as nails now, fire in his eyes and molten steel running through his veins. Davis looked into those eyes and must have known the party was over. But he hung in there, anyway.

"I don't even *know* anybody named Kitty Reynolds," he said.

"Why'd you leave Vero Beach?" Bloom snapped.

"I was sick, I told you."

"Who phoned you there Sunday morning?"

"Phoned me? Nobody. Who says . . . ?"

"Your first sergeant says you got a call there at nine o'clock on Sunday morning. Who *was* that, Mr. Davis? Was it Michelle Harper?"

"Michelle? I hardly even *knew* Mi—"

"Calling to say she'd spilled the beans the night before?"

"No, no. Why would . . . ?"

"Calling to say her husband was on his way to Miami . . ."

"No, hey listen . . ."

". . . looking for you?"

"No, that's wrong. Really, that's . . ."

"Looking to *kill* you, Mr. Davis?"

Davis said nothing.

"Were you afraid he'd found out about The Oreo, Mr. Davis?"

Davis still said nothing.

"Afraid he'd kill you because he knew about The Oreo?"

He was silent a moment longer. Then he said, "Oh, Jesus."

"*Was* it Michelle who called to warn you?"

"Oh, Jesus," he said again, and then, almost as if he were glad to have it over with at last, he buried his face in his hands the way Harper had done in this same office almost three weeks earlier, and began weeping as he told us all of it from the beginning.

The tape unwound unmercifully, and the recent past was suddenly the immediate present.

13

Bonn.

This has been the capital of the Federal Republic of Germany since 1949, its population doubling to 300,000 once it became the seat of government. In sits on one bank of the Rhine, facing the Siebengebirge—the Seven Mountains—on the opposite bank. Adenauerallee, named for Dr. Konrad Adenauer, the first chancellor of the new democratic state, runs almost parallel to the river. It is said that Adenauer's single vote caused this formerly quiet university town to become the new capital, and that his vote was premised on the region's climate, supposedly genial to aging men.

The climate is rainy.

It rains here almost six months out of the year.

It is a rainy night in November, two years ago.

The setting is a bar in the baroque old quarter of the town, near the Kennedybrücke. Davis is sitting at a table with the blond cabaret singer who is his date, waiting for Harper to arrive with the young girl he has fallen madly in love with, the nineteen-year-old named Michelle Benois, whom he'd met in a bar earlier this month. She comes in on his arm at a quarter past seven. Her long black hair cascades around a face that is beautiful but a trifle too made up. She is wearing a black cloth coat, and beneath that a clingy red dress cut low over her breasts and hugging her ample hips. He recognizes her at once for what she is: there are enough of them in Bonn. Georgie Harper has fallen in love with a hooker. (In bed with Davis later that night, the blond singer asks, *"Ist das Mädchen eine Hure?"*)

He is surprised when Michelle calls him at the barracks the next day. She says she must see him. He thinks at once that business must be slow, too much free stuff being handed out to the servicemen by willing young *Fraüleins*. But he agrees to meet her later, and in a small bar near the Hofgarten, she tells him that she doesn't know what to do about Harper. He has fallen madly in love with her, but of course she doesn't care for him, how could anyone return the love of such a *"monstre,"* she says in French, such a monster. She is not referring to the brutality Davis later attributes to him. He admits to us now, as the tape relentlessly records his words, that he *himself* was the one who'd used his billy on any drunks they picked up ("I told you it was Georgie 'cause I figured that'd make him beating her up seem more likely, do you see?"). Michelle is referring instead to Harper's *looks*, the apelike *appearance* of this *"monstre véritable,"* she says again in French.

They linger in the bar for close to two hours while she pours out her heart to him. He is thinking he would like to score with her, but not on her terms. He has never paid for it in his life, not at home, where his wife Leona is waiting for him to complete his four years of active duty, nor here in Germany either, where it can be had free just for the asking. He knows what her business is, but he broaches the possibility of a freebie, anyway, and is surprised when she readily agrees to it. In a hotel room on Koblenzstrasse, they make passionate love for the first time.

"I didn't know she was going to get crazy later on," he tells us now.

He continues seeing her. Harper knows nothing about their affair; Harper is blissfully in love with a girl who's been hooking in Bonn ever since she was thirteen, when she fled Paris and the bourgeois existence she shared there with her French father and German mother. Davis doesn't care *what* she is; in fact, her expertise is something new to him. There is never a moment in bed with her that he isn't learning something he has never experienced before. On New Year's Eve in Bonn, she pleads illness to get out of a date with Harper and instead arranges a small surprise for Davis. When he shows up at the hotel room she has booked in advance, she is waiting there with a voluptuous black girl who, like herself, is a hooker. "*Bonne année*," she says and introduces Davis to what he will later remember as his first "triad."

"That was the *real* beginning," he says now. "The real beginning of The Oreo, the beginning of everything."

It is *Davis*, not *Harper*, who leaves Germany without calling Michelle. He considers her nothing more than what she is: a whore with a splendid bag of tricks. He is eager to get home, not to see his wife Leona, whom he considers something of a drudge, but instead "to feast on some *soul* food" (words he also attributes later to Harper), "the general black female population." He does not know at the time that Michelle will follow him to the States in three months.

Nor does he know she is pregnant with his child.

She arrives in Miami shortly before Easter last year. She is wearing the same black cloth coat she'd been wearing when first he'd met her in Bonn. The weather is balmy and mild, but she is bundled inside her coat, trying to hide the swell of her pregnancy from the prying eyes of strangers. She does not have an address for Davis; he had refused to give her one before leaving Bonn. But she knows where to find Harper, who'd been asking her constantly to marry him and come live in the States with him. She goes first to the address Harper gave her in Bonn, but only to find out where she can locate

Davis. Harper's mother will not oblige her. Michelle must ask questions all over town before finally she can present herself on Davis's doorstep with the announcement of her pregnancy and the threat that she will drown herself if he does not marry her. This will later become an inside joke between the lovers, and Michelle will recount with sly pleasure that these were the exact words she said to *Harper* when finally she proposed to him in Calusa.

By then, she has already undergone an abortion in Miami. The abortion is Davis's idea.

So is the suggestion that she marry Harper.

"I told her he was a hard-worker," he says now. "Told her she'd be getting herself a free meal ticket and meanwhile, you know, we could pick up where we'd left off in Germany. No reason for us to stop seeing each other, I told her. Business as usual. Georgie was a fuckin dunce, he'd *never* know what was going on between us."

It might have remained that way, George Harper might never have found out about the continuing love affair between his wife and Lloyd Davis, if "circumstances" (as Davis now defines them) had not changed somewhat.

"It was Michelle's idea," he says. "Michelle was always the one with the ideas."

The idea, as it occurs to Michelle in the month following her wedding to Harper, is that it would be nice to give her lover Lloyd a birthday present. His birthday is on the eighteenth of July; wouldn't it be nice to arrange a little present for him on the following weekend? She has by now become close friends with Sally Owen, and Sally has confessed to her several extramarital affairs that her husband Andrew is unaware of. Michelle, in turn, has revealed to her the continuing relationship with Lloyd, has shown her secret photographs of Lloyd, has described in detail what a fantastic lover he is, and now suggests—discreetly, to be sure—that it would be wonderful if the *three* of them could get together sometime, someplace away from Calusa and Miami, just the three of them. In the beginning, it *is*, in fact, just the three of them—Sally, Michelle, and Lloyd, a white layer of icing between two chocolate wafers. *This* is the true start of The Oreo, as they secretly refer to their triad, and never mind the black hooker in Bonn. The Oreo—*their* Oreo—begins on the weekend following Lloyd's twenty-ninth birthday, in a motel room in Palm Beach, where the women have told their respective husbands they will be on a shopping trip.

In August a year and more ago, Jerry Tolliver is shot to death by an overzealous cop, and a black woman married to a white doctor out on Fatback Key decides to form a protest committee. The committee later dissolves, and it is Michelle—*again*—who suggests at a social gathering one night late that month (her husband George conveniently off on one of his junk-selling trips) that it might be fun if the men present were to be blindfolded in turn and then asked to kiss each of the women in an attempt to identify which one is any given man's own wife.

"Michelle's idea," Davis says again. "She was always the one with the ideas."

Ironically, the socially concerned couple on Fatback Key join The Oreo several weeks later. Throughout the rest of the summer and fall, The Oreo continues to meet secretly. Kitty Reynolds is a part of the group by now. Sally Owen has begun making paintings symbolic of the sexual activity they share. No one can imagine that—with all this free-and-easy mind-blowing sexual exchange—any pair of partners might commit the unpardonable sin of actually forming a true relationship, actually falling in *love*! This is what happens to Kitty Reynolds and Andrew Owen. Sally, furious, drums them out of the circle of "friends," and shortly after that, The Oreo itself begins to disintegrate, the cookie crumbling, the icing melting. It is back to just the three of them now, the way it was in the beginning—Sally, Lloyd, and Michelle. It continues that way for almost a year.

And then—

Sunday morning, November 15.

Harper finds a painting that puzzles him, and when he

questions Michelle about it she confesses her love for Lloyd—
but delicately manages to avoid the entire subject of the
little orgies she herself originated and promoted and, in fact,
misses with all her heart. Harper, in a rage, leaves the house
at 2:00 A.M. and goes looking for Lloyd—to kill him.

"She called me there at Vero Beach," Lloyd says, "warned
me to watch out, he was on the way. When I got back to
Miami, my wife told me he'd already *been* there. I had to
split. I didn't want to get in a fracas with that fuckin' ape,
he'da crushed my skull with his bare hands. I kept thinking
about how Michelle could've been so *dumb*. I mean, we had
it all *going* for us, didn't we? The three of us? Sally . . . and
her . . . and me? So why'd she have to spoil it? I figured she
had to be taught a lesson. I mean, man, no damn hooker can
put Lloyd *Davis* in danger and get away with it. No way! I
went to Calusa . . ."

He goes to Calusa expressly to teach her a lesson. He lets
himself into the Harper house with the key Michelle gave
him months ago. He is half hoping he will find her in bed
with yet *another* man, the white doctor from Fatback Key
maybe, or anybody *else* who used to be in The Oreo when it
was still in full flower. But she is alone in the house when he
lets himself in at eleven-thirty that Sunday night. He hurls
invective at her, tells her she's nothing but a no-good whore,
tells her she's placed him in a position where he has to fear
for his life—what the hell is he supposed to do when King
Kong catches up with him? How the fuck could she have
been so fuckin' dumb?

"And then I beat the shit out of her," he says.

The moment his rage cools, he recognizes that he has only
compounded the felony. Once George Harper comes home,
once Michelle tells him that Davis beat her up, the ape will
go berserk. He goes up the street to Sally's house, and tells
her what he's done. She soothes him, comforts him, and he is
surprised to discover that his anger is rekindled in the form of
"a raging hard-on" (as he recalls it now) and that he desires
Sally with a passion he has never truly felt for her before. It is

after they've made love that Sally comes up with an idea.

"It's always the chicks who come up with the ideas," Davis says.

What if—and this is only an *idea*, Sally tells him—but what if Michelle was to say *George* beat her up? What if she was to go to a lawyer, everything nice and legal, and tell him *George* did it? The cops would put him behind bars, wouldn't they? I mean, for beating up a woman? Don't they put you behind bars for that? Gain a little time, anyway, Lloyd, while you figure what to do next, am I right? Meanwhile, you better keep your ass out of sight. If George catches up with you—

It is Sally who calls Michelle early the next morning, to suggest that she first contact a lawyer she knows, and then go to the police to make the false complaint against Harper. By then, Davis—who has been hiding out in a Calusa motel room—is beginning to worry.

"I mean," he says now, "what if they let Georgie go? Wife-beating isn't such a big deal, is it? Suppose he got *off*, suppose he came looking for me again, what then?"

He gives this a great deal of thought. It continues bothering him. He cannot risk George Harper finally catching up with him. He knows what will happen once that gorilla finds him. But how can he possibly avoid him forever? Sooner or later—

And then the idea occurs to him.

What if Michelle was . . . murdered?

Moreover, what if Harper was *blamed* for the murder, the same way he was blamed for the beating?

Wasn't it possible to work it in a way that would make it seem Harper had done it? Make sure Harper was put away for good, or else fried in the electric chair? Either way, Harper would be out of the picture, and Davis himself would be home free.

Monday, November 16.

Harper is still in Miami, searching for his wife's lover. Davis goes to the Harper house, lets himself in with his key again, apologizes to Michelle for what he did to her the night before, ascertains that she has already been to the police to blame the beating on her husband, and then suggests that they take a little drive out to Whisper Key, make a nice fire on the beach maybe, patch up whatever quarrel's still between them, just the two of them, like it used to be in Bonn. Little kissy-facey by a roaring fire, okay? Maybe a little kinky sex on the beach, okay? In preparation for the kinky sex he has suggested, he takes from the glove compartment of his Thunderbird a pair of black leather gloves. He is wearing these when he removes the five-gallon can of gasoline from the shelf in Harper's garage. He is wearing them when he takes a pair of wire hangers from one of Harper's clothes racks. When Michelle asks him what he needs the hangers for, he replies, "To poke the fire with, honey."

On the beach at Whisper Key, when he tries to bind her hands with the hangers ("Little kinky sex, right, Michelle? You always *were* into kink"), she recognizes his full intent at last, and runs from him in fear. She is already naked, their "patching up" of the quarrel between them has already proceeded that far. He chases after her, drags her back up the beach, slaps her until she is limp and can no longer resist, binds her hands and feet with the wire hangers, douses her with gasoline, strikes the fatal match, and runs off into the night.

"Home free," he says.

At least until Thanksgiving Day.

On Thanksgiving Day, George Harper breaks jail, and Davis is forced to go into hiding again. He comes back to Calusa. But he has not reckoned with Sally Owen. At Sally's house on Monday afternoon, November 30, she tells Davis she suspects he's the one who killed Michelle. She says, moreover, that she might just go to the police one of these days to tell them all about it. He does not know whether she is teasing him or not. They are in bed together, she has just given him a blow-job worthy of Michelle herself. Is she serious? He simply doesn't know. But neither can he take a chance. He leaves the house "to go pick up some fried chicken" for their supper. Instead, he goes down the street to the Harper house, lets himself into the garage, and looks for a weapon there, something belonging to Harper, something that will link Harper to the *second* murder he has already decided to commit. When he finds the hammer with Harper's initials on it, he grins from ear to ear. He takes out his handkerchief, wraps it around the handle of the hammer, and then goes back to Sally's house again. She is at the kitchen sink when he comes in, filling a kettle with water for coffee. She does not turn when he says, "Hi, honey, I'm back." It is his belief now that she never even knew what hit her. The first blow crushed her skull, and the next one—as she was falling to the floor—she probably never even felt.

"I dropped the hammer on the floor," he tells us. "Another one for Georgie, I figured. My insurance." He looks up. He stares first at Bloom and then at me, and then he says, "I really blew it, didn't I? I mean, we had it all going for us, didn't we? How *else* in this town can blacks and whites really get together? Except in bed? I mean, Jesus, we'd found the *answer*, am I right?"

And suddenly, he is weeping again.

The state's attorney—Skye Bannister himself this time—arrived at the Public Safety Building a half-hour after the typed confession had been signed by Davis. Bloom was still there, of course. So was I. He was an exceptionally tall man, Skye Bannister, perhaps six four or five, with the appearance of a basketball player, reedy and pale, with wheat-colored hair and eyes the color of his name. He read the transcript in silence. Then he looked up.

"I never *did* believe that fisherman's identification," he said. "Man with veins on his nose is a drinker for sure."

"Will the confession hold?" Bloom asked.

"Can't see why not," Bannister said. "What are you thinking?"

"Entrapment," Bloom said.

"No, you were both very clever," Bannister said. He turned to me. "You thinking of entering the practice of criminal law, Mr. Hope?"

"Not particularly," I said.

"Don't," Bannister advised. "Got enough trouble getting convictions as it is." He smiled, and then turned back to Bloom.

"I'll have a man here in half an hour or so, do the formal Q and A. Good-bye gentlemen. You did good."

We were alone in the office again, Bloom and I.

"So," he said, "it wasn't Harper after all, was it? *Davis* was the beast we wanted."

"Was he?" I said. "Or was the beast really *beauty*?"

"What?"

"Michelle," I said, and then I left for the airport to pick up my daughter and Dale.